John Burnham Schwartz

CLAIRE MARVEL

John Burnham Schwartz is the author of *Bicycle Days* and *Reservation Road*, which have been translated into more than ten languages. His writing has appeared in numerous publications, including *The New York Times*, *The New Yorker*, *The Boston Globe*, and *Vogue*. He lives with his wife, filmmaker Aleksandra Crapanzano, in Brooklyn, New York.

Also by John Burnham Schwartz

Reservation Road

Bicycle Days

CLAIRE MARVEL

CLAIRE MARVEL

a novel

John Burnham Schwartz

VINTAGE CONTEMPORARIES

Vintage Books

A Division of Random House, Inc.

New York

The Library of Congress has cataloged the
Nan A. Talese/Doubleday edition as follows:
Schwartz, John Burnham
Claire Marvel: a novel / John Burnham Schwartz
p. cm.
ISBN 0-385-50344-X
1. Political science teachers—Fiction. 2. Graduate students—Fiction.
3. Loss (Psychology)—Fiction. I. Title
PS3569.C5658 C57 2002
813'.54—dc21
2001044413

Vintage ISBN: 0-375-71915-6

Book design by Caroline Cunningham

www.vintagebooks.com

Printed in the United States of America
10 9 8 7 6 5 4 3 2 1

For my brother Matt

That is my home of love; If I have rang'd,

Like him that travels I return again.

—SHAKESPEARE, SONNET 109

CLAIRE
MARVEL

PART ONE

o n e

THERE WAS BEFORE HER and now there is after her, and that is the difference in my life.

I will begin here because there can be no other beginning for this story. It was the middle of May, 1985. I was walking along Quincy Street on my way to see a professor one Monday afternoon when the weather turned suddenly. The sky broke open and rain poured down. I sprinted for cover, my book bag thudding against my ribs, reaching the Fogg Art Museum just as the rain became a torrent.

There was a rushing sound as I ran, and a flash of golden yellow.

I reached the museum's low front steps. Standing there watching me from under an umbrella the color of buttercups was a young woman.

"I hate to be the bearer of bad news. But the Fogg's closed Mondays."

Still breathing hard from my sprint, I shook my head. Rain the size of Tic Tacs was pelting me; water was leaking out of my hair and down the back of my neck. I rubbed a sopping shirtsleeve across my face.

She began to laugh, not unkindly. Against the gray stone building and storm-darkened sky her pale face gleamed like bone china.

"Sorry," she said after a while.

"It's okay."

"It's just that you're really, unbelievably wet."

Raising the umbrella a few inches higher, she offered me a place beside her.

I hesitated. Hazel eyes alive with amusement; a refined nose above a mouth of promising fullness; straight brown hair falling to the middle of her back; a body slender and lithe. I kept glancing at her, then down at the ground. She wore sandals and the hems of her jeans were frayed and her toenails unpainted and a sexy, glistening wash of spattered rain shone on the pale tops of her feet.

I stepped under the umbrella.

"Better, isn't it? Bring your bag under, too. Don't want your great thoughts getting wet."

Her irony was nimble, inviting. I lifted the flap of my stuffed book bag and showed her my inventory: *Party Systems and Voter Alignments* (5th ed., 1967); *A Theory of Parties and Electoral Systems* (1980); *Political Parties and the Modern State* (1984). A well-thumbed paperback of Bellow's *Seize the Day*.

Also the current issues of *Foreign Affairs* and the *Harvard Gazette*, a spiral notebook, five ballpoint pens, a fluorescent highlighter, and half a roll of Life Savers. Everything damp, of course, from the rain.

Reading the titles, she raised an eyebrow but said nothing.

"It's all right," I assured her. "This isn't the first conversation killed off by my interests."

"Oh, I'm pretty sure Bellow's never killed anybody," she said, "except maybe one or two of his ex-wives." She reached for the book. On the cover there was a black-and-white photograph of the back of a man's head, no face, just a hat visible, a pale fedora with a dark band, the hat tilted up in an angle of recognition or perhaps even of wonder at a skyscraper rising in the background. "*Seize the Day*'s not bad," she said, slipping the book back into the bag. "But you should be reading *Herzog*. The others—well, I'm sure they're fascinating."

I began to close the bag, then changed my mind. "Want a Life Saver?"

She cocked her head skeptically. "Depends on the flavor."

"Butter rum," I said.

Brightening, she nodded—a girlish bounce of her head that sent a thrill through me. I peeled the damp foil back so she could take one.

"I forgot how good these are." She was rolling the candy noisily around her tongue.

I stood watching her. Her simple but vivid pleasure had its own kind of pull. Oddly elated, I told her a story about my grandfather taking me to Central Park to play shuffleboard when I was a kid. His propensity to cheat had led him to ply me with butter rum Life Savers so I wouldn't tell my parents. It had worked. A tale I pursued until I became excruciatingly aware of the drone of my own voice. At which point I faded out.

"Your arm must be tired. Let me hold that for you."

Passing me the umbrella, her hand touched mine. Her fingers were cool with the moisture in the air. My gaze hurried over the unbuttoned area of her shirt (man's dark red oxford, worn untucked) yet still managed to get hopelessly stuck on the edge of her black bra.

In a voice of deceptive calm I asked about her field of study.

"What?" she said.

The rain was thunderous. I repeated the question, this time raising my voice practically to a shout.

Art history, she yelled back, first-year Ph.D. with particular interest in Burne-Jones and the Pre-Raphaelite painters. Then without warning she drew three fingers across my eyebrows and shook her hand, loose at the wrist, until the water that she'd lifted from my skin flew off her fingertips like sparks.

"Thank you."

"Don't mention it."

She turned to watch a car passing on the street, its windshield wipers working frantically to beat back the rain.

｜ ｜ ｜

Too soon it ended. It wasn't the great deluge after all, coupled beasts driven onto the hastily built ship to voyage for a lifetime. No, a mere spring shower experienced by two relative strangers.

She extended her hand out past the golden canopy, probing for renegade drops. Her shirt cuff drew back, exposing elegant ringless fingers and a very white wrist.

"Well," she said lightly, "that was certainly an adventure."

She was smiling. But it was a distant smile, as if the connection we'd just shared, however fateful or fortuitous, was finished now. She took the umbrella from my hand and began to furl it. She was getting ready to leave.

"I'm on my way to see a professor," I announced simply to keep her there. "I hope he has a towel."

"I'm sure he'll appreciate your tenacity. 'Neither rain, nor sleet . . .' How does it go?"

"I think that's for postmen."

She laughed, turning her face up to the sky. Just then the sun was breaking through the cloud cover, silvered rays brightening the pothole puddles of Union Street and the fat beads of water sitting like fake jewels on the hoods of parked cars.

"I have to go," she said.

"I'm Julian Rose," I blurted out, offering my hand.

"You're pretty good company in a storm, Julian Rose."

She held my hand for a couple of seconds. Then, a smile at the corners of her mouth, she let it go. She turned and descended the four steps to the sidewalk, where she paused, looking at me over her shoulder. Her expression had softened, and for a moment I thought she would come back.

"I'm Claire Marvel," she said casually. "I'm at Café Pamplona sometimes. Afternoons. I go there to read."

With that she turned and walked up the street. I watched until I couldn't see her anymore.

t w o

I HAD BEEN ON MY WAY to see Carl Davis, Sherbourne Professor of Government and Public Policy, during his office hours. Although I was in his lecture class on American political institutions, I'd never actually met the man whose brilliant reputation preceded him like the prow of a destroyer. It was my hope that afternoon to introduce myself and persuade him to advise me on my doctoral dissertation. As it was, because of the storm, I reached Littauer later than I'd hoped. The door to Professor Davis' office was closed, and filling the bench in the hallway were three graduate students from my department.

Mike Lewin, a thirty-year-old Brooklyn native obsessed with Joseph McCarthy, looked up from a new book on Hollywood's blacklist and muttered, "Hey. Raining out?" His reddish hair was shaggy, his jaw bristling with the wildfire beginnings of a beard. Beside him, pretending to ignore us, sat Parker Bing. An incongruous pairing, I thought. Bing was from Greenwich. His idea of political life belonged to that anachronistic age of WASP class-worship and finals-club "gentlemen" best exemplified by his heroes Acheson and Harriman. He wore hats and bow ties and sometimes even suspenders, which he insisted on calling "braces." Through connections he'd already had a three-month stint in the State Department and preferred to acknowledge only those colleagues he deemed likely to find similar advancement.

The third student was a slender woman from New Delhi named Dal. I'd heard she was a champion squash player.

The bench was full, so I took a seat on the floor. My three colleagues were all reading diligently. I pulled *Political Parties and the Modern State* from my shoulder bag and made an attempt to join them. But I couldn't concentrate. My damp khakis chafed against my thighs and Claire's yellow umbrella kept breaking into my thoughts. Beneath it I'd stood with her, the rain buffeting the thin sunlike carapace above our heads. Already it was hard to remember what had occurred. What had I actually said to her? Had her comment at the end been an invitation, or just a dodge?

"See you," mumbled Lewin, shuffling by. He'd already finished his meeting with Davis. I looked up to see Bing striding into the office and the door shutting behind him. Dal's glance met mine and I raised my eyebrows but she hastily lowered her eyes to her book, a tome called *Grassroots Nation*, leaving me stranded once again with my thoughts about Claire Marvel.

The odds weren't in my favor, I reckoned. Meeting her had been a freak occurrence, some weird twist of meteorological fate. I'd go on being myself—brain-channeled, sometimes awkward, sometimes amusing; occasionally, in moments as radiant and evanescent as soap bubbles, something more than just smart. But mainly safe. Safety lay not in numbers but in the assurance that where one has already walked no surprises can lurk. There was the future to think about. This was our creed. Among hard-core grad students in government romance was considered a questionable sideline. A muddy source to be handled with extreme circumspection, it might taint the waters of pure, wonkish ambition.

Bing emerged from Davis' office looking smug. He offered Dal a curt nod, as if permission to enter were his to bestow, then walked past me without a glance. Dal gathered her things. She was pretty and moved with an easy grace. She walked into the office, closing the door behind her.

There are men who feel handsome, I assume; perhaps, on occasion, even godlike. I was never one of them. It's not that I was necessarily unattractive—no one had ever called me that. But neither had I ever felt myself the object of a woman's delighted aesthetic scrutiny, her unmistakable, unassailable desire. My girlfriends in the past had been few and far between and willfully indifferent to my physical presence. Or they'd been mentally absent, perpetually immersed in their weekly planners, seminars, and fencing classes. A condition which I with my innate cautiousness had always accepted and reciprocated, perhaps even understood.

I wasn't particularly athletic or strong. My body came in at just under six feet, a hundred and sixty pounds. My skin was a Semitic shade of pale olive. My short dark-brown hair parted quietly to the left. My eyes were brown and spaced widely to either side of a medium-to-large nose that, given old photographs of certain relatives on my mother's side, had to be considered something of a blessing. I had nice hands, my grandmother used to assure me, with long pianist's fingers; though musical talent had not accompanied this gift.

No, I thought, I wouldn't be going to Café Pamplona. It wasn't an invitation. There was enough potential disappointment in any given day without the need to add to the risks. Beauties like her—women with extravagant umbrellas—were inevitably, biologically engineered to seek out beauty in their mates. And so she would. Me, I'd play the odds. And the odds said No way. This wasn't habit, I tried to assure myself, just sound reasoning.

"Julian."

I looked up. Dal was standing there, serene, exotic.

"Should I go in?"

"I'd talk fast if I were you," she said in a bored voice. "He kept looking at his watch."

three

WHAT FLASHED THROUGH MY BRAIN as I heard the deep-voiced "Come in" and entered the spacious office with the cherry-wood desk and mahogany rocking chair were the old photographs I'd often seen reproduced in magazines of a youthful, strapping Ronald Reagan on his Santa Barbara ranch—splitting wood, mending fences, riding the range. Professor Davis was standing by the window. Of course I'd seen him many times in lecture, where he was known for speaking in Churchillian fashion for two hours without notes. But here in the intimate confines of his office he seemed altogether more imposing. Not quite fifty, tall—like his hero and "friend," the actor-cum-president, he possessed broad square shoulders and large powerful hands. He favored suits rather than the usual professorial tweeds. His salt-and-pepper hair was impressively full, his brows two thick brushstrokes made by a supremely confident artist. Behind rimless glasses his eyes were a piercing blue. And he had a leader's nose: meaty yet straight, with a hawkish boldness that on a man of less defined character might have been a cartoon.

He glanced at his watch. "Are you the last?"

"Yes, sir."

"Good. I have a plane to catch soon. In the meantime we'll talk. Have a seat. That's a Kennedy rocker, by the way. Don't worry, I won't hold it against you."

It was a joke, I figured, however tepid; but he didn't smile and so neither did I. I sat on the rocker. For himself he took a wooden armchair emblazoned with a faded Harvard insignia.

"Professor Davis . . ." I began.

"You're in my class," he interrupted, scrutinizing me with sharp eyes.

"Yes. I'm—"

"Don't tell me." His brow creased, the verticals deeply etched. "Rose. Something Rose. Am I right?"

I stared at him, not sure whether to feel flattered or alarmed. "Julian."

"What?"

"Julian," I repeated a bit louder.

"That's it. Charlie Dixon mentioned you to me. I'm looking for a research assistant. Is that why you're here?"

"Actually—"

"My last one was a disaster. Thought he was a young Voltaire." He scrutinized me again, as if I'd just that moment walked into the room. "You always sit on the left. Correct?"

"Yes, sir."

"Same seat. Don't tell me it's superstition—I don't believe in magic. Did you know Dixon recommended you to me? You did some noteworthy research for him, I believe."

I nodded. "For his book on Teddy Roosevelt and the election of 1912. Just the final section, the part dealing with the Progressive Party platform—direct senatorial elections, woman's suffrage, reduction of the tariff, the social reforms. That kind of thing. Actually, Professor Davis—"

"Have you read the whole book? Because Dixon sent me a copy last month, hot off the press, and I've had a look-through. Strictly between us, I think it's soft."

"Soft?"

"Don't worry, I don't mean you. Old Charlie's been castrated by his Liberal desires. This isn't serious political scholarship. Show Dixon a big fat government program—a sinkhole for the taxpayers' money—and what he sees is the proverbial tree of caring. Christ, all the man wants to do is hug it. TR would've taken the big stick to him in a heartbeat."

"Roosevelt saved quite a few trees himself," I couldn't keep from pointing out. "Proverbial or not."

"It's not the saving I necessarily object to, it's the hugging," Davis said. "I'm all for saving—the Constitution, that is. Remember: Conservative stands for conservation. You're not some hugging Liberal, are you?"

There was a faint, appraising smile on his face but the voice underneath was hard as pavement. He was looking at me as if measuring me for a suit or a coffin.

"I'm a Democrat," I answered. "But I don't hug."

"You've got balls, then?"

"I like to think so."

Davis' smile broadened slightly, and for the first time in his presence I felt myself relax.

"You want the job?"

"You're offering it to me?"

"I am. On a trial basis, of course."

"Of course. Yes, absolutely, I want the job."

"Good."

There was a pause. I breathed out, glanced around. Behind Davis, between two windows gloried with timeless views of the Law School, there was a wall of photographs of himself with various kings of the Republican establishment: two with Reagan, three with Meese, one each with Weinberger and Shultz. Several had been taken on a golf course. I'd heard it said that his friendship with Meese, which dated back to Reagan's failed '76 presidential campaign, was the key to Davis' career. Early in Reagan's first term he'd used his pull with the attorney general to gain access to the inner circle of the president's unofficial policy advisors—where, by all accounts, he remained. He spent two days a week in or around the White House. His Conservative politics I sincerely disagreed with, but his talent and success I felt compelled to admire.

"Actually, Professor Davis, I was hoping I might be able to talk to you about my dissertation as well."

"There'll be plenty of time for that." He looked at his watch again and rose from his chair. "Let me see. It's 4:17. At 7:30 I have to be dressed for dinner at the Jefferson Hotel. The attorney general will be there. What odds do you give me of making it?"

"Slim to none."

He smiled with evident self-satisfaction and I saw that I'd just walked into his punch line. "That's the problem with you Liberals," he said. "No vision."

"Better blind than wrong," I shot back.

He paused; behind his glasses his eyes appeared to harden to sapphires. I waited with half-caught breath to see where my tongue had landed me.

Finally, he reached out and laid a hand on my shoulder. "I have a car waiting outside," he said in an avuncular tone. "Ride with me to the airport and we can talk details."

four

HE WANTED TO MEET AGAIN at the end of the week, following his return from Washington. There was a book he was
writing for Random House, currently titled *Congress and the
Constitution*, and a possible memoir. He'd be lunching at the
Faculty Club Friday but would have an hour free in the afternoon. Let's meet for coffee, he said. I asked him where and
with a challenge in his eye he told me to choose the place. My
first test.

Café Pamplona wasn't at all the sort of place to take someone like Davis; not if you wanted to impress; not if you had an
ounce of sense. It was a hangout for Euros and would-be Euros dressed in black. A certain Left Bank cool, not power, was
the currency there. He would hate it on sight.

I arrived an hour early. A Spanish-style café vaguely Moorish in decoration, low-ceilinged and cramped, down a few steps from the street. The narrow ground-level windows were all sealed shut and the air was thick with cigarette smoke. The round marble-topped tables were occupied by dark-clothed bodies and pale faces, Claire's not among them. For three days I'd been unable to stop thinking about her. Now I found a spot in the corner, ordered a cappuccino, and sat watching the entrance, vividly imagining the moment when she might walk through the door and see me and break into a huge smile. Ridiculous, of course. Foolish, idiotic . . . still, I sat watching.

There was plenty of time. Time to study an odd kidney-shaped puddle of water left on my table by the previous occupant; time to consider the question of my dissertation and how I should present myself to Davis.

He arrived promptly on the hour. His entrance made the café smaller. It was his legacy to leave others with a diminished personal landscape yet still with some unarticulated sense of the heightened possibility of their lives. Today his suit was navy blue and his tie yellow. He might have been a CEO or even the Gipper himself. He approached my table refusing to bow to the architecture, his head passing just inches beneath the nicotine-stained ceiling. Handing me a legal folder of impressive girth, he declared, "My manuscript," and eased himself into a chair.

"Fifty percent done. I thought you should read what's there before we move ahead."

The waiter sidled over. Davis ordered a double espresso

and requested that the table be cleaned; with a swipe of cloth, the puddle disappeared.

He took a look around. "Quite a little hellhole you've got here," he said amicably.

I grinned with relief.

He told me more about the book he was writing. Even by historical standards, he argued, the Democrat-controlled Congress was overreaching in its attempts to thwart the president. All this smoke-and-mirrors bullshit about Iran-Contra was nothing but an excuse, he declared. A certain amount of partisanship was fine and expected, a product of human nature; but there was this slip of paper called the Constitution. We finally had a man in the White House who honored it and understood the ways in which it was designed to keep America strong. The current Congress wasn't simply *against* Ronald Reagan, it was intent on distorting the literal words and institutional prerogatives expressed in the Constitution in order to bring him to his knees. His book, Davis claimed, contained a timely historical analysis of such irresponsible legislative gamesmanship and a powerful argument against it.

He sat back, his face etched with certainty. I finished my cappuccino and dabbed at my mouth with a paper napkin. I was seeing, far more clearly than I had at our first meeting, the huge gulf that separated our political beliefs and our views of the world.

He seemed to be waiting for me to comment and so I did.

"One could also argue that it's the president and his self-aggrandized view of executive power that's out to bring Congress to *its* knees," I said.

Davis stared at me until a willowy flutter of doubt ran up my insides.

"Now listen," he snapped. "We don't have to agree on all the details. But we have to come together on the basic principles. *My* principles, to be precise. Otherwise, you understand, the deal's off."

"I understand."

"And do we agree on those principles, Julian?"

I hesitated. Looking at him, weighing the possibilities. Envisioning my father's disappointment had he been witness to this moment. Disappointment not at the squandering of professional opportunity but rather at the unseemly desire to sell out. Though with characteristic reticence he would have abstained from passing explicit judgment on me.

Then I told my new mentor what he wanted to hear.

"Good." Davis swallowed the last of his espresso and checked his watch. "So tell me a little about yourself."

I looked away. Through the closed windows I saw the disembodied legs of people walking in both directions. I thought how badly I'd wanted Claire to witness my collegial meeting with Professor Carl Davis of Harvard and Washington, and a mist of shame briefly clouded the bright vision of my future.

"I'm from New York," I said. "After Columbia I spent two years working at the Council on Foreign Relations. Then I came here."

"Right. Dixon told me." Davis' tone had turned buoyant; he seemed relieved to have gotten through the preliminaries and was eager now to close any gaps between us. "You must have studied with Gordon Klein at Columbia," he said.

"He was my thesis advisor. And I took his course 'Legislating Freedom.' "

"Gordon and I go back thirty years. He's my son Peter's godfather." Davis' expression was confidential. This minor personal connection we happened to share was significant to him. In an easier, more welcoming tone of voice he inquired, "How old are you?"

"Twenty-six."

"Peter's a bit younger." He paused, regarding me with an almost paternal eye. "The other day in my office you mentioned your dissertation."

I nodded.

"Tell me about it."

I cleared my throat. "I intend to deal with various incarnations of the Progressive Party, their consequences and significance," I began. "The elections of 1912, '24, and '48. Especially '48, with Wallace running for president—this time challenging the Democrats, not the Republicans. He gets endorsed by the Communists and the American Labor Party, attacks Truman for not working with the Soviets to end the Cold War, argues for repeal of Taft-Hartley and the reestablishment of wartime price controls. Political suicide, right? Still, a million votes in the general election made clear that without the Progressives there was no way in the world Truman would've made it by Dewey. Then the whole thing went bust. The Progressive Party more or less evaporated. Where'd the voters go? That's what I want to get at. A million people isn't small change. Professor Davis, I want to write about the continuing presence of a legitimate third-party political movement in

America, an invisible, shifting group of voters that's been waiting in the wings for forty years, looking for a viable option. The
spring below the surface. I want to shine a light on that force
and its long-term political consequences."

I sat back, breathing hard.

"Interesting," said Davis. "I think you might be onto
something. . . ."

His tone seemed truly encouraging; a prospective protégé
could have hoped for nothing more. It was his attention I'd
lost, perhaps some time ago. He was staring past me, toward
the entrance, and he was utterly absorbed in what he saw. I
turned to follow his gaze. And so I discovered that while I'd
been talking Claire Marvel had entered the café and stood,
now, just inside the door.

five

"WELL, IF IT ISN'T JULIAN OF THE STORM."

She was dressed as she'd been four days ago—sandals and faded blue jeans and an untucked cotton shirt. Though she was even more beautiful than I remembered. I stood up as if hauled by the collar.

To Davis she said, "Your friend and I had the pleasure of meeting in a tempest. He was nothing short of heroic."

"What she means is she let me stand under her umbrella."

"I can think of worse places to be," murmured Davis.

He was looking at her intently, a faint smile working the corners of his mouth. With an odd feeling of reluctance I made the introduction. "Professor Davis, this is Claire Marvel."

He rose and took her hand. "A pleasure."

"You're Julian's professor?"

"I am. And now, I guess you could say, employer."

"Really," Claire said with a raised eyebrow; with a start I realized she was teasing him. "Are you somebody famous?" she went on in a jesting tone. "Should I know you?"

"Only if your world is politics and government." Davis' voice had assumed a grave rhetorical modesty.

"Do you consider art political?" A challenging smile had come to her lips.

"Not in any legitimate sense, no," Davis replied.

"Then we come from separate worlds."

"In that case I suppose it's my good fortune to meet you under any circumstances," Davis said with a smile of his own. He checked his watch and laid a five-dollar bill on the table. "Now if you'll excuse me, I'm afraid I have a meeting. Julian, if your choice of female company is any indication, you have a brilliant future ahead of you. In the meantime read the manuscript and get back to me. I'd like to push ahead full throttle on this thing. And with regard to the dissertation, the answer is yes."

"Thank you, Professor Davis."

"Carl. Don't thank me. Just work your ass off and make us both look like winners. Please excuse my French, Miss Marvel."

"I always excuse the French, Professor Davis."

A look of admiring astonishment fleetingly crossed his face. Then he got hold of himself and, remembering to check his watch a last time, took his leave.

We stared after him; he was one of those men who seemed to leave a wake. When he was gone we sat back down.

"An ego the size of Wyoming," was Claire's facetious verdict. "Yet weirdly charming. I take it from his comment about art he's not exactly a lefty?"

"Let's just say he counts Ed Meese as one of his closest friends."

"And you set him straight?"

"He's the one who generally does most of the talking."

"That's not how it looked. I watched you delivering your pitch. Very impressive hand gestures."

"I was telling him about my dissertation. You make it sound like an act."

"Not an act. I'm just making a distinction between mind and body." She reached for my hands, which were resting on the table. Her touch made the hairs on my arms stand up. "I'd trust these hands," she said.

Her gaze was direct. I couldn't imagine hiding, even if I'd wanted to.

"You're blushing," she said. "Are you always so easily embarrassed?"

I didn't answer. With an apologetic smile she released my hands. After what I hoped was a dignified interval, I removed them to the safety of my lap.

The waiter appeared bearing a mug of peppermint tea and a large chocolate chip cookie. "Lunch," explained Claire. It was three in the afternoon. She put a piece of cookie on the table in front of me and took a bite herself, chewing slowly.

"How old were you when you first became interested in politics?" she asked.

"Political science," I replied. "There's a difference—I'm not out to become president." I ate the piece of cookie. "I was twelve," I said.

"Twelve? Shouldn't you have been out playing stickball?"

"I wasn't any good at sports. Stickball included."

"Chess, then. Or looking after your pet rock."

"I wasn't cool enough to have a pet rock."

"Seriously," she said.

"I'm being serious. Something happened when I was twelve. Something that got me interested in the meaning of politics and the political system in people's lives."

"Something to do with a girl?"

"At twelve? In my dreams."

She was leaning forward, listening. So against my better instincts I went on. I told her the strange unfashioned truth: that the way in for me—the witch in the wardrobe—was model rocketry. I'd been hooked at an early age. The whole shebang: Sputnik, NASA, Yuri Gagarin, Glenn and Armstrong. Then a minor home-equipment malfunction, a run-in with the police, a memorable old woman from Budapest. And so, ta-dum, was the course of my life changed.

I glanced up: she was still listening. So I went on. I told her how at age twelve and a half, with money saved from a year's worth of allowances and odd jobs, I bought an eighteen-inch balsa-wood rocket from a catalogue. I built and painted this interplanetary vehicle in absolute secrecy—everything geared toward a big spring launch out my bedroom window. The building across the street was a few stories lower than ours. And my plan—simple yet daring—was to aim the rocket above the opposite roofline so that after blastoff it would arc over all obstacles in its path and end up drifting down into the Hudson River on its little built-in parachute.

I told her how, after weeks of prep, the big day arrived. A clear day with no wind; perfect conditions such as have stirred entire nations as they sit watching history made on their television sets. Careful not to fall out, I opened my bedroom window as far as it would go and aimed the launching pad. Then I lit the fuses and jumped back to watch from behind a chair. The fuses went squirreling rapidly up into the rocket like Roman candles—then a double explosion, and the rocket blasted out the window! My sense of triumph was indescribable—until I saw what was actually happening. The explosions hadn't been simultaneous. The first had jolted the nose to the left; then the counterforce of the second had depressed the altitude. Now the rocket was flying directly toward the building across the street at warp speed. The noise, meanwhile, had brought people to their windows. Mostly old folks and housewives. It was afternoon. One old woman in particular was looking out her window on the sixth floor and observed what she thought was a flaming, heat-seeking missile zooming right for her heart. She began to scream. Who could blame her? She screamed so much one of her neighbors called the police. She was still screaming when the rocket crashed into the building just above her window and dropped, smoking, into the window box of pansies that, it turned out, was her pride and joy. It also turned out—all this my parents learned later from the policeman who interrogated me—that this woman was a Jew from Budapest who somehow had managed to survive the war, the Holocaust, and countless other tragedies and degradations; who decades ago had made it to America and the Upper West Side, wife of a camp survivor, the mother of two and grandmother of three, and, recently, a widow; who loved her neighborhood and the lox at Zabar's and her window box of pansies with the kind of fervor and gratitude that can come only through a lifetime of suffering.

"Oh no," said Claire.

That wasn't all, I said. About a month afterward I spotted the woman on Broadway, outside Fairway. She was small and hunched, with a face so wrinkled that the sum of it all was a kind of radiance: from out of this thicket of tortured history her eyes, brown and deep-set, took in everything that moved. Her shopping bags she pushed slowly down the sidewalk in a wheeled wire basket. I followed for a couple of blocks, trying to gather my nerve to approach her. Not far from her building I overtook her, told her who I was and what I'd done. For some time she stood sizing me up with those eyes that had seen much of the worst that human beings have to offer. Finally with a nod she said, "You may push, if you like." And so, pushing her shopping cart, I went home with her. Into her building, up the elevator: she said not a word until we were standing outside her apartment in a hallway that smelled of cooked cabbage and vinegar. "You may come in, if you like." And I went in: a railroad flat, long and narrow, stained with shadows like resin, one room leading into another, depressing, yet also homey, full of things—books, black-and-white photographs, stuffed pillows, candles stuck in dried pools of wax, many things I couldn't even name. At the back the kitchen. She made tea with spoonfuls of jam in it and gave me three small chocolate rugelach to eat.

"After that, I went back to see her fairly often," I told Claire. "Some days her joints were so bad it could take her five minutes just to sit down. In Budapest before the war she'd studied piano and had a dachschund named Gustav. She never gave a thought to history or politics. But in New York she became an exemplary citizen. She read the newspapers cover to cover and knew the names of every local politician and never missed a chance to vote. The next November she asked me to take her to the polling station. By then she already needed help getting around. She was in the booth a long time. When she came out I saw she'd been crying. I asked if she was all right. She said, 'One day you'll know how important this is.'"

I stopped talking. A knot of grief had lodged in my throat. I was surprised, all of a sudden, to discover other people in the room, conversations, the hazy drift of smoke; a man with a terrier on his lap; a woman dealing a deck of tarot cards.

"What happened to her?" Claire asked.

"One day I came home from school and there was an ambulance in front of her building."

＊　＊　＊

Outside, there on the curve of Bow Street, we stood close, breathing the same fresh air, feeling the warmth of sunlight on our faces. Spring. My thoughts reeled. Was this the same person I'd met only days ago?

Claire plucked a bit of brown fuzz from my cotton sweater; it floated to the ground like a minuscule toupee.

"Here we are," she said, "on this beautiful afternoon."

A faint smile infused her face with the inward light of a dream. Then, raising her eyes to mine, she kissed me on the mouth. An explosion of heat—I shivered as though burned and half turned away to gather myself.

"Julian Rose," she murmured into my ear. "What are you thinking?"

I turned back to face her. Ready, now; such terror, I was discovering, had very nearly the same effect as courage.

This time the Fogg was open. Past the security desk (the portly middle-aged guard greeted Claire by name) we entered the roofed central courtyard of the museum: an Italian palazzo with monastic impulses, resplendent yet austere—dark mahogany benches, arched colonnades through which the galleries could be reached.

I followed her across the courtyard, under a stone arch, and into a small, square gallery lined with nineteenth-century British pictures.

She said, "He grew up in Birmingham. Never saw a great painting till he was a teenager. At Oxford he met William Morris. Then at twenty-six, on Ruskin's dime, he took his first trip to Italy. He'd never imagined such beauty. When he finally saw it he stopped being afraid of failure in himself."

Before a large gold-and-sepia-toned watercolor she halted. A plaque at the bottom of the frame said, *Sir Edward Coley Burne-Jones—1863—Love Bringing Alcestis Back from the Grave.*

Two women in golden robes were arranged in close proximity—Alcestis on the right, head bent slightly, eyes glittering as though bejeweled, gaze angled toward the ethereal winged goddess who is leading her back from the underworld. Love's wings were diaphanous, delicately outlined in blue. A shell like a blood-red scallop rested above her left breast. And though she faced ahead her gaze was visibly focused off to the side, away from Alcestis, into a middle distance.

"Maybe Love is looking at the husband," Claire speculated quietly. "Maybe he's waiting there just offstage for his wife, who sacrificed her life for him. Missing her so much that he can hardly stand to wait another minute. We'll never know. But that's what I think."

She paused. As she'd been speaking her face, her whole body, had taken on a melancholy aspect that I had not seen in her before; her head was bowed and her shoulders slumped. A long minute of silence ensued. Then an echo of footsteps and voices reached us from the courtyard, pulling her out of her reverie, and with sudden intensity she continued.

"Ruskin bought it and lectured on it at the Royal Institution in 1867. He described it as having a 'classical tranquility and repose,' and he was right. But that's not why I fell in love with it. I fell in love with it because it's beautiful and the husband's not in it. He's invisible, everywhere and nowhere. You feel his sadness and hope and waiting permeating the picture—the way love permeates things in real life. It's sad and beautiful. The women are like two stories that have come together on a journey to tell a single story, and even though we think we know how it's supposed to end, there's a mystery in their differences that makes us wonder. I believe in that."

She was silent again. Not an echo penetrated the invisible walls that her words had built around our place in front of the canvas. And yet I was still hearing her voice. It was inexplicable. As if listening to her I had turned over a beautiful painting in the museum of my heart; and found on its reverse side, hidden from the world's cold gaze by no more than a fragile deception, another painting, more original than the first, more mysterious, and far more beautiful, at least to me.

MY EYES OPENED. There was a taste like a spent dream in my mouth and a net of shadows on the ceiling. A street-lamp's careless light spilled around the edges of the window blind.

Questions. Where was I? Whose room? I lay as if dead. Until after a long moment's drop into the void, a cupboard creaked open in my mind and the hours just passed with her came tumbling out—

The arched footbridge between Dunster House and the Business School. Late afternoon. We stand at the center as a Boston Whaler passes underneath, casting the brown water of the Charles into shivering waves. The owners' lily-white arms

waving, fists holding cans of Miller Lite, Steely Dan on the
boom box singing "My Old School," raucous shouts and frat-
boy challenges—I hold Claire's hand as if to protect her from
something, though I have no idea what. The boat skims away.
Joggers and bicyclists on the riverbank path, rush-hour traffic
on Memorial Drive. The sun by now huge, low, nearly gone. I
am still holding her hand as we stroll beneath haloed streetlights far up Kirkland Street to her apartment. Even my own
sense of credulity is strained by these events. Yet it contin-
ues, we aren't finished here, she emerges from a closet-sized
kitchen with glasses and bottle. "The good news about the
champagne is it's French," she announces. "The bad news is
it only cost six bucks." Then, glasses charged, we sit together
on the russet-colored flea-market sofa with the Balinese
sarong draped over the back. She tells me that a great-aunt
on her mother's side was Danish and that as everybody knows
the Danes are blessed with a gift for the art of toasting; a
gift that has come down to her (the only thing of any worth,
Claire insists in a calm yet bitter aside, that has passed
through the maternal line of her family) in the form of this
toast, now, between the two of us. Whereby, led by her murmured instructions, we raise our glasses and without ever
breaking eye contact stare at each other over the rims saying,
"Skoal, dear Julian"; "Skoal, dear Claire." And that is the whole
of it.

  And I can't say why or how, but to me these stilted, formal
phrases sound like ancient invocations; vows that must at
all costs be kept. And every brilliant idea I've ever had has
begun to fail me; one by one I watch them drop from my

grasp until I am bereft, without recourse or plan. It feels like freedom. I lean forward and kiss her. The moment passes between us like a current. She tilts back, her face close, her fingers buried in my hair. Already her eyes have begun to lose focus. We kiss again—and now as she pulls away I see in the dim light of the room that her eyes are opaque pearls of brown and green and gold. And that sound in the air—whispered, urgent, permanent, in a voice familiar and strange—is her name, and I am calling it.

She was looking at me, her head propped on her hand, her hair an aura, darkly luminous, around the shining depths of her eyes.

"He wakes."

Her voice was hushed, dusky; it must have been three or four in the morning. The same sheet that partially covered me snaked around her legs, ending at her hip. A wash of stray light the color of antique brass glowed on the curve of her exposed skin.

"Hello," she murmured. "You look kind of stunned."

"I guess I'm not used to being watched while I sleep."

"By anyone?"

"By you," I said.

Tipping her head forward, she kissed me. "Thank you for saying that. Are you feeling all right?"

I reached out and brushed the hair from her face. "Better than all right."

She smiled, a match struck, vanquishing shadows. I sat

back against the wall, the sheet slipping below my waist. I began to pull it up but she stayed my hand.

"Wait. Don't I get to look?"

I lay back, trying not to think too much—a fantasy condensed into a moment that was also an eternity, her hand resting halfway up my left thigh. Seconds and minutes. Hours. Already thinking too much. How was it possible that this was still the same day? How was it conceivable that I was where I now found myself? Whose hand was this? Too many blessings. Enough to make a habitually wary and skeptical man afraid, this sudden altering, for no logical reason, of the accepted laws of the universe.

"Okay," she said lightly. "That was a treat."

I was silent. But I did not cover myself again with the sheet.

Then it was my turn. She sat up and the sheet fell away. Her naked body, lithe yet full, absorbed the room's shadowed refractions until she was burnished. The time passed too quickly.

She reached down for the bottle of champagne on the floor. "There's an inch left."

"I don't need it," I said.

"There's need and there's want." She poured the last of the champagne for herself and set the bottle down.

"I can't help it," she continued. "My father taught me never to waste."

At the mention of her father her voice seemed to lose altitude.

"Well, mine taught me never to be the first person to clap

after a performance," I said. Then I paused, staring at the shadows on the ceiling, caught in the undertow of an old, unnameable sadness. "He has a problem with being noticed."

Pressing her hand against my cheek, Claire brought her lips to my ear and whispered, "It's too late for you. You know that, don't you? You've already been noticed."

seven

In the morning she was gone.

My head was pounding from the champagne. The apartment was quiet. For the first time I observed her room. Around the tattered window shade daylight edged in, yellowed as though dirty; there was a poster in French of *The 400 Blows*; the sheet was in a tangled knot at the foot of the bed. I lay in a state of foggy rumination. Suddenly anxious, I raised myself onto my elbows—but my throbbing head was a painful distraction. I eased it back onto the pillow. It was Saturday, I seemed to recall. Soon I was asleep.

When I woke next, the headache was less severe; the light in the room was more white than yellow; the air was hot.

During the night, I remembered, she'd fallen asleep with her head on my chest; against my cheek her hair was a dream of softness, granted to me while awake. Her breathing slowed, then evened, as she dove into the depths of herself, taking me with her. A gift of some kind, I somehow understood. And yet I could feel myself resisting. Years of habit: even as a boy I'd been no good at receiving gifts, never seemed able, like my sister, to appreciate a gesture of pure feeling without subjecting it to some awkward form of scrutiny. Guilt and a convoluted practicality had been my watchwords. At eighteen, opening a birthday present from my mother—a leather-bound set of *The Decline and Fall of the Roman Empire* that had belonged to John F. Kennedy during his Harvard years—I thoughtlessly told her that she shouldn't have done it, it was too expensive. To which my mother, her eyes black with hurt, replied bitterly that if that was how I felt she would take the books back. Which she did. I never saw that set of Gibbon again. Presumably it was resold, and so it became the quiet pleasure of somebody with a bigger heart than mine to run his hand over the same gilt-edged pages that the future president had fingered. In my past were other stories like this—in which, one step removed from the emotional truth of the moment, I had misread another person's loving intentions. Perhaps had my own nature been as vivid to me as the historical figures in books, I might have gained some insight into my condition sooner. As it was, resting in Claire's bed with her head on my chest, for once I felt convinced of the lifelong cowardice of my doubts. Here she was, hardly knowing me at all. Why should her reasons matter? Her trust—unfathomable to me— was to give herself to sleep in my arms. My trust was to remain awake, never losing sight of her, never wanting to.

Slowly now I sat up in bed. A new day. I was myself again, and alone. To my night with Claire I had brought a host of ignorant suspicions about the relative accountability of the heart, both hers and mine—all of which returned now in force.

I dressed, opened the bedroom door, and was hit in the face by a wall of daylight. My hands flew to my eyes to cut the glare.

"You must be Julian," said a husky voice. "I'm Kate Daniels. Claire's roommate."

I blinked, fighting to see into the living room: a tall, muscular woman with Slavic cheekbones and clear blue eyes was sitting on the sofa, surrounded by sections of the *Boston Globe*. Her short blond hair had a greenish tint. She wore denim shorts and a V-neck T-shirt and her feet were bare.

"It's almost noon. I was starting to worry you might be dead. Want some coffee? There's a pot in the kitchen."

"No thanks."

"Claire's gone. She left a note. She was sorry."

"What happened?"

"A message from Alan. Her father's had some bad news. She had to get to Stamford right away."

I was silent. And perhaps it was my expression but Kate's attitude toward me softened visibly. Pity, followed by an almost imperceptible sigh. As if she'd just realized that I wasn't the usual overnight guest, no Lothario, just a tourist who without guidebook or common sense had stumbled blindly into the wrong country and now must be handled with diplomatic compassion.

"Alan's her brother," she explained patiently. "Twenty-

eight, five years older than Claire, lives in San Francisco.
Stamford's where they're from. Her father owns a car dealership there."

"Did her note say anything about when she might be
back?"

Kate shook her head.

"Could you give me a phone number there, Kate? I'd really
appreciate it."

"Sorry." This wasn't the same thing as saying she didn't
have it, I was meant to understand.

I looked away. Through a half-open door a glimpse into the
second bedroom: a crimson-and-black gym bag sitting atop a
trimly made double bed. Kate's room. I knew nothing about
this place or the people who lived in it.

"I'm going to get my things," I said.

I retreated into Claire's room, shutting the door after me.
Silence once more. My head was throbbing again and a nausea that might have been no more than regret was eddy-
ing around my gut. I sat down on the bed. On the floor at my
feet were tokens of our night together: the black knot of her
panties; her velvet hair ribbon; the empty bottle of champagne.

I found my shoes and put them on, careful how I moved.

When I came out again Kate was standing just beyond the
bedroom door.

"You seem like a nice guy, so I'll level with you. Her dad's
just been diagnosed with lung cancer. They're really close
and she's going to be devastated. You should know that heading in."

I brushed past her. "Thanks for everything."

"I'm not finished," Kate said. "She's my best friend. I adore her. But I still don't have a fucking clue what she's going to do from one day to the next. That's how she is. I just wouldn't want you to have any illusions about how it's all going to turn out. For your own sake."

I turned and looked at her. "I appreciate the concern. But I wouldn't worry about my having illusions."

eight

SO IT BEGAN. Life without her. A week without word from her
became two. Then three. Exams cast a general hush over the
college, followed by commencement and reunions; a conflagration of human noise and heat. Then silence once more over
the campus and the Square, the flames of euphoria fading
quickly into exhaustion and a swampy nostalgia. The under-
grads went home.

When I had tried to reach Claire through a Connecticut
operator I was told that the Stamford number for Marvel was
unlisted and by law could not be given out; she was sorry. Not
as sorry as I was, I told her.

Imagine being offered a rare delicacy the like of which you
believe you'll never have the opportunity to taste again.

Wouldn't such a condition overcharge the senses, warp the stakes of feeling? Force you to taste with an unhealthy, perhaps crippling expectation of fulfillment? Wouldn't, afterward, memory be called forth with a distorted sense of urgency?

To remember the taste. To never forget. To know the taste with a certainty that could never be taken from you.

In which case, if you were someone like me, you might berate yourself for having foolishly, hungrily desired the taste in the first place. You might, in the days and weeks following your first and only night with a woman named Claire Marvel—days and weeks during which the phone doesn't ring and the mail delivers nothing but the usual crap and the ache around your heart that originally felt like a premonition is gradually solidifying into a steel-lined bomb shelter—you might just conclude that you'd made a terrible mistake. Might grow desperately angry. Might try to forget, get back to square one, to the impossible zero (discounting, of course, Zeno's Paradox), where for more than twenty-five years you'd been living peacefully, if not always happily, in studied oblivion of any tastes whatsoever.

Before her.

I threw myself into my work.

My undergraduate teaching was finished for the year; all my attention turned to Professor Davis' work in progress. Three hundred and seventy-five pages of undeniably lucid conservative ideology hammered out in a prose notable for its frequent use of the first-person singular, as well as its unshakable confidence in its own historical significance.

I read it twice. On the first pass I wrote my comments on a legal pad accompanied by corresponding page numbers and bibliographical references. On the second I winnowed my queries down to ten and transferred them to yellow Post-it notes which I inserted into the manuscript. As I saw it at the time, my job was to appear politically savvy and intellectually scrupulous in Davis' eyes without causing him either to doubt my loyalty or to balk at what he might perceive as impertinence. It seemed to me that a few critical notes would be more palatable to him than dozens. So, as agreed upon, I crafted my brief observations in such a way as to almost entirely suppress any evidence of my own feelings about the subject at hand.

My work was well received.

Summer. Clear, hot days, everyone down by the river—rowers and lovers, pedants and geriatrics, mothers with babies. Animals to the water hole and the whole human parade.

In the long, slowly cooling evenings I sat with my landlady, Mary Watson, in the front garden of her rambling Brattle Street house. My apartment was on the second floor, with its own entrance. Occasionally Mary and I would pass an hour or so together at the end of the day, reading in companionable silence as her obese Blue Persian waddled mewling at our feet on a leash.

"Misha's just like a little dog," she observed one fair evening in late June. Her voice was old New England, singsongy on the vowels. It wasn't the first time she'd offered such an opinion.

"Dogs can be trained," I said.

"Don't be narrow-minded, Julian. Misha *chooses* to ignore us. It's a sign of his independence and self-possession."

"Some of the world's biggest despots are known for their independence and self-possession, Mary."

"Now you're being ridiculous. Come here, Misha dear. Come to Mother."

Lurching forward, Misha threw himself against Mary's purple stockings and began aggressively rubbing. His purring, amplified within his capacious belly, was deep and undulating in rhythm.

"I've always found feline mating rituals fascinating," I said.

Mary sniffed. "Don't be cruel. Misha's testicles were removed ages ago. It was a trauma I'm sure he doesn't wish to revisit."

I bowed my head. "Apologies to Misha."

"I will relay them." She stroked the cat's obscenely arched back. "See what a little dear he is? Gus, there you are. I was beginning to worry."

Gus Tolland, in his seventies, dressed in a sage-green high-waisted suit of a bygone era, emerged from the house carrying a tray with a martini shaker and two glasses. A widower himself, he'd been the best friend of Mary's husband. They'd been together now—drinking martinis, watching *Hill Street Blues* and *Dynasty*, and taking semiannual trips to Europe—for more than a decade.

"Sure you won't have a drink, Julian?"

"No thanks, Gus."

He set the tray down on the low iron table and began

pouring the clear diamondlike liquid evenly into the glasses. He spoke with a mild lisp and walked with a slight limp. His real life, Gus liked to say, began not on Beacon Hill, where he'd been born into a prosperous Boston family, but in France, where during the last months of the war he'd ended up playing clarinet in an Army band led by a gifted young jazz pianist named Dave Brubeck. They'd performed for the troops all over the European front; once they'd even opened for the Andrews Sisters. A lean introspective boy in youth, the war had woken in Gus appetites and joys he'd sensed in himself but never officially recognized. And now, decades later, with so much behind him, it was his privilege to have a martini and let his thoughts wander back: the band, on their way to a gig, getting lost in the Ardennes behind enemy lines; the jamming with Brubeck on the back of a truck otherwise filled with chickens. The girls! It was a piano, leaned on by the formidable derrière of a woman from Nantes, that had rolled over his foot and given him the limp. It wasn't his intention to make light of the war—too many of his friends had died—but Christ, once back home and conscripted (this time for life) into the family law firm, never had he missed anything so much as the waking dream of those days, mornings when he woke hearing, over the drone of turbines and the brave whistling of homesick men, the constant rhythm and jump of jazz in his head.

Mary said, "Gus, Julian has been amusing himself at the expense of poor Misha's vanished testicles."

"Has he, now?" An eyebrow amiably cocked, Gus handed her a martini. His age-spotted hand shook, spilling some of the drink onto the grass. "Well then, I'd hate to hear what he'd have to say about me when I wasn't around."

"Oh, a great deal, I should imagine."

They shared a private smile.

Mary picked up her book again—P. N. Furbank on E. M. Forster—and Gus, hitching up his pants, sat down with his drink and his memories.

Above our heads birds sang boisterously in the trees. The old trees, thick with leaves, on the old street. This was the beginning of the Golden Mile of manses that stretched almost to Fresh Pond Parkway. Longfellow had lived nearby, Hawthorne too. H. H. Richardson had designed houses for the rich. A sense of original privilege, of enlightened remove from the heedless, hectoring pace of the unreflecting multitude, persisted here as an embodiment of exalted New England stateliness and the founding ideals of Harvard itself. Ideals meant to be irrefutable, I supposed. A stateliness oppressive, it often seemed to me, for being so certain of its claims.

A low stone wall with an iron gate surrounded Mary's garden. Across the street stood a more recent building made of plain red brick—a general dorm for grad students, many of them foreign, who had nowhere else to stay. The dining hall was on the ground floor. During the long winter months when daylight was as scarce as wartime rations and the city was dark by five o'clock, I'd stood in my bedroom spying down through the windows at the big hall lit like a sunken stage. The stark wooden tables occupied by solitary men and women—grown students like myself—who routinely ate their dinners while reading.

"Gus and I are planning a little trip to the Veneto," Mary said.

I looked at her. Her glass was empty and her eyes brighter and two gentle blossomings, like wilted rose petals under rice paper, had appeared on her cheeks.

"When?"

"We leave the fourteenth, I believe. Is it, Gus?"

"Fifteenth," Gus replied, swallowing the last of his drink. "The fourteenth's Bastille Day."

"So it is! Of course, that's France and has nothing to do with the Italians. Well, the fifteenth, then. We return on the fifth."

"Sixth," said Gus.

"The sixth of August. It's a Palladian trip. I've always wanted to see the villas. And now we will. Won't we, Gus? Not that you particularly care about Palladio. But we're not getting any younger."

"Speak for yourself," Gus said.

"All right. *I'm* not getting any younger. Soon Gus will be hitting puberty. He'll find Misha's lost testicles and dance till the cows come home. Forgive me, Misha! Anyway, Julian, you won't mind taking care of him while we're away?"

"Who, Gus?"

Gus began to chuckle.

"Misha," Mary said sternly.

I grinned. "I won't mind, Mary."

"Thank you. I know I'm biased but he really is the best company. I've always found it impossible to be lonely with Misha around. I hope he'll be the same comfort to you."

"Julian isn't lonely," Gus objected.

Mary didn't say anything. She just patted my arm and asked Gus to mix another shaker of martinis.

As scheduled, they left on the fifteenth. Mary had written out a detailed explication of Misha's daily regimen. Included were afternoon walks on the leash around the neighborhood, fifteen-minute "play sessions" with a catnip-filled mouse, and the addition of a special gravy to his Tender Vittles.

So it happened that late one July afternoon I was once again sitting in the garden, this time with a copy of Karl M. Schmidt's *Henry A. Wallace: Quixotic Crusade, 1948* on my lap. Much of my summer had already passed like this. For it seemed better, or at any rate less worse, to sit alone in an old woman's garden than to sit with sunbathing couples on the grassy banks of the Charles.

The day had not gone well with Misha. First he'd managed to lose his catnip mouse—I suspected him of eating it— which meant that I was going to have to locate another before Mary's return. Then he'd refused either to walk or be carried on his afternoon constitutional around the neighborhood, forcing me to drag him by the leash the entire way.

He sat now, in the listless heat and fading light of late afternoon, on the lawn chair as on a throne, cleaning himself. Every pass of his paw over his fat pushed-in face represented a little sneer of disdain in my direction.

"Misha," I told him calmly, "you are a pampered piece of shit."

Glancing up at that moment, I felt the breath freeze in my throat. Claire was standing on the other side of the low wall in a blue dress patterned with flowers, her skin tanned, her dark hair streaked auburn by the sun.

"Quite a beauty," she said. "That cat."

"Actually, he's Himmler with fur. How's your father?"

She didn't reply. There was a gate but she ignored it; I watched her step over the wall. The dress rose to the tops of her thighs before slipping back again to touch the thumb-sized indentations of muscle just above her knees. Her hair tumbled across her face. Her skin wasn't pale as I remembered except where two narrow strap marks strayed across her shoulders and the delicate bones of her clavicle. Then she was over. Reaching Misha's chair, she began to scratch him between the ears, and in no time had him purring like an opium junkie.

"What've you been up to?" she asked.

There was a breeziness to her tone that I didn't believe, given the circumstances. *You've been away seven weeks and four days without calling,* I wanted to say. *Do you have any idea what that feels like?* Instead, I held up my library book on Wallace.

"The usual?" she said.

"What else? Now tell me how your father is."

"Not very well." Her gaze settled past me, onto the front of the house. "Though his weight's started to come back. He says he's returning to work by the end of next week and damn anybody who tries to stop him. That means me." She paused, holding her head very still. Tears had appeared from nowhere, floating in her eyes like pure light. "They say hair grows back differently after chemo," she said. "Is that true? He had beautiful dark hair before. He thinks it'll be white when it comes back. Is it true?"

"I don't know, Claire."

She nodded. On an impulse I reached out and took her hand. For a few moments she returned the pressure. Then, gently, she let my hand go. When she spoke again her tone was a few degrees harder; the shine in her eyes was gone.

"I feel as if I should be wearing one of those skull-and-crossbones signs. I'm a danger to myself and others right now."

"Is that a warning?"

"It's a confession."

"What's the point of confessing to me, Claire?" I said, unable to keep the anger out of my voice.

"Because I trust you. I don't know why. I just do."

I said nothing. Some light of my own was going out in my heart, like a beacon sinking into black water; and I stood watching it.

She said, "You're misunderstanding me."

"I think I'm understanding you perfectly."

"Listen, Julian. I loved our night together. You made me happy. Happier than I've been in a long time. But my father's very sick. He may be dying. And if you and I were to get seriously involved now, with the way things are, I'd end up killing it somehow. I know I would. And you'd end up hating me."

"I would never hate you."

"Yes, you would. And then I'll have lost you for good. Don't you see?" The luminous cast of imminent grief was back in her eyes; hardly seeming aware of what she was doing, she reached for my hand. "And I don't have the strength now, or the courage, to risk losing you for good. I can't explain it. Just be my friend, Julian. Please. Be my friend."

nine

YOU SIT WITH HER IN THE CAFÉ, back corner table, eyes rimmed with smoke, her hair pulled back in a velvet thinga-majig, her fingers turning the pages of Georgiana Burne-Jones' *Memorials*. Snippets she reads to you as, red and black ball-points in hand, you methodically work your way through Pro-fessor Davis' latest installment, easily a hundred pages (how can he write so fast?); and there is the persistent presence of her foot resting idly against your ankle beneath the table; and there is her voice reading, now and then in a quite credible English accent, the words of the still-living (at the time) wife for the dead husband-artist, words of sorrow and joy, pro-claiming how every minute with him contained the life of an hour; and you have not touched her, you think, really touched her, in four months, ten days, and sixteen hours, and don't know if you ever will again.

_t e n_

A SATURDAY MORNING IN NOVEMBER and I stood bent over
the gate to Mary's garden, scrubbing at layers of rust with a
piece of steel wool. Hearing a car horn, I looked up to see
Claire's red Volkswagen Bug pulling up in front of the house.
I stopped what I was doing and went over.

"Come for a ride?" Claire said.

I held up the steel wool. "Can't. I promised Mary."

"Come on." She leaned over and opened the passenger door.

"Where?"

"It's a surprise."

We headed south, Mass Pike to the interstate. The Bug a vi-
bratory instrument of surprising intensity; we had to shout to

hear ourselves. At Providence we turned east, crossed the bridge past Fall River, then southeast onto a local road that ran through Tiverton. In a village called Four Corners we stopped to buy turkey sandwiches and bottles of cream soda. A gray-shingled shop sold homemade ice cream. An iron-works offered hand-forged gates and fire screens. A mom-and-pop travel agency advertised resort vacations in Tahiti, Aruba, Cancún. We went on. Into Little Compton, the houses turn-ing progressively larger and the fields marked by gray stone walls. It had rained recently and the grass was green, the air fresh as a new continent. Wisps of cloud tempered the cool autumn sunshine. The road hit a rise and now we could see cows standing in acres of pasture stretching in gently undu-lating hills down to the river in the distance. Through the open windows we breathed in the whiff of summer camp long gone, bus rides and packed lunches and wet bark and lichen-covered stone, an old country of perpetual arrival. Around a series of turns the water appeared beside us as if conjured: a cabin hardly bigger than a doll's house bore a flag proclaiming the Sakonnet Yacht Club, though no boats were to be seen.

The point of land curved and narrowed. Into view came a ramshackle warehouse and behind it the haul poles and torn rigging of a fishing trawler. Claire stopped the car. The air smelled of fish. On three sides now there was nothing but water; on the fourth a cairn of broken lobster traps, a seagull sitting atop it like a sphinx.

"We're here," announced Claire, as the bird lifted off, hov-ered, resumed its place, watching us one cold eye at a time. Other gulls circling now, reeling above us, piercing the air with their cries. She reached for my hand.

We didn't remain there long. The promontory wasn't our real destination, I sensed, but some uncertain point of entry—sun and salt, breeze-licked whitecaps, a tidal pull into a past about which I knew little. Beside me in the car, staring out through the windshield as if the ocean itself were a celluloid memory projected onto a screen, Claire had a melancholy air. Something was overtaking her—as I'd seen it overtake her before, standing in the museum, lying in her bed. Her hand lay slack in mine until, rousing herself as though waking, she abruptly started the car. We drove back to the main road and stopped again, this time in front of a long gravel driveway.

She got out and I followed. She walked quickly now, energized by some new spirit of investigation. The driveway ended at a white clapboard house with slate-blue shutters. Two large oaks fronted the property, at their feet brilliant-colored leaves like burning drop cloths. To the left stood a garage with both doors closed; to the right, bordered by Japanese maples, stretched a lawn as square and green as a croquet pitch. A beautiful place, yet forgotten. No cars rested in the driveway. All the windows of the house were shut. A bird feeder hanging from a branch by the front door was empty of seed; as we watched, a blood-red cardinal alighted on the aluminum perch, pecked in vain at the feeding hole, and flew off.

"Claire, whose house is this?"

"It used to belong to my mother's parents." Her voice was excited, girlish. She was right up close to the house, trying to see in a front window. "The living room was here. On Christmas Eve we'd gather around the fireplace while my grandmother

told the story of Jesus in the manger. I'd sit on my father's lap
with my head tucked under his chin. What I loved was hearing how all the different kinds of animals stood together like
friends."

Abruptly she stepped back from the window, her eyes
darkening. "That was a long time ago. It looks different now."
She turned and marched around the side of the house.

By the time I caught up to her she had reached the low
back porch. Again she was spying into the interior, this time
through a glass-paned door cut into a large sunlit kitchen.
From the top half of the door her hollowed-out reflection
looked back at her; she had to shift her head continually in an
effort to see through it.

"What is it you're hoping to find, Claire?"

Without taking her eyes away from the door she said, "For
my thirteenth birthday my father brought me a dog from the
animal shelter. I named him Buzz because he was gold and
black and small like a bumblebee."

Her tone was brooding again; her head drooped; she would
not look at me. She cupped a hand over her image on the glass
until it disappeared.

"One morning about a month later I woke early and
couldn't find him," she said. "The house was quiet. Too quiet.
I went downstairs, and my mother was standing in front of the
sink there. This door was open. It was supposed to be kept
closed so he wouldn't run out to the road. She knew that. I
asked her if she'd seen him, and she turned and looked at me.
I'll never forget that look. She was telling me she knew. Then
she started yelling. She said she was sick and tired of having

to keep the door closed all the time, she refused to live cooped up like an animal for the sake of a dog, not on a beautiful summer day, and if my dog was too fucking dumb to be trained not to run into the road it was no fault of hers."

Claire turned to face me.

"I found him a quarter mile up the road, curled against the cemetery wall," she said. "He'd been hit by a car. Somehow he'd dragged himself. When he saw me he began to whimper. His hip was crushed and his stomach was bleeding. He died in my arms."

It was afternoon. We stood on the perfect lawn as the sunlight thinned and an autumn chill spilled ink from the woods behind the house. A pair of robins hunted for worms in the grass. Beside me Claire seemed mired still in that long-ago scene with her mother, the violation of a trust that could never again be set right. Her arms were folded across her chest and her gaze was fixed on nothing.

We were almost touching. I wanted to throw her a line and haul her to safety, if I could. To press my hand against her cheek. Failing that, there were only words to fall back on, to attempt to tell her, by way of my own limited experience, that the darkness in which she now found herself was not an eclipse.

I said, "My mother and I don't really speak anymore."

Claire looked at me.

And I told her about the day, four years earlier, when my father returned from work to find an empty apartment and three

white envelopes lying on the kitchen table. The envelopes—
one addressed to each member of the family—were thin. I
still had mine. The letters were typed, a paragraph long, the
same words for each of us. She was in love with another man,
had been for a long time. She couldn't go on like this. She was
sorry. She loved us and always would. She hoped we'd understand in time. She would send her new address once she got
settled.

"She lives in a Houston suburb now. He's an orthopedist."

"Do you miss her?"

"I miss believing in her," I said.

A long silence then. Claire's expression intense, collabora-
tive. She smiled gently.

"Come on. I want to show you something."

She turned and began walking toward the woods. I followed. As we neared the edge of the lawn a path grew visible,
narrowly forged through the trees and strewn with dead leaves.
The air, blocked from the sun and dank with humus, turned
cooler. Our footsteps trod softly over the layered ground. In
our noses was the scent of the vegetation.

I walked behind her. Thinking not about my mother but
about my father. Quiet, mild man. Once immortalized out of his
earshot by my older sister, Judith, as "Clark Kent minus Super-
man." Had he ever even raised his voice at us? I couldn't remember. Though he must have. Kids, after all, did stupid and
dangerous things—ran into streets without looking, fell from
trees, stepped on shards of glass, got crushes on girls who
wouldn't give them the time of day. He must have raised his
voice at me, at least in warning. But I couldn't remember.

Though the man I knew wasn't inclined to shout. If a problem was discovered, his first instincts went inevitably toward reason and compromise. For nearly four decades he'd been with the same publishing house, beginning as an assistant editor in adult trade, a die-hard lover of literature. But when, five years after he'd joined the firm, his employers urged a move into the textbook division, he'd complied without a murmur. At his retirement recently he was given a crystal paperweight and a pension half the size it should have been. A history of neglect exacerbated, one might have speculated, by his physiognomy: his wide kind face was the very emblem of modest decency; his fine limp hair was of no distinctive color. His pale gray eyes were clear of the accrued resentments and morbid regrets typical of men in late middle age; but clear too, it had to be said, of the determined will and potential fierceness that make men remembered after they're gone. Perhaps I'd grown up vaguely ashamed of his benign acceptance of the status quo and the smallness of his footprint on the earth.

And yet for much of his life my father had done all right, according to the rather modest terms he'd set for himself: marriage, kids, career. Until a few years ago, that is, too late in the game to defend himself, when the woman he'd loved and trusted and depended on had left him without so much as a word of tenderness. A quarter century in the making, and then a single paragraph had crushed him as if he were built of nothing more substantial than paper. After which he was by definition flat. Even his own past—especially this—would from that moment on appear like a perilous mountain. And he was no climber; he would lie down. I knew, because I'd observed him from up close. Had for almost two years after college moved in with him in that dusty prewar co-op whose furniture, books, china, and pictures he had chosen with my mother.

Yes, I'd roomed with him again, driven by filial compassion. But when he'd failed to get up—when, day after day, I watched him hugging the floor of his memory like a boxer who's thrown the fight—I'd fled to Cambridge as if my life depended on it, and not looked back. As if in his stunned misery he'd become a stone gorgon, capable at a glance of turning me to stone just like him.

. . .

Ahead, now, a flare of daylight: the path gave out onto a small wooden dock at the edge of a saltwater marsh. Here the sunshine was intensified rather than thinned, the water deep blue. Between two rocky islets more than a hundred swans floated, princely confections in a still parade. Visible on the far shore was a strip of scrub brush and beyond that a whiteness that must have been beach. In the distance, hazed like a mirage, lay the ocean.

I stood with her on the dock. Behind us there was an overturned Old Town canoe, the handles of two paddles, still shiny with varnish, poking out from underneath. Algae had stained parts of the dock green and water had rotted it; we stood a bit unsteadily, as if on the deck of a slowly sinking boat, and listened to the soft lapping of the marsh. Running some fifty yards out to our right was a cluster of desiccated cattails in the middle of which, raised above the water on a square wooden platform and partially camouflaged by reeds and tall grasses, I was able to make out a duck blind.

"Hunters?" I said.

Claire nodded. "True story. My brother had an air rifle and used to go around shooting squirrels and birds, pretty much anything that moved. My father tried to make him stop. But Alan was thirteen and either a natural sadist or he'd just seen too many Dirty Harry movies. Eventually Daddy had to take the gun and lock it in the linen closet upstairs. Later I found where he'd put the key and started plotting my revenge. I was going to show the little macho freak. One day while my parents were in town I looked out the window and saw him tossing a tennis ball to himself on the lawn. I went and got the gun. It was still loaded—Daddy'd forgotten to empty the pellets. I went over to the window and took careful aim. Then I shot him twice in the ass before he ever knew what hit him." Claire burst out laughing. "God, it felt good!"

I gave her an appraising look.

With a tough-girl grin she demanded, "How about you? Ever shoot anybody?"

"No, but when I was ten I burned the hair off Judith's Barbie. Ever seen a bald Barbie?"

She laughed. Then, glancing away from each other, we entered a long silence. Invisible threads connected us—as if we were Siamese twins, sharing origins, necessities, desires, fates. This was the law of bound hearts: separate us and only one, at most, would survive.

Up again rose the liquid whispering of the marsh against the dock, while the rustling of the breeze through the cattails sounded like fingers combing a wheat field. A swan began to beat the blue water with its wings. Massive, improbable wings. Began to walk on water, gathering speed. And Claire, as we sat watching, without a word reached out and laid her hand against the side of my head. Her touch was electric. I remained still. The swan achieved liftoff, beat the air, seemed to create the air, banked, curved, and flew off for the far side of the marsh, where the ocean was. She took her hand away. When it was gone the hard beating of my heart was all that remained in my ears—as if the earth's elements had recombined, become one indivisible thing which was her. Then that sound too began to fade. I grew aware of some critical moment having passed without my grasping it, and of Claire standing beside me on the dock, still close, yet now angled away.

Then she turned to me.

"Another true story. My uncle proposed to my aunt on this dock," she said. "He was over from Brown for the weekend, paying court. Her parents wouldn't leave them alone. Then it was late Sunday and he had to be getting back. So, desperate and preoccupied, he took her for a walk down here. She was naive and didn't see it coming. She'd brought her camera. Took her time like a tourist, peering through the viewfinder at everything. That was how he appeared to her—next to her here on the dock, so close she couldn't quite get him into focus. He was blurry, fuzzy at the edges. It all kind of embarrassed her. As if it was her fault somehow that he wasn't crystal clear, she must have been doing something wrong. It *confused* her. Then suddenly he blew up. He said, 'Just put the

goddamn camera *down*, Ellen, for chrissakes!' And because
it was 1959 and she was a woman who didn't know any better, she put the camera down. And that's when she saw him
clearly for the first time. Really saw him, his big blue eyes totally inward-looking, focused only on the question he was
about to ask, not actually seeing her at all. Blind to her. She
knew this. Yet two minutes later she'd accepted him. And
three years later they had two kids."

"And the marriage?"

Unsmiling, Claire drew a finger across her throat.

Thinking about my parents, I said, "It's hard to understand
the choices people make."

"Not hard, Julian," Claire replied with sudden vehemence.
"Fucking impossible. The choices most of us make, most of
the time, make no sense at all."

She seemed angry, staring out toward the ocean. Seeing
perhaps—she must have seen—that the day had declined
subtly, the sunlight was no longer brilliant over the marsh, the
water was no longer so blue; that large numbers of swans, following that intrepid first one, had begun to fly away.

Thinking about my parents had depressed me. "I like to
think people like us won't make the same bad choices our parents made," I said.

"And I like to think there aren't any people like us," Claire
replied. "I guess for my sanity I need to think it. That we're ba-
sically blank slates. That the choices we've already made and
will end up making—what we do with our lives, what I'm saying to you right this second—that all of it's the story, our original message to ourselves and the world, getting written all the

time, again and again, till one day it just covers us like an epitaph. . . ."

She leaned over and kissed me, briefly but feelingly, on the mouth.

"And then I guess we'll know. Or someone will, Julian, if you and I aren't around anymore. Someone will, if not us. How it all turned out, I mean. What the odds were. How we did."

SHE WROTE CHECKS with a black Waterman fountain pen, a gift from her father, in emerald-green ink. Her signature was arguably the most voluptuous aspect of her character; debts were to be obliterated by the name of Claire Marvel. Which was perhaps the point—the presence of funds could be a spotty business with her. She might go from broke to flush, or flush to broke, in a matter of days. The money, like the pen, came from her father, who sent it without his wife's knowledge; and who was embattled during these months, for his cancer had returned.

Every weekend now she spent with him in Stamford. I never accompanied her; she never asked me to. She made it clear she wouldn't appreciate my calling while she was there. What I received instead of an invitation were letters, written in the familiar green ink, sometimes as many as two a day. Claire imbued my mailbox with the sense of deliverance it had been lacking. Letters of all lengths, scrawled on folded sheets of lined paper torn from a spiral-bound notebook, composed at any hour of the day—though usually, I guessed, while her father rested; for whispered between her lines was a reverent, grieving hush.

By the time they arrived in my box, she would already be back in Cambridge. Mondays, Tuesdays, even Wednesdays I'd be reading what she'd written a few days before in her father's house. And so her moods reached me belatedly, mountains whose troughs and peaks I was coming to know, like a climber in the dark, by feel rather than by sight. I scaled them with a careful sort of greed, pausing over each new turn of phrase as if it might prove the key to her. It never did, of course, but I wasn't disappointed. Real knowledge had many faces, I was discovering; it wasn't literal. There were aspects of her in everything she did or thought, more so in the discrepancies and contradictions that lit her mind like sparks. With time that fall and winter, it came to make a strange kind of sense that the Claire of the letter I read on a Tuesday morning should be so much warmer or cooler or angrier or more tender or more hopeful or more heartbroken than the Claire I saw in person that same evening.

twelve

I GIVE NOW THIS MAP OF OUR DAYS.

Afternoons at the café. Short days growing shorter. Through street-level windows boots seen tramping soundlessly in powdery snow. Inside, smoky warmth and the illusion that this place had been built just for us.

Today I sat buried in Davis' manuscript, which seemed to be growing as exponentially as our great nation's budget deficit. The man was a writing machine. This left me little time to work on my dissertation. It was December and I was still wrestling with the introduction, trying to winnow down the scope. Davis, fount of industry that he was, had time only to advise me to "pick your locus, Julian, and stick with it."

Pick my locus . . . ? In my dictionary a locus was most interestingly defined as "a center of intense concentration"; also, in mathematical terms, as "the configuration of all points whose coordinates satisfy a single equation."

I looked up. Claire was studying a painting by Dante Gabriel Rossetti in an illustrated monograph on the Pre-Raphaelite artists. Our table cluttered with empty cups and gritty with cookie crumbs. She was bundled in a heavy sweater red as a fire truck, and a beige muffler wrapped around her throat. Her elbows rested on either side of the book, an index finger tapping at the corner of her mouth. And so my locus was picked, as it were, and I had no choice but to stick with it.

One afternoon Davis strode into the café. It was the sort of coincidence that makes even the biggest skeptic a believer—Claire and I had just been talking about him. She'd asked what sort of mentor Davis was turning out to be, and I'd replied that he was prolific, productive, ambitious, occasionally brusque; but also fair and sincere in his wish for me to get ahead. He was a better person than he liked to make out, I said. And here he was in the doorway, peering through the smoke, head nearly touching the ceiling, wearing a navy cashmere overcoat and black leather gloves and carrying a black leather briefcase.

He navigated the cramped room to our table.

"Been calling you all day, Julian. Now I know why. Hello, Miss Marvel. Pleasure to see you again."

"We were just talking about you, Professor Davis."

"Were you."

"According to Julian, you have a big heart. All that tough-ness is just for show."

"Is that right? Then clearly, I'm not working him hard enough."

"Not true!" I said.

Everybody smiled.

Opening his briefcase, Davis produced a sheaf of typed pages.

"I talked to the folks at Random House this morning, Ju-lian. They couldn't be happier with what they've seen so far." He handed me the pages, then put his hand on my shoulder. "I told my editor about you. A man named Fox. I said you were top material. He intends to keep his eye out for your work."

"He may need both eyes," I said. "There's not much to see."

"That will change." With a quick smile he glanced at Claire. "So you're the one who's keeping him from his work?"

"I don't suppose you ever get writer's block," she said, re-turning his smile.

Davis laughed. "Not me."

Then he turned and left us.

Evenings at the Brattle Theater: retrospectives of Cassavetes, Kurosawa, Hitchcock, Buñuel. I was no connoisseur. My job was to buy the popcorn while Claire staked out the seats. Side aisles she preferred, life at an angle. Though once settled she liked to sit high, her coat folded under her, like a queen or a bus driver. And silent—her fiercest condemnation was re-served for people who talked during the film.

Afterward, we'd have drinks at Casablanca, sitting side by

side in a wicker cabana chair. Our interpretations of the film just watched were almost always different. She stared at a movie screen much as she did paintings in the Fogg, utterly absorbed by color and line. Dialogue, sound, music—nothing aural could compete with the images, if they were original and beautiful enough. Her expression then belonged not to an art historian but to an artist; a traveler who through circuitous wandering has stumbled upon an uncharted place beyond explanation.

This, of course, was not my way. I believed in the existence of empirical truth. It was hard for me to bump up against anything without immediately supplying or reaching for a definition.

One night after watching *The Birds*, I told her how I'd been struck by Hitchcock's deft narrative construction. But Claire, though she'd grasped the plot clearly enough, wasn't interested in its twists and turns. What had mesmerized her was the visual patterning of the birds themselves, black against gray sky, as they swarmed—a stroke of genius all the more notable, she insisted, for being beyond the artist's initial conception or control. Another evening, after *Ran*, she emerged so moved by the extended dream of images, the battle scenes like long ribbons of color melding one into the other, that she appeared visibly altered: her eyes dimmed as though from sensory exhaustion, her lips imperceptibly stung.

Mary's living room, with fireplace roaring, was the best-heated part of the drafty old house. By invitation, this became our library. The Widener Reading Room was soon a distant necessity, for there was no fire there and no Gus to offer glasses of mulled wine when the afternoons turned dark. Besides, the older couple seemed to enjoy having us around. In Claire, Mary discovered a young woman who had been to, or at least read about, most of the great museums; who unlike myself knew what chiaroscuro really meant. ("The arrangement of light and dark elements in a pictorial work of art," said my dictionary. "Also called *clair-obscure*.") And Gus meanwhile found a new and appreciative set of ears into which he might murmur, with occasional inventive flourishes, some of the Top 40 tales from his book of wonders. Between January and March he played for her benefit every Dave Brubeck album in his huge collection of LPs. And in that warm, gold-lit room, Claire sat and listened. With older people, I was learning, she could be disarmingly courteous, even humble; could pay the sort of attention that made them feel invigorated about the time remaining.

"Julian," said Mary one day as we stood waiting for the kettle to boil, "she is a lovely, unusual young woman."

"Yes, Mary, she is."

"Do you have intentions?"

"Intentions?" I almost smiled. The kettle began to sing and Mary turned off the burner. "Yes," I said. "I have intentions."

"Then I wouldn't wait. That's my advice, for what it's worth."

"It's worth a lot, Mary. Only it's not quite as simple as that."

"It never is," said Mary.

In March Claire drove down to Stamford for one of her week-end visits, but this time didn't return. There was no word from her until a letter arrived in my mailbox on the following Thursday:

Sunday

They say it's in his liver now. Other places, too. That's what they say. We've moved a hospital bed down to the living room. A hired nurse will come six days a week. Josette, from Martinique. Daddy lies there, half his old weight. The look on his face says he knows the joke's on him. Other times he's in too much pain to look like anything I recognize. I love him so much I'd kill him if he asked.

Tuesday

My mother took to her bed today, complaining of "symptoms." She is a diva with a head cold, the kind who can't be counted on to show up. The kind who can't stand attention being directed at anybody else—even at her husband, who is dying. I won't forgive her.

There's a Burne-Jones you've never seen. A portrait of his wife. He never exhibited it during his lifetime, supposedly wasn't satisfied with it. Though I think he was wrong. Her moral courage and her fierceness in love are there. Her eyes are the most exquisite gray. Their children are in the background, the son painting at an easel, like his father. In the foreground Georgie holds a book of herbals, open to the page for pansy, with a real pansy there like a bookmark. The other name for pansy was hearts-ease; it symbolized undying love. This was the flower she later put on his grave. Heartsease. My mother has no right to behave like this. She has never put his heart at ease. She's done nothing all their lives together but make him heartsick and uncertain, and he has stood it and stood it and stood it. Well, he won't have to stand it much longer. Then who will she blame?

Two weeks later she left a message on my machine saying to meet her at the café.

When I arrived she was already there. We hugged longer than was usual for us; she seemed reluctant to let me go. Her face was thinner, her eyes large and bright. Once we sat down her hands would not stop fidgeting with a manila envelope that lay on the table.

"How is he?" I said.

She shook her head.

Deep in our separate thoughts we sat watching her fingers tapping the envelope.

Finally I said, "You should have let me come down and be with you."

"I don't want you to see him like this." Suddenly she looked up. "I told him about you."

I was pleased, but didn't know what to say.

"Julian, will you do something for me?"

I told her I would.

Opening the clasp, she emptied the contents of the envelope onto the table.

I was staring at two plane tickets, round-trip between Boston and Paris.

Claire said, "A long time ago, before he was married, my father spent time in a house in France that belonged to family friends. He's been telling me about it. His memory's driving him now. He says that time in France was the happiest of his life and he wants me to go back there for him, while he's still around to hear about it."

She reached across the table for my hand and held it tightly in both of hers.

"Julian, please come with me."

thirteen

WE FLEW INTO CHARLES DE GAULLE at eight in the morning, eyes bloodshot and heads heavy from the wine served free on the flight. It was the middle of April. There had been rain in Boston when we'd left, but over Paris now the sky was clear, cool as an underground spring.

Her father had arranged our trip with the scrupulousness of a man who knows this to be his final production. A road map and a two-door Peugeot awaited us at the car rental agency. In Claire's pocket were keys and handwritten directions to the house in the central south of the country where Lou Marvel had stayed once, for a month, in his early twenties; and the name of his old friend, Leland Conner, to whom the property had since passed. Conner and his French wife would be out of the country, we were told, but nonetheless had offered us their house while they were gone. We planned to stay two weeks.

This was my first time in France but Claire had been twice before—Paris, Nice, Aix-en-Provence. The region we were heading for was the Quercy; the department was the Lot, pronounced with a hard *t*.

By request Claire drove first, which put me in the passenger seat with the map. With some confusion I managed to navigate us around the Périphérique de Paris (a hangman's noose of traffic) and onto the autoroute, south toward Orléans.

Then full speed ahead. Claire was a fearless driver, working the clutch in quick bursts, punching between smoke-belching camions and testosterone speedsters. Our car hummed like a bee.

The metropolis fell back as the big open fields of the north reclaimed the land on either side of the autoroute: vast tracts of green, enormous fields of mustard like planes of sunlight. Looking out at the swaths of vibrant yellow, Claire said she was reminded of how Matisse, like van Gogh before him, was born in French Flanders, near the Belgian border—beet fields and smokestacks, the old forests leveled by factories, the Prussians marching across the flats, the cold and damp. A hard, dour northern light of muted pigments and even more muted hearts. And then how both painters in different ways had spent the rest of their lives moving ever southward, toward the sun and a brighter, more expressive palette unfettered by bourgeois convention. Matisse's father was a seed merchant. There were no artists in his family nor in the town of Bohain-en-Vermandois; no model for the son's imagination.

When Matisse returned home thirty years after leaving, his old neighbors still spoke of him as a failed law clerk.

Claire fell silent.

She was wearing yesterday's clothes—father's old sweater, jeans, hiking boots. Perhaps it was the light that made her eyes shine so—as if some autonomous and morbid vision were alive within her. Seen from the side, she appeared on the brink of tears, the nascent lines at the corners of her eyes like faint hieroglyphs of sorrow or penitence.

We reached Orléans by noon. In the old part of town, where Joan of Arc was martyred and all was made of stone, we found the Café des Pierres, still looking as Claire's father had remembered it: a dark, timeless room on a cobbled side street, filled with bundles of wood, a crackling fire, and the smell of grilled fish. A lunch of trout and white wine, tarte Tatin and coffee. At the end of the meal the old couple who owned the place stopped by our table. Claire spoke French to them. I could understand only half of what was said, yet even with my high school vocabulary I sensed her gift for the language. She used it with secret joy, managing to imply both confidence and a polite deference. She gave each word its own, new light.

Then it was my turn to drive, and our car hurtled back onto the autoroute. To either side the fields stretched out, brown and green and yellow. The odd château spied like a private realm in the distance. The ceaseless, cumulative roar of engines and the billboards of cartoon ugliness. In places the autoroute paralleled the high-speed train tracks; when a train went shooting by with a vacuumed whoosh, all the cars on the road seemed to be standing still.

And then Claire, folding her coat into a pillow, curled up against the door. From the corner of my eye I watched her drift off to sleep. She grew still, her legs tucked underneath her, her hip inches from my hand.

Two hours passed. I was tired yet very much awake, driving to the rhythm of her breathing, seeing France out of every window as she might have seen it. The open farmland of the Loire was giving way to the hill country of the Limousin and Périgord. Here were geologic boundaries where earlier there had been only the man-made divisions of agriculture and industry. Red-tiled roofs were beginning to appear in pockets of land that refused to lie flat.

At Brive-la-Gaillarde, as we left the autoroute and turned southeast, she woke with a start.

"Where are we?"

"No idea, really."

She smiled drowsily, picked up the map, gave it a cursory glance, shrugged, and dropped it at her feet. As a general rule she ignored all maps and instruction manuals, considering them the propaganda of the confused. Arching her back against the seat, she stretched. Then she rolled down her window a few inches, sniffing the air.

"We're getting close. I can smell it."

I lowered my window too. The afternoon was clear and cool. The road was a country road, narrow and winding. It curved and dipped through sparse-wooded hills with fields arrayed down their sloping backs. Pastures were framed by limestone walls. There were few shadows on this land. Those that existed appeared ancient and fixed, birthmarks of creation. In the shaded hollows flocks of Roman-nosed sheep huddled together, and on the steepest slopes grapevines hung from their crosses like crucified children. There were plum orchards and solitary walnut trees growing in fields of raked bare earth with ragged lines of crows sitting on the gnarled black limbs and discreet herds of cows waiting in mud for their deliverance. The air smelled of all of it.

Claire said, "Now I know why the French call this region 'la France profonde.'"

As she spoke we were descending into a valley. A narrow gray-blue river appeared on our left. The road ran alongside it and soon we began seeing occasional white signs written with unpronounceable names—not towns, we saw, not even villages, but hamlets consisting of a few houses, stone walls, a yellow postbox, a donkey or two; and the belled sounds of the animals.

In time the river ran through the center of a market town. Here Claire suggested we buy food. I pulled to a stop on a main square girded by medieval houses darkly striped with creosoted timbers. We got out and stretched. It was late afternoon; the outdoor market was long closed. A few red-faced old men in blue work clothes stood chatting under a plane tree. They stared at us, then resumed their conversation. Otherwise the square was empty.

But shops were open. In a food market that might have been someone's parlor we bought fresh eggs, tomatoes, onions, lettuce, cornichons, pâté, strawberry preserves, butter, milk.

Then we found the baker, wine merchant, cheese shop—where Claire asked the old woman for cabécou, white disks of the local goat cheese. The word itself sounded freshly made on her tongue.

We loaded our provisions into the car, and set off on the final leg of our journey. The river flowed out of the other side of the town. Across it the early-spring sunshine lay thin and slanting. And the spindly poplars that grew alongside the banks could be seen too on the water's mirrored surface, round leaves turning like coins. Following her father's directions, we drove over a primitive bridge and turned left, then right, onto a road that wound its way up a mountain. The ascent was slow, circuitous, beautiful. The wide valley was splayed out behind us, first one angle, then another. High on a plateau the climb ended. We turned right again and proceeded slowly down a single-lane road flecked with sheep droppings, between lichen-covered walls and compact fields.

A plain white sign. A hamlet of six old houses. And at the back, standing apart behind a low wall, two structures made of stone: a barn in the shape of an ancient granary, built up the slope, with a tiled roof like an oversized hat; and a simple two-story house with a steeply pitched roof and blue shutters. Beyond the buildings there was a raked field of walnut trees. Then, gradually descending all the way to the valley floor, there were more fields and walls, and the distant, dreamlike, gray-blue gleam of the river.

fourteen

THE INDELIBLE MOMENT OF ARRIVAL. Stepping through the doorway with Claire as if it was ours. The ancient house. Dust in the air, cold in the stones, cobwebs shivering at the tops of windows, scars and slants of furniture, the warping of the floor beneath its covering of worn straw matting.

Claire stood in the center of the open room, her eyes radiant, turning from one object to another with rapture on her face.

The hearth was tall and wide. A cast-iron bucket a yard deep held moss-covered logs of plum and walnut. The mantel was set high as a man's head, burled and not quite level. Claire ran a hand over it, searching yet absent, as if looking for something whose shape she couldn't remember. Then she turned and stared out through the glass panes of a back door to a small terrace—perhaps imagining the delicious meals we'd eat out there, if the weather was warm enough. Though the weather wouldn't matter; we were here, had traveled all this way together, had left everyone else behind.

She did not seem to notice the thick coating of dust that her fingers had picked up from the mantel, how nothing in the house was clean. She stood in the light that came in from the valley. And when she turned and asked me how I felt, I could smile and declare honestly that I was happy too.

Then up the creaking, ladderlike stairs to stand with our bags on the landing between the two bedrooms and the bathroom. An unavoidable moment—the bigger of the rooms contained a double bed while the smaller held a narrow single. Yet we hadn't envisioned this possibility or discussed it and we paused now, too awkward to catch each other's eye.

I stood debating with myself. Exhaustion, the long journey, a too-familiar cloud of romantic uncertainty—all this made me numb. Should I step forward or hold back? To set myself up for rejection now could mean the end of something. On the other hand, if I refrained from forcing the issue, perhaps she might feel compelled to reach out.

"I'll take the single," I said.

"You're sure?"

The question was too quick. I'd made it too easy. Disappointment brought the full weight of my exhaustion down on me and I turned away. Lifting my suitcase, I stepped into the room with the single bed.

There, standing with head ducked under the eaves, I heard her drop her bags in the other room. Heard her as she opened the tall windows that looked out over the valley. Heard through the thin wall that now divided us, the complex silence of her listening.

We'd agreed in advance that neither of us knew how to cook. Nevertheless I made an omelette for our first dinner—plain, empty as a fist, in the inelegant shape of something dropped on the floor—and we ate it at the lopsided kitchen table with slices of the thick-crusted local bread and half a bottle of a rough Cahors.

The kitchen was large and drafty. Nothing about it was remotely modern. The floor tiles were scuffed and pockmarked. From one corner of the ceiling curled a strip of flypaper still dotted with the wizened corpses of bygone summers. The dishes were chipped, webbed with hairline cracks. The refrigerator was half-sized and slope-shouldered. The gas stove had the sturdy rounded presence of an old pickup truck.

At the end of the meal, raising her glass, Claire awarded me two "Marvel" stars for my effort. She held out the promise of a third. I bowed, looking up at her through the flame of a candle stub, and in a phony French accent gave her my Hippocratic culinary oath: *First do no harm*. She laughed. Her face flickered and shone, her cheeks were red. We'd kept our heavy sweaters on against the chill.

After dinner she was the first to go upstairs. I remained by the fire, poking the gnarled, slow-burning logs with a stick. Soon I heard her running a bath, the old pipes filling the house with their crotchety deliberations. I thought about the meal we'd just eaten and how afterward—contented, exhausted, quiet—we'd stood together at the stained white sink and washed the dishes. There were all the mundane aspects of her life about which I realized I knew little—how she put on lipstick, rode a bicycle, took a bath, opened a present, folded a shirt—and which appeared suddenly illumined now that we were here alone, living together: a series of prosaic firsts that felt like love letters and that I wanted to catalogue for myself as though they belonged to me.

The pipes fell quiet. I opened the back door and stepped out onto the terrace. The night was cold and clear, every star in it bright enough, bold enough, it seemed, to be a planet.

She would be getting into her bath.

Not a sound could be heard, not a voice. Washed by the Milky Way, the walnut trees were the black of shadows.

I climbed the stairs to the landing. The bathroom door was ajar an inch, steam suffused with artificial light swirling lethargically out through the gap. Unable to stop myself, I put an eye to the opening, and saw through the pearled air a corner of the tub, and her bare wet foot resting there.

"Julian?"

Startled, I jumped back—before catching her tone, a sleepy, heat-drugged murmur, minimally amplified by the bath in which she lay. Her luxurious calm reached me, and I relaxed. And the sound of the water too, a sinuous, glassy ripple as she moved.

"Looks like an opium den in there."

"Mmm. This may just be the best bath I've ever had in my life."

I remained on the landing, staring at the inch of her bare foot. Then the foot disappeared. I heard her lean forward. The tap came on, trickle of water into water. After a minute there was a long sigh of contentment, and the tap was shut off.

From out on the landing I said good night.

"You're not going to sleep?"

"I'm exhausted."

"Stay and talk."

I was silent, waiting.

"Please," she said.

I sat down on the landing, my back against the outer wall of my room, unable now to see any part of her. The floor was cold. The house was still. There were just her occasional liquid movements coming through the door like a private language.

I tried simply to be. To listen to the sounds of her. To find contentment. Instead, inexorably, I began to think about the single bed in the darkened room behind me and the pair of light blue cotton pajamas that earlier I'd folded and placed neatly on the pillow.

An image of my father long ago, dressed in pajamas and robe, came to me unbidden:

He bends down at the front door of the apartment. When he rises, he's holding a copy of the *Times*. That's all. He is perhaps forty. His loosely worn slippers make a shuffling sound as he walks, already murmuring aloud the day's news—Vietnam, the Black Panthers, the Six-Day War—back along the hallway to the kitchen.

It is always the same; only the news changes.

And I wanted to get up now and take my carefully folded pajamas and tear them to shreds. But there was a cold draft on the landing and all through the house, everywhere but where she was. So I stayed, on the wrong side of the almost-closed bathroom door, and brought my knees up and hugged them, and watched the steam curl out through the gap and disappear above my head.

"Julian?"

"What?"

"What are you thinking about?"

The sound of her moving in the water, and then the tap coming on again. I rubbed my hands over my face. My exhaustion was like a weight pressing me down. Through the doorway at the other end of the landing I could see into her room: a suitcase on the floor, clothes already flung about, a home-made lamp on a table, the bulb shining over the double bed.

"Pajamas," I said.

"What about them?"

Her tone was serious and true. I leaned my head back against the wall.

"They remind me of my father."

She said nothing. The tap continued to run, a thin trickle, and my face began to burn with shame.

"There's a poem by Rilke," she said. "'Archaic Torso of Apollo.' Do you know it?"

"No."

"I think it would mean something to you."

"What's it about?"

"About?" The impatient, watery flutter of her hand in the bath. "Well, on the surface you could say it's a poem about a Greek statue. But that doesn't tell you anything."

She leaned forward. I still couldn't see her. The tap continued to run, and around her body I imagined the water rippling in circles of light. More than anything, I wished I could see her.

"It begins with the poet speaking to the statue, to the god alive in the art, inside the white marble," she continued, the energy growing in her voice as she spoke. "He calls it 'you,' describes it to itself. And we're so sure we know who he's talking to, who the 'you' in the poem is. We're reading along and saying to ourselves 'How beautiful, how true,' feeling all safe and wise and poetic. Then suddenly, in the last line, he blows it all to pieces. He says, *You must change your life.* And now we understand that he's not talking to the god in the marble any longer, or to Art, but *from* them, straight into our souls. I was eighteen. I'd never read anything more urgent in my life. It was like being grabbed by the throat and shaken."

Her story finished, she turned off the tap, lay back heavily as if she'd just realized how tired she was. Now the house was as quiet as if it had been empty.

And in that quiet, out on the landing, my frustration began to grow.

"And have you, Claire?"

"Have I what?"

"Changed your life."

She exhaled in annoyance. "Life isn't a switch you turn on and off, Julian. Love isn't."

"Who's talking about love?"

She was silent.

"I said who's talking about love, Claire?"

"I am." Suddenly her voice was small, hardly recognizable.

"Well, I am too."

Through the door came a new silence, more potent than speech.

I sat thinking. How it was she who'd mentioned love first. How she seemed to be waiting, the door still between us, for me to act. And I imagined that if I reached for her I would find her where she lay waiting in the water, and my fingers would glide over her bare wet skin until every inch of her, every crook and hollow, would become mine. I would vouch for her with my life.

But the silence wasn't long enough. While I sat dreaming, Claire pulled the plug.

She rose, I heard the water sliding off her in sheets. Her naked arm flashed across the gap in the door, then back again, trailing a cotton robe. When the door opened fully she was dressed in the robe, the belt loosely tied, holding her long water-dark hair in her hand.

I got to my feet. My body was stiff from sitting so long on the cold floor, and I cleared my throat self-consciously—like a man who, after years of silence, intends to start singing again.

In the end, though, all I said was good night.

fifteen

I WOKE LATE THE NEXT MORNING, alone in the narrow cot beneath the pitched roof, and looked out the square window at the tongue of mist covering the valley floor.

Downstairs, the open room smelled of woodsmoke. Morning light broke through the east-facing windows in long, slanting shafts. Airy cobwebs like the ghosts of old ladies trembled at the tops of the tall windows, and the yellowed newspapers used for insulation during the winters were visible at the tattered edges of the straw floor matting.

Through the open doorway I saw Claire at the kitchen table, reading a paperback. A bowl of coffee steamed in front of her. Her hair was tied loosely back and her face held pale light from the window. She smiled as I entered the room. "Good morning."

I asked what she was reading.

She held up the book—*La Cousine Bette*. "About an old spinster who sabotages her niece's one chance at true love," she replied with a touch of irony. "Balzac in his romantic mode. Nice way to start off the day. Sit, and I'll make you breakfast."

Putting the book aside, she stood up and moved to the stove. Shirttails stuck out from beneath her red sweater and her hiking boots were streaked with fresh mud.

"Looks like you've already been out," I said, sitting down at the table.

"I have, and it's beautiful. Around here it's still the sixteenth century." She lit a match, turned on the gas; a low flame appeared under a saucepan of milk. "How'd you sleep?"

"Not bad."

There was a pause.

"I had a strange dream," I added.

"What sort of dream?"

When I hesitated she turned around and looked at me expectantly.

We were bundled in furs on a dogsled being pulled across a snow-covered tundra, I told her. She and I. We came to the coast. Not an arctic coast; more like Cape Cod. Sitting on the beach was a raft made out of planks and old tires. She wanted to take it, but I worried about our chances. She persuaded me. Soon we'd shed our furs and dragged the raft down to the water. The waves nearly swamped us. But we made it. Time passed. We were becalmed in the middle of the ocean. Not a ripple or wave or boat. Then a moment when I called her name and as she turned toward me she slipped and tumbled

off the raft, disappearing beneath the water. She didn't surface. There was nothing. Many times I called her name. Then,
in seconds that were like years, I began to grieve. My grief
filled the dream until it was everything—until another moment when I turned my head and she was simply there again,
alive in the water, waving to me. Mute, stunned with happiness and relief, I steered the raft over to her. I was reaching
down to pull her to safety when I woke up.

There, I said. My dream.

Claire turned away. She switched off the burner under the
saucepan. Into a small bowl she poured the hot milk and black
coffee from a hexagonal metal pot. Steam rose. She added two
lumps of sugar, stirred, then passed me the bowl without a
word. I had no idea what she was thinking. Was she offended?
All I had told was the truth. I studied her back as she cut
an inch-thick slice of bread. The saw-toothed knife cracked
through the crust as if it were wood and crumbs flew halfway
across the room. She slathered the bread with butter and
strawberry preserves and served it to me on a plate.

Only then did she look at me. A long look, hinting at an intimate smile. And I believed she understood my dream; that
she'd been listening.

She leaned back against the stove to watch me eat.

I took a bite. The thick crust gave the bread a chewy heft
while the preserves made it sweet and comforting. The coffee
had a dense, sobering consistency leavened by the sugar and
frothy milk. I held the bowl in both hands and sipped slowly,
my eyes closed, relishing the warmth running down through
me, savoring the earthy sweetness.

"I like the way you close your eyes when you taste things," she said.

I opened my eyes. She had moved and was standing with her back to the window.

Behind her daylight flooded in; the mist over the valley was gone. In the backdropped glare the subtleties of her expression were lost to me. With the bowl held before her in both hands, her face and body in silhouette, she might have been a saint painted on the wall of a village church to encourage the supplication of the devout. But the warmth of her gaze I could feel. And this perceptible difference in her today: how she looked at me without hurry, with tenderness and care.

"Everything tastes wonderful here," I said.

She smiled. "Our secret."

I got to my feet. My heart was stumbling over itself and my mouth was dry. The house seemed to be waiting for me to declare something more than a dream.

"Claire . . ."

But I never finished. Coward. I saw that her eyes had dropped to the floor—as if she knew what I wanted to say and was embarrassed for me.

"Nothing. Thanks for breakfast."

I walked out of the room and kept going until I was outside. I tried just to breathe. To find in each breath the end of the long winter and the beginning of spring—the day just begun; the sun blocked by the house; the dew gleaming on blades of grass in the dank shade; the mushrooms as white and round as marbles; the ground holes made by snakes.

To the left of the door there was a stone bench—a slab of rock smoothed and hollowed by millennia of hard weather. Seeing it, I heard Claire's voice in my head: *la France profonde*. Ancient France, true France, she'd said, earthy France, feminine and wise at heart, its spirit that of a woman so real that she has become immortal and cannot be changed by the vagaries of time.

And here, now, this bench—solid, archaic, inexplicable. Above it, climbing the house, a swath of early roses. Pale pink flowers not yet opened, petals packed tight, all desire tamped down, waiting and hoping to be born.

I heard a sound. I walked up to the gate and opened it and stepped out onto the road. From the left, about half a kilometer away, a blue truck was approaching. I watched it come. Almost an event, in a place like this. It moved slowly, puttering. I tried to remember the feeling I'd had waking just an hour before—the assured sense that simply being with her could be enough; the discipline to stop myself from wanting more. Because it was the endless wanting that would break you, I thought. The constant craving for a love that might never be fulfilled that would bring you low, bit by bit, until one day you'd no longer be able to recognize any part of yourself.

The truck had three wheels rather than four; it looked like the runtish offspring of a small pickup and a tricycle. The man driving it was somewhere between seventy and a hundred. He wore blue coveralls and a cloth cap. He did not so much as blink as he went by.

At lunch we were fine again, full of laughter. Claire teasingly recounted an adventure she'd had that morning, before I'd woken up.

"I found a dead rat."

"A rat?"

"In the kitchen. Right here on the floor. Dead. There must've been some poison around. Rigor mortis had set in. The poor disgusting thing. It died with this horrible rictus grin on its mouth, showing its sharp little teeth. I took a handful of paper towels and picked it up by the tail and took it out to the terrace."

"The terrace?"

"Why not? Rats are biodegradable, aren't they?" By now she was barely hiding a mischievous grin. "Anyway, I swung it like a kind of bola and let go. It had good velocity on takeoff. But you know that tree? The tall one, about ten feet from the terrace? It hit that."

"What?"

"Not the whole tree. Just a limb. And because of the rigor mortis it was pretty much frozen in the shape of a hook. So when it hit the limb, it just kind of hooked on."

"It's still there?"

She couldn't help herself: she was laughing. "Want to see it?"

"Maybe later."

After lunch, though, the rat was forgotten; there was something else. Early that morning she'd gone investigating the property and discovered that the house, built into the side of a hill, had a natural cellar—to which Claire, having rummaged through a chest of drawers in the living room, now possessed the key.

We descended the stone steps that curved around the house till we came to a wooden door.

Inside, the cellar was as cool and damp as earth—cooler, because of the massive wall of limestone. Spiders' webs made opalescent tracks across the quavering beam of our flashlight. The floor was strewn with chunks of stone, broken chair legs, empty gas cans, an armoire door, a rusted washing tub. Claire shivered. "So much history." In front of us a reflection gleamed: an enormous glass jug lay cracked on the ground. I took her arm and steered her around the jagged shards. Small steps, our bodies leaning imperceptibly against each other. Her hand cold but the rest of her warm. The flashlight beam illuminating one object, then another—a visual excavation, oddly stirring. The cellar a book of forgotten poems broken by time into dusty words like mementos in a trunk.

We came to the back of the underground room. Claire tilted the light up against the wall that was built into the hill. "This is what I wanted to show you."

From floor to ceiling, its rusted, attenuated limbs like the shadowed heights of some buried toy city, rose a metal wine rack. The beam of the flashlight shone through it, casting a netlike pattern onto the rough stone behind. Only a dozen or so bottles remained. While Claire held the light I carefully extracted one, rubbing it against my corduroys to remove the dust. According to the label it was a 1964 Pomerol. In the bed underneath was a 1962 St. Estèphe, and beneath that a 1966 St. Émilion Grand Cru, and beside that a 1965 St. Julien.

Around these were others without labels, home-bottled, each capped with a hood of red sealing wax that was brittle and cracked though still garishly bright, like an old prostitute's lip-sticked mouth.

One by one we carried the bottles out of the cellar and up the stairs to the house. Some of the wine would be stupendous; some of it would have turned. It hardly mattered. To us it was a major archaeological discovery. For the rest of our trip we would dine like ancient kings.

And we would stand in the barn where she took me next and stare at the dust-blackened windshield of the 1940s Ford van that in another life had been laid to rest here and never brought out again. The sediment of time had worked an embalmment: seen from outside, the vehicle, so still and resolute, gave evidence of a state of unearthly physical perfection. As did everything we encountered that afternoon: the sky passing over our heads through the holes in the three-hundred-year-old roof—eyes of celestial blue looking down on us, in shafts of mote-drenched light like stalks of dry rain; the lingering smell of animals from the dark hay-filled stalls beneath our feet, where the animals no longer were; the old tools hanging on the walls, their wooden handles worn smooth by somebody's hands, and waiting for another's.

sixteen

SHE'D BROUGHT WITH HER a spiral-bound notebook filled with Lou Marvel's recollections. This was our bible, consulted daily over breakfast—her father's dictated words transcribed in Claire's handwriting, the phrases all the more evocative for being terse and stenographically compacted. Sitting at the kitchen table reading aloud this compendium of mundane fact and remembered feeling, I unexpectedly caught some inkling, like the faint rhythmic pulse of his character, of the young man he once had been and of his daughter's love and despair:

> *Wine man's name Raoul.*
> *Fresh trout from woman outside Martel. Look for sign.*
> *Once found whole snakeskin.*

Statue of Black Virgin, Rocamadour—relig. pilgrimage—
looks like a Giacometti (???: did Giac. ever come & see?).
Vicinity: ruined fortress—11th cent.—Knights Templars?
From right spot on clear day see 20 châteaux.
Old phonograph. Records. Ella and Louis. Scratchy
tunes & plum eau de vie. Summer—light till 10.
Corinne—French, beautiful. Walked the causse w. her.
Married. Still think about.

She'd sat beside his rented hospital bed in the living room
of the Stamford house, she later told me, jotting down his
memories. And what surprised her was how fresh it all still
was to him, particular and distinct. As though it wasn't the
past that had gotten abstracted and fragmented by life, but
rather the present.

.   .   .

The ruined fortress we found on our eighth day, an hour's walk
from the house. It stood high on a promontory, on the hard
limestone upland called the causse. From a one-lane paved
road we followed a dirt path in the direction of the ruin. The
land here was desiccated and unforgiving, savage with stone.
A donkey stared at us with sly, questioning intelligence from a
walled square of hard-bitten pasture. We stopped to feed her
handfuls of grass, and then walked on.

It was a fortress still, though the only thing it protected
now was the past. You could see where the power had been—
the vertiginous path winding down the mountain, wide enough
at the top for only one invader at a time; the forty-foot walls
and fifteen-foot hearth; the archer-slit windows that could

see, like the eyes of God, every castle and château in the region. But nature was king now. Sky owned the roof. The hearth was a void. Two stories up, a small tree grew out of a crushed chimney. Loose boulders of sun-bleached limestone littered the tall grass between the decimated though still upright walls: white against green, skeletal though resonant, like the shattered marble columns of the Parthenon. It felt as old as that.

We wandered around for a while, quiet, stepping into and out of enormous ceremonial rooms cracked open by time. There were no other people. The weather was fair. It was exhilarating, but haunting too. All the feasts and declamations, the wild game sizzling in the hearth, the arrogant and fearful staring out at a world full of enemies from windows that no longer shaped the air.

"Ghosts," Claire said. It was the first word either of us had spoken.

We sat down on a ledge of grass at the tip of the promontory. Behind us stood the ruin like a cliff face from which we'd turned back, hiding us from all sight but our own. Before us lay the valley, the castles and châteaux like stone islands in an ocean of chlorophyll; while across the entire breadth of the country the Dordogne River was a sun-gleamed snake, curved and deceptively quiet. Birdsong rose up from the trees that grew at impossible angles on the steep hillside below us. And from far off the droning of a tractor faded in and out.

"He'll be happy we found this place," Claire said.

That morning she'd called her father and told him all that we'd seen and done during our first week. She was thorough and patient in her telling. And when, far sooner than she expected, he confessed to being too exhausted to continue the conversation, she consoled him in a firm and loving voice. "All right, Daddy, I'll call again tomorrow. You rest now."

Afterward, she'd stared at the phone for a long time. It was black plastic with a white rotary dial and sat on a three-legged table under the stairs.

Out over the promontory a small hawk was circling.

Claire said quietly, "He sent me here so I won't see him die."

She began to cry. I reached out and slipped my hand under the soft column of her hair. Her nape was warm, almost feverish. I left my hand there, gently massaging her neck, until, like a fighter surrendering, she tipped her head back against the pressure of my fingers and closed her eyes.

Late that afternoon we found the woman who sold fish. She must have been eighty, living in a stone hut by a stream. She scooped a net into the dammed-up pool of the stream and came out with two shimmering rainbow trout, and with quick brutality struck them headfirst against a rock and wrapped them in newspaper.

As we were leaving she reached out a trembling hand and touched Claire's cheek. "Ma belle fille," she whispered.

Tears sprang to Claire's eyes. She grabbed the old woman's fishy hand and kissed it.

seventeen

ON OUR NEXT TO LAST DAY WE packed a lunch of bread and cheese and wine into a knapsack and set off to walk the causse.

There are stories still read in books and told in cafés about men who walked the causse from one end of the Lot to the other. Those were the old days, when the more remote fields were sparsely fenced, if at all, and any shepherd might find himself out on the hard bare upland as on some separate earth—grass and soil spread thinly over stone, ruins of stone, animals in thrall to stone. A barren plenitude. In winter stone held the cold like a vow; in summer it embraced the heat like a vendetta. The only protection from the elements were the odd stone huts built by shepherds long gone. You might walk for hours amid limestone rubble and hear nothing but the howling wind or the parched grass crackling in the heat. You might yearn like an exile for random proof of other living creatures—kites gliding high on precisely feathered wings, spoor of fox, a distant oratorio for sheep with bells. The snakes, called vipers, were gray as bilgewater and just eighteen inches long; yet step on one, two hours' walk from anybody, and you would not be coming home for supper. All this was on the causse on any given day. There were more fences now, it was true, and more machinery. But the feat of walking alone from one end of the upland to the other could still be managed. It was still possible, in this country, to disappear willfully back in time. To disappear period. It was a paradise of solitudes.

＇   ＇   ＇

We didn't make it all the way to the end. Perhaps there was no end. We walked through the morning, ate our lunch sitting under a tree, fell asleep with our shoulders touching. Woke, smiled at each other, walked back.

We were silent much of the time. Words were becoming superfluous.

Reaching the house, she went into the kitchen to make coffee. I went upstairs, my legs aching, and started running a bath.

She was still in the kitchen when I undressed and eased myself into the steaming tub. I slid down until the water covered my shoulders, thinking how things between us had changed.

＇   ＇   ＇

I came out of the bathroom wearing a towel. She was standing in the doorway of her bedroom.

"Today was the most beautiful day. I wanted to thank you."

I looked at her. Words came to mind, but they were just words. Out on the causse, napping with her under a tree, I'd dreamed a silent dream of a shelter made of stone, with a rounded roof and no door. She was inside, and I was walking back to her across the miles of forgotten fields. She was waiting for me. I didn't know where I'd been. I only knew that I was coming home to her.

"You don't have to say anything," she said finally. She turned and went into her room. After a moment I went into mine. On my pillow she had placed one of the pale pink roses that grew above the stone bench in front of the house. Its petals were open. It must have bloomed only in the last day. I picked it up, careful of the thorns, and held it to my nose. The scent was delicate and young.

I turned. She was there in the doorway of my room. And I watched her come forward, her hands already reaching.

e i g h t e e n

THAT NIGHT IN THE BIG OPEN ROOM the fire had burned down to embers. Our dinner was eaten, the dishes neglected, the bottle of St. Julien drunk to sediment. The night was black beyond the dusty windowpanes. Ella Fitzgerald and Louis Armstrong were singing "They Can't Take That Away from Me" on the antique Phillips turntable that, following instructions in Claire's notebook, I'd found wrapped in a musty blanket in a cupboard outside the kitchen.

At first, in deference to my complete lack of dancing skills, Claire guided me in a slow circle, treading water on land.

Through "Gee Baby, Ain't I Good to You." Through "I Won't Dance." Through "It Ain't Necessarily So." Through "A Fine Romance."

I loved it anyway. I loved all the steps I didn't know. I loved the awkwardness which with each subsequent song became more like an embrace, until our separate movements began to feel like one joined act, which was the dancing. I loved the two beautiful voices—one clean and limber and high, birdlike in its nimble airborne maneuvers; the other deep and rasped and lived-in though powerfully tender, a friend of the earth— two voices alternating, calling out to each other, talking, singing. I loved feeling that I had the right to hold her. I loved every one of the places where my body touched hers: our hips and thighs, her head on my chest, my left hand over her right, my other hand pressing the hot small of her back.

On and on. Through "Stompin' at the Savoy." Through "A Foggy Day." Through "Don't Be That Way." Through "Summertime." Through "Cheek to Cheek."

Then the phone rang, and Claire lifted her head from my chest. She stepped back. The song continued to play but now the room had been cast down into silence. We stood frozen like figurines on a music box. Her face had lost its color, her eyes were aimed at the floor. Her nostrils were dilated and I could see her chest rising and falling with each breath. She stood like someone woken from a trance, thinking very hard, just beginning to feel the terror of it.

The phone rang again.

"My father," she whispered.

"I'll get it."

She grabbed my arm. "Please don't." She turned and crossed the room. I realized that the record was still playing and I walked over and shut it off. Then the phone rang again, a sound loud enough to shatter any peace, and she answered it and learned that her father had died that afternoon.

n i n e t e e n

OUR PLANE TOUCHED DOWN in Boston in the late morning. Neither of us had slept on the flight. We came through customs and out through the double doors to stand dazed before the small crowd gathered there—parents, and parted lovers, and men in rumpled black suits holding cardboard signs with names scrawled on them. And even before I saw the tall man about my own age who stepped forward to greet us—the man with her coloring and her cheekbones and her long white wrists—even before I saw him and began to grasp his claim on her, I felt the difference, the wrenching displacement, of being back in the world again. As if France and our lives there, our intimate promising lives, had been dreamed by me.

Alan Marvel strode quickly forward, straight to his sister. They hugged, their arms tight in a cradle of wordless exhausted grief, while I stood angled slightly away.

Then Claire opened her eyes, lifted her chin off his shoulder, and stepped back. It was what she'd done in France when the phone had rung during our dancing, I thought; how she readied herself for pain: opened her eyes, lifted her chin, stepped back—out of one life that must have seemed to her a dream, and into this other life that was bitter and more real. She was here, now, with her brother, already turning forward to face the shadows that lay ahead. While I was still back in the old place, with her in my arms.

Alan Marvel picked up her suitcase. "Ready?"

"Alan, this is Julian."

"Sorry." Awkwardly we shook hands. I told him that I was the one who was sorry—about his father. He nodded vaguely. My name meant nothing to him; he'd never heard of me. His eyes, hazel like hers, seemed instead to regard me from some remove. Stepping away, he turned to his sister again and repeated, "Are you ready?"

Claire was silent.

"Everybody's at the house," he said. "The funeral's at three. We should get going."

She nodded absently, but turned to me.

"Julian?" she said.

That was all. My name uttered once, almost whispered, an unmistakable upward inflection at the end. Though in her eyes an urgent, vulnerable intensity I'd never seen before, a silent plea of some kind.

And yet I stood before her and did nothing. Because her brother seemed to own her then, to know her with the unspoken completeness that I had foolishly begun to think was mine. I watched him take a step forward and put a comforting hand on her arm, silently urging her back toward a private world of home and family, and it was like having a door closed in my face, putting me on the outside.

And so I looked away from her.

It wasn't much, but it was everything. An unseeing glance of no more than a couple of seconds, a hesitation not of feeling but of habit, a lifelong compulsion to gather my forces in the face of any potential rejection, to assess and weigh odds so as not to make an even greater mistake. I looked away at nothing, and only then did the possibility occur to me that she might be asking me to step forward too. To step forward and come home with her, as lover and friend, to help her face what she did not feel strong enough to face alone.

But by the time I looked back it was already too late. Withdrawn was her unspoken plea for comfort, and with it some abiding belief in me. A blunt disappointment now shadowed her eyes like an eclipse; I had betrayed her.

"Claire . . ." I said.

"I'll call you." She stepped forward and kissed me coolly on the cheek. Then she turned to her brother. "I'm ready."

As I stood watching, she took his arm and walked away. She did not look back. The electronic doors parted and I saw taxis lined up and two porters in orange ponchos. It was raining, I remember. Then the doors closed and she was gone.

For a long time I stood there.

I stood as though in a trance, remembering a little boy in a state park in New York. Summer. Standing in that park in front of a wall of stone, a boulder the size of a small hill with a sheer vertical granite face, and Judith telling me I could never climb it, and my telling her she didn't know what she was talking about. What I remembered, though, was not the climbing, but rather finding myself already partway ascended, about ten feet from the ground and twenty feet from the top: in limbo, without ropes or physical skill or knowledge. My hands gripping the rock face, my sneakered feet splayed like a duck's, my pelvis jammed as flat as I could make it, one side of my face kissing boulder. Too afraid to move, to climb or descend, to speak or cry out. Loving that rock, and hating it.

Judith, exasperated, calls out to me: "Scaredy-cat!" But I'm frozen. And eventually, with a theatrical accusatory sigh, she gives up and goes to get my father, who, with my mother, is sitting at a picnic table by a stream, some hundred yards away.

Alone, a strange calm descends. My body maintains its grip with no less urgency, but my heart, which like some tiny jackhammer has been powering through my chest into the rock, begins to settle itself. Poised between two places, two states, I begin to imagine staying there indefinitely, moving in, like some new creature roosting in the cliffs.

I hear my father before I see him. Because, for the first time in my life, I am above him in the actual world. If I were to open my eyes and look down, he would appear small and insignificant. I *know* this. And yet my eyes remain closed—the right because it's plastered against rock, the left because of this strange calm that has graced me while alone.

And then my father says my name. Doesn't call or shout it, just says it in his usual voice—a voice quiet but not calm, unhurried but not in command. Julian, he says. I keep my eyes closed. Julian, he says, don't move, whatever you do don't move. And in his voice I hear the fear. He doesn't know what to do, hasn't got a plan. For some reason he's not like other fathers. Experience hasn't toughened his heart and made him strong, but drained him and left him afraid. I can hear it in his voice.

I open my eyes, let go. The fall is quick and merciless.

twenty

I TRIED TO REACH HER. Again and again during the next few days I called the number in Stamford only to get her father's voice on the answering machine—a sound that, no matter how many times I heard it, never failed to send a chill through me.

But the machine was full and wouldn't take my messages.

Five nights later, in the faint hope that she might have returned without telling me, I showed up at her apartment.

It wasn't Claire who greeted me at the door, but Kate. Looking past her into the living room, I saw that the door to Claire's bedroom was closed.

"I can't get through to her, Kate. How is she?"

"How you think she'd be. Not here and not good."

"When's she coming back?"

"I don't know."

"What about her classes? Her exams."

"Lost," Kate said. She tilted forward, studying me. "You look terrible."

"I haven't been sleeping," I admitted.

Kate shook her head pityingly. "Jesus, Julian. All right, come in and I'll make you some tea."

Depositing me on the sofa, she disappeared into the kitchen. She was wearing Penn State athletic sweats and plastic shower slippers—relics from her undergraduate days, when she'd placed fifth in the 200-meter butterfly at the NCAA swimming championships. She still moved with the fluid power of an athlete. Yet as a conventional jock Kate wasn't entirely convincing; over the months I'd discerned in her a bluff tenderness and wary vulnerability. In Cambridge she spent her days openly besotted with a fellow Ed School student named Marcy. And once I'd seen her break into sobs after a painfully stilted phone call to her parents—conservative Republicans from Bethlehem, PA, who she was sure would never accept her if they knew she was gay.

Nonetheless, her penchant for blunt honesty could be sobering.

She returned from the kitchen carrying two steaming mugs. I asked her where Marcy was.

"Dinner with her parents."

Seated on the sofa, we sipped our tea. She'd left the bags to steep indefinitely and the taste had turned metallic.

"Did you go to the funeral?" I said.

"Of course I did."

"How was it?"

"It was a funeral. Sad. Maybe a little maudlin. Her mother made a truly unfortunate speech. Otherwise it was mostly just sad." She paused. "You should have been there."

"Did Claire ask you to come?"

"She didn't have to," Kate said pointedly.

I was silent.

She let out a sigh of frustration. "Can I say something here? Sometimes watching you two fail to connect makes me want to scream."

"That's not how you felt a year ago."

"I was skeptical then. I didn't know you. Your biggest mistake was winning me over. Now I'm frustrated."

"Not as frustrated as I am."

"Listen, Julian, you've got to step up to the plate. Not tomorrow—today. She needs you and you're blowing it."

"I'm trying."

"Bullshit. You're sitting on your hands. You want to be sure it's all going to turn out roses before you commit. Well, get this: you can't be sure. You'll never be sure. In my book, sure's for everyone who doesn't care enough."

*   *   *

I didn't sleep that night. In the morning I canceled a meeting with a student and rented a car. As I drove along Storrow Drive to the Mass Pike the sky was the color of lead, a wind was rising, and there were tiny whitecaps on the Charles.

Passing Wallingford, Connecticut, it began to rain, a light spring shower that by Bridgeport had turned into a squall. I drove squinting through the windshield, wipers on high, hands gripping the wheel until they ached. By Stamford the rain had lessened. At a Mobil station just off the exit ramp I asked directions to Willow Road.

A leafy suburban block, middle to upper middle class, houses big but not huge, the odd swimming pool set off to the side. I parked on the street outside number 14 and sat in the car with the engine off. Her house was a two-story neo-colonial of dark brown wood, rain-soaked and cheerless, with a front lawn and a garage at the end of a short driveway and, to the right and a little behind, a modest pool still covered with its winter tarp. A brown Mercury Cougar was parked in the driveway.

I got out of the car. The rain was a drizzle now, a ghost of its former strength. The temperature was mild. I hadn't thought to bring an umbrella or jacket. Still, for a few moments I stood with my face turned up to the sky, so full of longing I was afraid of myself. The rain fell on my body with the muted, whispery sound of secrets. Then I walked up the driveway.

I rang the doorbell and waited. A middle-aged woman with brassy hair opened the door and glared at me as though I were a confused deliveryman.

"Yes?" she demanded. Her eyes were at once blurry and hard and her aquiline nose was veined from drink.

"Mrs. Marvel," I said, "I'm Julian Rose."

"Who?"

"Julian Rose."

"How do you know me?" she demanded harshly.

"I'm a friend of your daughter's, Mrs.—"

"I said how the hell do you know who I am?" she shouted.

"I don't, I . . ."

She turned on her heels. Through the open door I heard her stomping up stairs. Silence then, except for the eerie whispering of the rain. My hair was stuck to my temples, my shirt was damp and steaming; had I come for any other reason, I would have fled.

Then the known sound of her feet on the stairs, approaching.

She appeared in the foyer dressed in old pajamas and socks, her hair a tangled nest and her eyes visibly dimmed.

"Julian," she said in a dull voice that I hardly recognized. "What are you doing here?"

I hesitated. During the trip down I had planned what I imagined would be an appropriate apology. But standing before her now everything vanished but instinct.

"I'm sorry I wasn't with you for the funeral," I blurted out. "I should have been. I wanted to be."

Her head tipped up, her eyes and voice waking angrily from their stupor. "Then why weren't you?"

"I was afraid."

"Afraid of what?" she demanded.

"Disappointing you. Which is exactly what I've done." I took a breath. My hands were trembling and I gripped them in front of me. "I'm a fool, I was wrong, and I'm sorry. I'm asking you to forgive me."

She said nothing. She stood there thinking. Her gaze was oddly deliberate, as if she were seeing me through the haze of our disparate griefs. The waiting was a torture. Then, almost imperceptibly, she nodded once. Relief of a kind coursed through my body, easing fear and urging hope toward the daylight. My arms opened and I stepped toward her.

And for a few seconds it worked. She held me as I held her, fiercely, emboldened by the resilient force of our feeling, our arms silent benedictions of an unbreakable bond.

Then she went cold and still. Cold in my arms, stilled by some new thought or decision. Shaking her head, she stepped back, murmuring, "No."

"Claire . . ."

"No, Julian. I can't. I'm sorry. I don't have it in me right now to make everything okay. Maybe when I'm feeling stronger." She paused, her eyes welling—until, with a clench of her jaw, she willfully hardened them to glass. "I really appreciate your coming down," she concluded formally, as though I were but the stranger her mother had assumed me to be. And then she stood there, staring at her feet, waiting for me to leave.

twenty-one

I RETURNED TO CAMBRIDGE, and for a while did not attempt to see or speak to her. I hung back in the shadows of desire, thumbing thoughts of her like worry beads, her grief as visceral to me as my own longing.

Through Kate I learned that Claire was still in Stamford. And so at night I lay awake for hours imagining her in that house, that childhood room whose bookshelves and private corners I'd never seen. I imagined her on her bed hugging her knees and weeping.

I thought about her so hard that a paralyzing confusion spread like a cloud over my life. Until I could take no real action toward her at all, could do nothing but think about her.

Inaction is not the same thing as patience. It is instead a kind of perpetual waiting room, a sterile holding pen for un-lived desire, a negative sanctuary. You wait and wait, but the receptionist is very stern and, somehow, the appointment book always full. To make matters worse, crowded into the adjoin-ing cell like so many desperate immigrants, and separated from you by nothing more than the thin permeable wall of your own fear, are all the anticipated rejections of your life. You would think it might be noisy in there, but you'd be wrong. It is totally silent. There's a small Plexiglas window through which you can study these things, this silence, if you have the inclination and the nerve. And eventually, if you have been a diligent enough student and not wasted your time in dream-ing, you come to understand that it is not the rejections that make this a prison, not the defeats, but rather your own grim expectation of defeat; not life but its bodily outline drawn in chalk, where the body should be but isn't, where it once was, this ingrained cowardly pessimism, this relentless betting against love and instinct. This is where the silence comes from.

twenty-two

IT WAS NEARLY THE END of the school year. The days were growing warm and balmy as I sat in Mary's garden grading final papers for my section in Davis' course. My number 2 pencils were honed like scalpels, the stack of papers neatly arranged.

Back in March, during long office hours at Café Pamplona, there'd been the gratification of helping my students choose their paper topics. This was teaching, after all, guiding, putting spark to the kindling of curiosity and seeing what sort of fire burned. Learning as a blaze of light.

But here now, alone and at a loss, it seemed suddenly preposterous to think of myself as a force of illumination. By afternoon I would find myself erasing comments I'd written on papers that morning, doubling back in my tracks, scribbling revised thoughts over the shadowy corpses of previous ones—reminding myself with each new scratch of the pencil of my own tenuous hold on certainty.

It was little wonder that my own work was crawling along at an enfeebled pace. For every new chapter of *Congress and the Constitution* that Davis typed I seemed to produce, like some hair-shirted monk in a cell, but a single elaborately illustrated footnote for my dissertation. Viewed in thin light, my introduction might have appeared promising: the full scope of my argument laid out with clarity and boldness; my intellectual arsenal made apparent, with a surprise or two cannily held back for the conclusion; the Progressive movement in American political history never again to be seen the same way. This was not inconceivable. The problem, of course, was that the introduction was all there was.

And Davis, for all his lip service in support of my publishing future, had offered no concrete help. On the contrary, I had the growing suspicion that he was all too content to keep me buried in the landfill of his tremendous output, toiling away like some beleaguered clerk, thereby ensuring that I would never produce anything consequential of my own.

One afternoon he called and asked me to come by his office. I arrived expecting the usual handout of fresh pages, but instead saw two cardboard manuscript boxes sitting on his desk beside a bottle of single-malt whiskey.

"I think this calls for a toast," he said. Opening a drawer, he brought out two glasses and poured a finger for us both. "To *Congress and the Constitution*," he declared. He was beaming.

"Congratulations, Carl."

We drank.

"So," he said. "Think you can get your notes to me by Wednesday?" It was Friday.

"Actually, Carl, I'm right in the middle of grading papers. How about a week from Monday?"

His smile, without altering physically, took on a noticeable stillness. "It's my course," he said calmly. "I give you permission to hand your papers back late."

"I'll do my best," I replied.

I carried the boxes home. Three pounds, 767 pages. I made a pot of coffee, finished grading my students' papers at four that morning, slept a couple of hours, then began reading through the big man's book. And when I finished early in the week I humbly offered him the last remnants of my months of research, throwing in a few random notes of minor criticism. How intelligent and well written, I concluded, which was true, undeniably, even if his "Reagan Revolution" was not my idea of a revolution. The poor and homeless, the disenfranchised, the minorities—the needs of these people were everywhere assaulted in this mammoth volume. Though at present I didn't have the stomach for a fight. And so my editorial remarks did not reflect my true beliefs, and my mentor's satisfaction with my work remained, I believed, undimmed.

· · ·

Then without warning it was June, commencement week, alumni reunion week: the big dollars rolling in, the crimson flags raised high, the pomp and circumstance, the invocation before the convocation, the protective ropes removed from around the quadrangles of freshly seeded grass, the departmental festivities and familial celebrations, the private dining rooms at Locke-Ober's, the gowns rented, the suits and dresses bought on Newbury Street, the champagne drunk, the sun taken by the river.

Every year before graduation, Davis threw a cocktail party at his home for some of his colleagues in the government department and the Institute of Politics, and a few carefully chosen Beltway insiders from Washington. The governor usually made an appearance, and a Kennedy or two. There had been sightings in the past of high-ranking members of the Reagan administration. And Davis' old pal Kissinger could be counted on to show his perpetually tanned face, casting a Mitteleuropa glamour over the assembled guests and ensuring at least a mention in the *Globe*.

When I next saw him, Davis assured me I was invited, and even suggested the date I ought to bring.

"What about your friend . . . ?" he said, snapping his fingers to himself, as if her name were there at his fingertips awaiting instant recall. It was all just there for him, I thought darkly, all of life's essential information all the time, constantly being sorted through that prodigious brain, an endless returning to the well, a perpetual orgy.

I'd come to his office on a Saturday morning to discuss his next project. Now that the political book was done and the publication date set, he wanted to get going on the memoir. There was a lot of fascinating material from the early part of his career, he assured me, half a dozen file cabinets alone in the basement of his house, the house he was currently renting since the divorce from his wife last winter; and there was a lot of stuff too in his mother's house back in Scranton, an entire garage full of documents, memorabilia, trophies, letters, photographs. Enough certainly to keep me busy all summer from dawn till dusk, if I was inclined. A researcher's heaven. And that was just the early years. This one would be fun. The last book had been business of a kind, but this would be pure pleasure, including the fat contract he intended to get for it. Possibly instructive too, if he said so himself, would be the experience, digging up touchstones of a life spent thinking about government and its consequences, its ramifications and contradictions and meanings, yet spent also in the thick of things, the front line, in politics, the two sides, ideas and action, the branching of these great rivers and then the uniting of them in one man's life, thus far. It would be a hell of a time, he said, wouldn't it, working together, the two of us, on a book like that.

The day was hot. The tall twelve-paned window was wide open to the breeze and Davis stood before it, his hands loosely clasped behind his back, looking out at the Law School.

"What's her first name again?" he asked.

"I don't know who you're talking about."

"Sure you do. Your friend, the marvelous Miss Marvel."

"Claire," I said, to get him off my back.

"That's it. Claire. How'd it end up with her anyway? Are you two together?"

I didn't answer. It had never been our habit to talk about personal matters and I did not want to start now.

"Unless, of course," he added, "you'd rather not discuss it." He cocked his head and looked at me as though I were being oversensitive, squeamish.

"There's nothing really to discuss."

He raised his eyebrows but did not comment. For a while, drawing his own conclusions, he returned to gazing out the window. I saw birds out there, a squirrel climbing a tree. Then he said, "Well, all the more reason to ask her. It's going to be a hell of a party, for one thing. It always is. And if you won't ask her for yourself, then at least do it for the *party*." He stressed the last word to make the pun evident, and then turned and shot me a clubby grin. "Because I'll tell you, nothing makes the old boys happier than a pretty face."

twenty-three

IT ALL STARTS SPEEDING UP NOW. The story. One moment I am here and it all seems remote; the next she is right in front of me, she is everywhere, and I am back in my old life, years younger, scurrying around, prostrate on my bed, getting excited, getting depressed, trying not to fear anything, holding my head in my hands, holding my head high, being stupid, being brilliant, making decisions, making choices, all of them wrong—and yet filled, filled with such ardent love, such good intentions, and such resilient hope.

· · ·

She agreed to come to the party as my guest, an acceptance that sparked in me an optimism I hadn't known in weeks. Though there was something she had to do that afternoon, she added, an appointment she chose not to specify, which would make her a little late. She would meet me at Davis' house, if that was all right. And I said that it was.

The day arrived. I dressed in my bathroom, in front of the chest-high medicine cabinet that was my only mirror; in order to see my bottom half, I had to back out of the bathroom and stand on the bed. My blazer was a crisp navy blue, my pants a summer-weight gray flannel, my tie, which I had tied and retied three times, a light paisley from Liberty of London. My loafers were spit-shined. I moved from bathroom to bedroom to bathroom, peering and crouching, tugging at cuffs.

I didn't feel unlucky. There was nothing evil today in the sleeping stars or the moon, it seemed to me, or even in the mirror. And so, checking my watch for the tenth time that hour, intending above all not to arrive at the party earlier than was appropriate, I strode out into the bright afternoon with my spirits rekindled. It was a typical late-spring Cambridge day, a day of privilege and beauty, sunny and fair but not too hot, the air graced with the sweet green notes of grass and privet.

I walked. It wasn't far. I came off Brattle Street toward the river. And from half a block away I began to hear it—a clench-jawed, drink-smoothed murmuring. I had never been to Davis' house. It was not one of the old ones but modern, with a generous front yard enclosed by a picket fence. And it was in that yard, above the arched teeth of the fence, as in some kind of white-collar barnyard, that I observed the crush of partygoers.

Then I was in that crowd, among them, and there was no more distance or perspective to be had. I was up close, flat against it, where nothing could be gleaned but the stark angles of people, facades like snapshots, clothes, outfits, blues and pinks and whites, wrinkled linen and pleated cotton, the wild glances of sunlight off a hundred champagne flutes. A uniformed waiter handed me a glass. I swallowed half of it and tried to get my bearings. Everybody was there, just as advertised: the governor, short and large-headed and dour; only one Kennedy, but at least it was Teddy, the patriarch, who in event-terms counted for two; a major real estate developer and Republican fund-raiser; and the state's junior senator, with his noble visage and stellar war record. And Parker Bing was there, of course, in a straw boater and white bucks, conversing intently with the deputy secretary for Near Eastern affairs, a fellow Fly Club member, who as I watched slipped a leather-backed memo pad out of his pocket and wrote something down—no doubt Bing's number, I thought, turning away in disgust and almost bumping into Mike Lewin, my Littauer comrade-in-arms, who muttered, "Did you get a load of Bing's hat?" I said I had and he shot me a gallows grin. I asked if he'd seen Davis yet and Mike shrugged, gesturing across the sea of heads to the other side of the yard. "Probably over that way. And don't miss Kissinger holding court by the shrimp boat."

I swallowed more champagne and checked my watch, wondering when Claire would arrive. I'd already lost track of how long I'd been at the party. Fifteen minutes? Half an hour? Telling Mike I'd catch up with him later, I headed off for the far shore, looking for her, beginning suddenly to feel the anxiety of it, hoping that somehow, someway, I'd be able to whisk her out of the party quickly, get her alone. Perhaps for the first time since France we'd have dinner together. And late into the night we'd sit declaring to each other all the feelings we had not yet declared, the hard-to-say feelings, perishable because true. Feelings that had to be spoken now or else thrown away. And I would not allow them to be thrown away. For the life of me I would refuse. . . . So many people, I was musing, as I emerged from the backside of the throng of partygoers. . . . And yes, the shrimp boat was there, just as Lewin said it would be, but Kissinger wasn't in it. Though he easily might have been, I concluded, for it was a kind of Chinese junk made of plastic, with a cargo of pink boiled shrimp piled high above the gunwales, and miniature wooden barrels of cocktail sauce. Egregious, I thought, turning away—and saw nearby, at the edge of the big yard, a hammock strung up between two trees, with an esteemed professor of political philosophy sprawled in the netting, asleep.

I stepped through the front door of the house and into the foyer. Immediately the murmuring of the crowd was left behind, replaced by interior quiet and shaded repose. I stood listening. From the back there came faint sounds of the catering staff at work in the kitchen, and the strangely comforting smell of brewed coffee.

At that moment, drifting out of the living room, I caught the sound of Davis' voice. Not his usual speaking voice but softer. Not the words but the tone—no less forceful for being lowered, still uncanny in its confidence, though something lighter in it today, I thought, quietly jaunty, like that of a man at a party, late at night, in smoke and haze, telling an intimate joke—

Then Claire laughed, saying distinctly, "You did not! I can't believe it."

I entered the room. My own forward motion was a shock to me. They were alone, standing to the left by the windows, close together but not touching, like lovers in a drawing-room play. She was wearing a pale green linen dress and high-heeled shoes and she was as beautiful, as ravishing, as I had ever seen her.

Their heads turned at the same moment.

"Julian!" she exclaimed in surprise. Her face was flushed. As she spoke, I saw her take a step back from him.

"Julian," said Davis in a more restrained voice. "There you are."

I looked only at her. "How long have you been here?"

I saw her hesitate. The room was still and quiet, and in the stillness she seemed to be debating with herself whether to tell me the truth.

"When I came in Carl was standing by the gate," she said. "We got to talking and he said he had a Gwen John. . . ." She made a halfhearted gesture at a small painting on the wall beside her. "I lost track of the time. I'm sorry."

"How long have you been here?" I repeated in a harder voice.

"Half an hour."

"No. I would've seen you arrive. I've been here over an hour and I didn't see you."

"Are you calling me a liar?"

"I just want the truth."

"The truth! My meeting got out early and I came right over. I came because you asked me to. And if that's not good enough for you, then you can go to hell." Suddenly she was livid, shouting. "Do you hear me, Julian? You can go to hell!"

Now Davis joined in. "Julian, listen to her for Christ's sake. What she's saying is obviously the truth."

At the sound of his voice something inside me cracked. "Nobody asked you, Carl."

"What did you just say to me?"

"I said shut up, Carl. Nobody asked you."

"You've just made the biggest mistake of your life," he said in a low voice.

"Claire," I said.

But she turned her back on me. Which was the last thing I saw before leaving.

twenty-four

THROUGH THE WRONG SIDE of the peephole I saw a light come on. A shadow approached, unbolted locks, then the door opened and he stood in the doorway, in his pajamas and robe, squinting into the light.

"Julian?"

"Dad."

It was past midnight. A pillow crease marked one side of his face. His hair stood up like the wind-torn crest of a wave. He reached out and laid a hand on my shoulder. "Has something happened? Are you all right?"

The worry in his voice and the weak, questioning touch of his hand caused a bubble of sadness to rise up in my chest; my whole body tensed with the effort not to give in to it. My father misunderstood this, or perhaps not, because he quickly pulled back his hand, as though afraid he'd offended me.

I told him that nothing had happened.

He nodded. Then, looking down, he noticed my suitcase and the concern began to lift from his face. "You've come for a visit?"

"If it's all right."

"You know it is. When was it ever not all right?"

"I caught the late train. I should have called first."

He studied me, the corners of his pale eyes starting to bunch again with worry. "You're really all right?"

Secretly he wanted an answer that would explain things, but not too much.

"I'm just worn out, Dad."

After a moment he nodded.

I followed him into the apartment. Smells of old rugs, wood, potted plants, bric-a-brac. Years of Kraft mac and cheese, Stouffer's frozen, Jell-O pudding cups, canned soups. Piles of papers, the faded useless manuscripts of old college textbooks he'd edited, their versions long since revised, their figures and theories and declarations no longer sound, and yet here preserved and collected, offered their own museum. Strata of anxiety, ninety-nine percent of it untold, closeted, held mute, stoically and for years, all the years of sitting by himself, married and divorced, eons of woolgathering. And books, not to be forgotten, easily over a thousand volumes, fiction in the living room, biography in the master, philosophy and psychoanalysis in the little study at the end of the hall that once had been my bedroom, books like paving stones to a quiet man's fortress.

Through all these essences, remembered and literal, I followed my father, his slippers scuffing the worn floorboards, the belt of his robe dragging.

We came to his study, my old room. He switched on the light. "I would have cleaned up if I'd known you were coming. But it's been . . . well, it's been a while, hasn't it."

"Yes." It had been ten months since my last visit.

I set down my suitcase. The room looked almost as it had always looked. An old corduroy sleeper sofa where, during my teens, my bed had rested; his desk, now, where my desk had stood. Otherwise the same. Change had never been his friend. He was like a man who, try as he might, could not get a weather report—not on TV, not in the papers, not in any almanac—and so regarded the ever-shifting sky with incredulity and suspicion.

"That old sofa," he said, shaking his head.

"Do you still have the number for that chiropractor?"

He laughed softly, touching my shoulder, shyly glancing at me out of the corner of his eye. We stood looking at the room. The silence was familiar to him, seemed to remind him of something. He took back his hand and asked, "Have you eaten?"

"No," I answered.

We went into the kitchen. This too was unchanged. When she'd gone to Houston, my mother had taken with her just her most personal belongings, her essential clothes and papers. As if there had been no joint enterprise here, no real union, ever. As if, for all those years, we'd been merely passengers in a lifeboat, lumped together by circumstance and the brute laws of survival, and then one day we'd landed, and she had climbed onto that new shore by herself and never looked back.

My father stood staring into the refrigerator, cold white light flooding out around him: no matter how long he stood there, we both knew, the kitchen would always be hers.

"Scrambled eggs all right?"

"Sure, Dad, but let me do it."

"No, no. You must be tired."

I removed the cushions and unfolded the sofa. I made the bed with the sheets my father had given me, and got undressed, and lay down in the dark.

A long night. The room airless, with just one small window that looked out onto an air shaft. My back ached from the steel crossbar that ran under the two-inch-thick mattress, and my mind would not let me go. Every time my thoughts began to return—to the day's events; to Claire and Davis standing together in that room and her turning her back on me; to the mistakes I had made and kept making despite my overwhelming desire not to; to the possibility, so awful to contemplate that it repeatedly forced my eyes open in the darkness, that she would never love me as I loved her—every time these thoughts came near, I tried to divert them. But I could not. There are some thoughts that can be manipulated in this way, ideas which seem to come from outside the self like choices waiting to be made. But there are other kinds too. Intuitions which, like water mysteriously seeping from the ground during a drought, are born so deep within the self that their source, finally, is beyond reckoning.

I stayed with my father all that summer. A placid time, still and flat, despite the city's racing pulse. The city hardly touched us. It was a time of known silences and familiar oblique glances—an interlude of implicit understanding to the extent that certain long-standing arrangements between us were maintained without argument, like an anachronistic treaty:

1. It was not to be assumed by my sudden reappearance that there had been any fundamental change in my thinking with regard to family.
2. Whatever general lassitude and rudderless deportment he observed in me at present was not to be interpreted or commented upon.
3. No more than half of all the movies we saw could be subtitled.

Oh, we were a pair, the two of us. He was sixty-three and prematurely retired and probably lonely and his days were his own. I was twenty-seven and heartsick and my days too were my own, utterly free, though I doubted very much if I could have given them away had I tried.

And so that summer passed.

twenty-five

IN SEPTEMBER I RETURNED TO CAMBRIDGE. Where nothing had changed, and everything had. Where early one morning I stood waiting for Claire outside her apartment building, and in the new light watched her walk slowly up Kirkland Street, her hair unbrushed, her clothes wrinkled. When she saw me she stopped, apprehension on her face, and crossed her arms over her chest as though she wasn't sure what I might do.

"You've been away," she said.

I nodded.

"All summer. Where were you?"

"I went to see my father."

Concern softened her face. "Is he all right?"

"Fine," I replied tersely. She was the one I wanted to talk

about, not my father. "I got back last night and came by to see you but nobody was there," I said.

The concern departed, replaced by a mask of defensive indifference. "Did you?"

"Yes. So I waited."

"Industrious of you."

"Only you never came home."

She said nothing.

"Where were you?" I demanded.

"What do you want me to say, Julian?"

"I want you to say you weren't with him. I want you to say you weren't with anybody. You were up all night in the library catching up on your work and you forgot the time. Or maybe you went to the late show at the Brattle and afterward decided you might as well stay up till breakfast. Or maybe, maybe you just got plastered and had a fling, some stupid one-nighter with some harmless idiot you couldn't give a shit about. That would hurt, but I could live with it. I'd survive. But not him, Claire. Just don't tell me you were with him."

"I'm not going to lie."

"Goddamn it, I don't want you to lie."

"Then what do you want?"

"You," I said. "I just want you."

She looked away. The sunlight slanted across us, already hot, and a small, shrill voice rose in my head telling me to walk away, that what felt unbearable now was only going to get worse. Then Claire sighed and looked at me again. And I thought, She is still here, there is still time, and I stood my ground like an ox or a tree.

She said, "He called after his party, wanting to talk. He doesn't understand how you could have turned on him like that, after all the support he's given you. And personally I don't either. It was cheap and cruel, if you want the truth, not to mention professional suicide. It's shaken him."

"You can't be serious."

"I'm very serious."

"Claire, listen to me. You don't know him. He'll suck the pleasure from your life and his ego will swallow you whole. A month with him and you'll feel up to your neck in sand. Just stay away from him."

"I don't want to stay away from him, Julian. It's already been a couple of months, as a matter of fact, and I don't feel buried. He's not what you think he is. You have no idea what he is. He's decent, kind, supportive. He listens to me. He's considerate and strong. Turned out my father was a wonderful man but not much of a businessman. He left quite a few debts behind him. The dealership needed to be sold right away. It was Carl who worked out the details of the sale and made it happen. Carl, not some lawyer, not my brother. Carl, because he cared. I'll always be grateful to him for that. I trust him, Julian. Trust him a lot. I may even be in love with him. So forgive me if I don't agree with your assessment. Now, if you'll excuse me, I'm going home."

Quietly, without fanfare or drumroll, I changed advisors on my dissertation. Professor Charles Dixon, whose tutelage I'd had before Davis', agreed to take me back. A small-nosed, balding man, tweedy and thoroughly academic, he was well respected by his peers. But he wasn't feared or envied. In almost every regard he was the antithesis of a political player like Davis. At our first meeting, over glasses of iced tea in his house, he asked me why I was interested in switching advisors. I replied that Professor Davis was away too often, a bit too oriented toward the White House and too professionally distracted for my interests and needs, which were more academic. Dixon looked pleased. He nodded approvingly, said yes, he could see how that might be so. He agreed to take me on. The first thing we did together was to work out a writing schedule.

My dissertation would have eight chapters. It was September, and I was still mired in the second. We agreed that I would turn in a new chapter every six weeks, which if all went well should see me finished in time to receive my doctorate at next year's commencement. Wonderful, we concluded, a wonderful prospect—and yet, imagining it, I felt nothing. There would be staying, or there would be going—a career sought after, hungered for, somewhere, by someone. Why? To what end? I no longer felt anything about it, if I ever had. And what, Dixon wanted to know, had I been doing in the way of applications for foundation grants and future teaching positions? It was hard out there, even for the brightest, he said, didn't I know that? And I said yes, I knew that, and we agreed that with the coming academic year I would radically step up my efforts in this area. And we went on talking and planning out my future. And somewhere in the neighborhood Claire went on seeing Davis, sleeping with him, falling in love with him. And soon I saw myself standing in a field alone, far from everyone I knew, with my arms out—a human sundial waiting for the sun, waiting to feel it on my back and arms, waiting for my shadow then to appear over the green grass, the perfectly delineated shadow, time held there in precise configuration; time told, for just that moment, in that shadow that was the absence of light.

PART
TWO

one

THE SEASONS TURNED. Through the leaf-strewn fall, through the day she married him.

Through the frigid winter, alarm clock ringing in the black mornings, the hiding under bedcovers, the sound of windshields being scraped, the steam of car exhaust, the handsome city pocked with gray scabs of frozen slush.

I turned twenty-eight.

Much to my surprise, I was not crippled outwardly. Mornings I woke and stood on my own two feet. Life, as they say, marched on. Every six weeks I continued to produce a new chapter of my dissertation for Professor Dixon's perusal. And twice every week I continued to lead a junior undergraduate tutorial on the philosophy of politics. Such elemental concepts as Democracy, Natural Law, Justice, Sovereignty,

Citizenship, Revolution, Marxism, Anarchy, Power and the State, Liberty and Reason as expounded by thinkers from Plato, Aristotle, Locke, and Montesquieu to Burke, Rousseau, Kant, and John Rawls. No exams, only papers. It was in helping the students determine their next year's thesis topics that I came to know them best. Two favorites stood out: Peter, gangly and unathletic, with a hearing aid (the result of falling through the ice one long-ago winter on a pond in his native South Dakota), who shared my interest in Teddy Roosevelt and the ambiguous legacy of the Progressives; and plucky, feisty Margaret, four feet ten inches tall in platform heels, who'd grown up working evenings in her parents' Korean grocery in Los Angeles, and who, when she wasn't quoting liberally from Georges Sorel's *Reflections on Violence* or Ralph Ellison's *Invisible Man*, was busy writing an allegorical novella about a rabble-rousing, bank-robbing Korean-American circus clown.

And twice in six months I went on dates, both times with women from my department: Megan, a blue-eyed ecoterrorist from Oregon; and Dal, the lithe squash champion from New Delhi. Neither relationship lasted long. By the end of our first dinner—at a Back Bay bistro, where I foolishly ordered the steak frites—Megan had already concluded that my commitment to the ecomovement was suspect. With Dal, however, the problem was not so much disappointment as a general lack of urgency. She moved to her own mysterious beat. It was she who'd asked me out, yet once at the Central Square Indian restaurant (and later back in her room), she couldn't seem to rouse herself to any heights of enthusiasm. The diffidence she'd shown me in the past had not been personal, I realized. It was simply her way with the world, the same supreme coolness of temperament that allowed her to go for—and hit—a three-wall nick at match point in the finals of the national championships.

And (speaking of which) Thursday nights at Hemenway Gym, after the varsity was done practicing, Mike Lewin and I played a regular game of squash. We weren't particularly skilled, but we were evenly matched. It was a routine that would continue until the first week of March. On that night I became a different person; or, to put it another way, I completed a transformation that had been in the works all winter long. Some bitter darkness was rising in me, a brutally competitive spirit taking root—no-holds-barred, win-at-all-costs. I didn't just want to beat my friend, I wanted to annihilate him.

Back and forth the match went, and by the end of the fifth set we were tied, leading to an overset. And then on match point I hit what I thought was a winning forehand. With triumphant satisfaction I watched the ball bounce once, twice— only to feel, a split second later, Mike's hand on my back, and hear him mutter, "Let." I turned on him in a rage. Mike Lewin never called lets, but he'd called one now, on match point. "You can't be serious!" I yelled at him—hearing even as I spoke a distorted echo of the words I'd said to Claire on the sidewalk outside her building. But Mike was indeed serious, and already stepping into the service box to replay the point. He was counting on the fact that squash was a "gentleman's" sport—the rules an honor code, combatants (even the most amateurish) schooled in the accepted politesse and obliged to respect the sanctity of the opponent's honest judgment. He knew we'd replay the point. And for that alone, just then, I hated him. A malevolent anger surged to my core from all the tributaries of those long months of disappointment. Before he could serve I slammed the flat of my hand three times against the white wall streaked with black ball marks, the noise a series of detonations that reverberated like gunshots through the court. Mike looked at me as if he'd never seen me before. Then he served and won the match. It was the last time we played together.

Spring arrived. In mid-April, after two days of rain, I walked into the Square on an errand.

The sun was out. The slowly drying sidewalks were thronged: bearded loiterers at Out of Town News, pierced rich-kid skateboarders from Newton and Brookline, coffee-nursing, clock-punching chess masters outside Au Bon Pain. The winter was over, as though just today, the air fresh and filled with a cacophony of sounds, machine and human, business and play, the fluttering of want ads on the kiosk by the T stop, the drag and slap of boarders hitting brick, a passing boom box, a car horn, the next big thing strumming guitar in front of Warburton's. Filled too with smells, with blueberry muffins, with hot dogs and mustard, with the astringent tang of rain evaporating off pavement, with the brackish, bracing scent of a breeze that seemed to carry the tastes of the river and the harbor beyond and the ocean beyond that, the memory of ships.

I checked my watch—I had twenty-five minutes to order my cap and gown for commencement and get over to Littauer in time to teach tutorial—and hurried into the Coop.

At the back of the main floor I joined a line of under-graduate seniors waiting to order their caps and gowns. A cheerful group, many of whom seemed to know one another: in the buoyant notes of their laughter and talk there was an expression of communal achievement, some binding stroke of good fortune. Cares had been lifted, a curtain pulled back, a limitless horizon revealed. Everybody was young. Like some stiff-backed elder brother, I eavesdropped on them for a few minutes, then pulled a folder out of my shoulder bag and began reading over my comments on Peter's final paper:

Peter:
First, don't be disheartened by all the pencil marks—overall, the writing here is excellent. This is no small thing. Second, I am full of admiration for the scope of your thesis. You went for it, didn't play it safe. Intellectually this bodes well, and I'm proud of you.

That said, while interesting and elegantly elucidated, your argument that TR was more tolerant, indeed compassionate, on matters of race than generally believed unfortunately fails to convince. You seem to have completely overlooked . . .

The line moved up. I checked my watch. More students had arrived, I was in their midst, three young men discussing their plans after graduation—a trip to Europe for one, the

Radcliffe Publishing Course for another, a job with Morgan
Stanley for the third. At the front of the line two stylish women
were leaning on a table where a patient Coop employee sat
measuring heads and writing down sizes.

The line shuffled forward. Putting away my papers, I
stepped up to the table and gave my name, academic department, and expected degree.

"Height?"

"Six feet."

"Sleeve?"

"Thirty-four."

The Coop employee wrote this down and stood and deftly
ran a tailor's tape around the circumference of my head.
"Seven and one-quarter," he said, and wrote this down too beside my name. "Will that be Coop charge, cash, or credit?"

I paid. The line had replenished itself; there seemed no
end to its enthusiasms. Checking my watch again, I saw that
I was on the verge of being late for class and hurried past the
chatting students.

Halfway to the exit I stopped in my tracks.

Inexplicably I had the feeling of being watched. Though
what was strange was that this wasn't threatening but somehow familiar and wanted. My heart raced as I scanned the
store.

I saw her then. She was standing across the wide room beside shelves of stationery with the rooted stillness of someone
who hasn't moved in a long while.

For a minute or more we stared at each other. Then, slowly,
she approached.

She was right in front of me. Her appearance was altered. Her pants and sweater and boots were expensive and
finely cut—a far cry from the faded Levi's and hand-me-down
sweater of last year. She wore lipstick, eyeliner, jewelry—
diamond engagement ring and gold wedding band, new silver
earrings, a new watch. Her hair hung attractively down her
back in a long plait. Her body and face seemed subtly fuller
and more womanly. She no longer looked like any kind of student. She looked grown up, adult, married, well off. And of
course, all the same, she looked beautiful, more than ever.

She started to speak but her voice caught. She cleared it,
began again.

"I've discovered something interesting," she said. "If you
ever want to avoid somebody, this city's as small as a postage
stamp. But if you ever really want to run into somebody, if you
really hope and pray, it's as big as an ocean."

I said nothing. It was a nice enough first line, a line she'd
probably even prepared, perhaps months ago, and we both
knew it. We stood at slight angles to each other, her eyes
roaming my face with an insecurity I did not associate with
her. I checked my watch. I saw her take in the gesture as she
was meant to—as if the appointment I had was more important than running into her again. I was trying to be cool, stoical, resolute. But in my mind the crowded store had been
gutted, become a cave for the two of us, and my mouth had
gone dry.

Anxiously she said, "You're late. You probably have a hundred places to be."

I stood looking at her. Seven months and a marriage lay

between our old selves and now. A lifetime. More than her clothes and hair were different. She seemed tentative, her old confidence shaken as though by some still-remembered accident.

"I have a class," I said.

"I don't want to hold you up. I just . . . I'm glad to see you, Julian. That's what I wanted to say." She touched my arm, then abruptly turned and began to walk away.

"Claire."

She stopped without looking back.

"It's just over in Littauer. If you don't mind walking with me."

ı ı ı

We went outside. Nerves up, heart rioting, static on the brain. It began awkwardly enough with silence, as if we'd forgotten how to speak to each other, which perhaps we had. Finally, sounding desperate, she jumped in and congratulated me on my doctorate.

"I don't have it yet," I reminded her. "I'm still writing the last chapter. Dixon may hate it and even if he doesn't there's the oral defense."

"You'll get it," she said. There was something in her voice— I couldn't be sure—something like quiet pride. She looked away. "Do you have . . . plans?"

"I'd like to teach," I replied. "But I don't have a job yet, if that's what you mean."

"No, I . . ." Flustered, she didn't finish.

A red light across from the north gate to the Yard; in silence we waited for it to change, then crossed Mass Ave. Passing the newly rebuilt guardhouse just inside the gate, Claire used it as a pretext to change the subject, to try again.

"Do you know," she asked me incredulously, pointing at the newfangled structure, about the size of an outhouse, with a uniformed security guard standing inside it, "how much that thing cost to build?"

I told her I had no idea.

"Twenty-five thousand dollars. Can you believe that? It's like those eight-thousand-dollar toilets the Pentagon keeps building. Harvard should be ashamed of itself."

Suddenly an old bitterness darkened the edges of my feeling, and I told her that there was no shame around here that I could see, not at Harvard or anywhere else.

Silence again. It persisted as we walked through the Yard. Already in the distance, above the high stone wall, I could see the paler stone facade of Littauer. We'd be there shortly, I thought, this would end; in two months I'd have my degree and probably never see her again. For the best, I told myself. Yet there, ahead, was Littauer. Davis and the world he'd made. His office with the tall windows and the view of the Law School and the Kennedy rocker and the brass nameplate on the door. I remembered the first day I'd met him, which was the first day I'd met her.

He is her husband, I thought for the thousandth time. Her husband.

I made myself speak, hoping to sound normal and well adjusted. "How about you?" I asked. "How's Burne-Jones?"

"Still a genius," she replied vaguely.

I said nothing. An image of our sitting together in the café, her books open on the table before her.

"Yes," she added, her voice turning harsh with self-irony, "he's still a genius, all right. But not me. I'm taking a leave of absence."

"What?"

"I've left school."

"Why?"

She shrugged, looking away.

"That's a mistake, Claire. You were good at it. You had a passion."

Her eyes met mine for a moment, then retreated. "I still do," she said. She paused, visibly upset. "It's just timing. Don't you see that, Julian? Everything's just timing."

"Bullshit, Claire. You don't believe that any more than I do. Go back and get your degree. Finish what you started."

"I will," she said faintly.

But her tone was equivocal and suggested the opposite. She wouldn't look at me. And this, more than anything she'd said, alarmed and pained me. Where was her old spirit? The Claire I remembered would at least have been defensive in the face of my telling her what to do, my challenging her. It was as though her assured mask of married womanhood were no more than a single coat of paint; while behind it, unplastered and unattended to, lay the same cracks and gouges that had always afflicted her. She'd been touched up, that was all, and the declarations of individual mind—the I wills or I won'ts—were just words to cover the difference. She wouldn't be going back to her studies, I realized. Burne-Jones would shrink until he was just another picture book on a table in her fine new house. She'd given up her claim on him, though not the passion that gave birth to it. And already she was bruised by the loss.

In silence we arrived at the steps of Littauer.

"How late have I made you?" she said.

I checked my watch: fifteen minutes late. "Five minutes."

Another minute passed. We continued to stare at each other. Between us the air rippled with unsaid words like waves of light. A strand of her hair came loose from her carefully constructed plait, and I reached out, tucking it behind her left ear.

She looked down, touching the tip of her shoe to the tip of my mine.

"You'd better go."

Neither of us moved.

I tapped my watch, put it to my ear. "It may be a little fast."

She smiled. My heart lifted. Then her mouth went too far, her composure broke, and her eyes filled.

"You don't know how I've missed you," she said, and began to weep.

t w o

SUPPOSE SOMEONE WERE TO SAY TO YOU: These are the happiest days of your life, right now, and they are already ending.
What would you do? You might craft yourself a credo, a phrase
to live by; might write the words REMEMBER THIS on an
index card and tack it to the wall above your desk. You might
practice meditation, seeking through the emptying of your
mind that state of mindfulness in which your life with its
many attendant contradictions might one day be appreciated
as it is, without questions of ownership or control. You might
fail miserably at this. You might turn your back on your desk
and the invocation (or imprecation) on the card, on the whole
static cowardly life of the desk, only to find that no other life
occurs to you, that you are *not fit* for any other existence;
and so, losing your nerve for the hundredth time, you might

retreat. The card would still be there on the wall, waiting for you. And you might once again sit gazing into the wake of all your feeling, a prisoner of memory, until before too long you realize that every one of your love poems to her has become an elegy, and every elegy, a love poem.

three

LEANING AGAINST THE DOOR when I returned from class was her umbrella. Not her, just her umbrella, yellow the color of buttercups. I unfurled it, today believing in my own luck over any superstition. It snapped open, sunlike, and a note fell out:

> *For you, this small patch of shelter, from me.*
> *Wherever you go.*
> *I love you.*

Her script was known to me. I'd seen it many times. As an intimate friend I'd sat by her shoulder and watched her scrawl and write, thoughtlessly and thoughtfully, on checks and applications, postcards and Post-its and letters.

Still, it was new. Rightward-leaning, idiosyncratically fluent, with tall *t*'s, loopy, elongated *l*'s and *f*'s, with crazy *r*'s and *s*'s like little accidents, and perfectly round *o*'s.

At the bottom, in letters more compact than the others, was her address.

I stood outside my door, key still in my pocket, reading the note again. And again. Even though I already knew it by heart.

four

WE TOOK TO EACH OTHER AGAIN as though we had all the
time in the world, and no time at all. This much I know: neither of us thought of it as an affair. It wasn't breakage but re-
newal, regeneration, the inevitable rectifying of past mistakes,
the passionate and just completion of unfinished business.
History and gravity and truth were on our side. We weren't
against anyone, but *for* ourselves. Davis wasn't our enemy.
When he was away—two nights a week ensconced in the Jefferson Hotel in Washington—he was, in a sense, our ally. When
he was home, he was simply an obstacle, a barrier, something
to avoid, no more personal to us than a fallen tree that we
must skirt, and skirt again, on our way to some private destination of our own. That he didn't know what he was—hadn't
yet felt the force of the storm that already had leveled him—
was not something we talked about.

Lying on my bed half asleep, I felt her get up. The floorboards groaned under her feet and in my mind, with the window light embered and whorled through the thin folds of my eyelids, I saw her fully and clearly naked. Then through the open door of the bathroom there came the unabashed sound of her peeing.

The toilet flushed and she came back into the room. Beneath her weight the bed dipped as though bowing. Facedown I felt the silky heat of her against the backs of my thighs as first she straddled me, then stretched out like my double, her body aligned with mine, her heart beating into me. The weight of her was nothing at all like weight.

Finally, she slipped off. The soft cool air touched the places where she'd been, raising goose bumps on my skin. Missing her, I turned and found her again.

Then she was tracing my mouth with her finger. Murmuring.

"What would you do if you'd never met me?"

I shook my head. It seemed unthinkable.

"I mean it."

"Probably sit on a bench somewhere for the rest of my life thinking how I was a person who'd never met you."

"Sounds stoical."

I kissed her fingers one at a time.

"Maybe."

"And sad."

"Yes," I said.

"What else?"

"I can't really imagine it. I'd be another person. With another name."

"What kind of name?"

I smiled. "Utterly forgettable."

She grew pensive. She began to stroke my hair.

"There's something I heard once. It came from an old man. He said, 'If you want to be remembered, put yourself in a story.'"

"Sounds like good advice."

She stopped stroking my hair and her eyes searched mine.

"Put me in your story, Julian."

"I already have."

We gave each other presents, unremarkable objects of personal history. As if with our newfound riches only impoverished things stripped of all gloss and affect would do.

Here is one. It sits on my worktable. A little gray stone with raised white lines.

She'd found it as a girl, walking on a shingle beach with her father. Later she'd remember how the stone had seemed to call up to her out of a sea of stones, as though meant especially for her, and how she'd had to let go of her father's hand in order to pick it up.

Since that day, everywhere she'd traveled the stone had traveled—tiny friend, talisman, hieroglyph. Until this morning, when she'd woken out of a dream of the two of us.

We were back in France, she told me, standing in the ancient barn, in front of the 1940s Ford van—whose headlights were lit, whose engine was running, exhaust billowing up like the breath of life. A vision that frightened her because there was no one inside the van and she did not understand how this could be. She began to cry in the dream, standing with me in the barn. I took her hand then and told her she must have faith. I kept repeating this. And finally, she said, faith was what she came to feel. Absolute faith in me. Which was why this morning, waking without me in her husband's house, she'd decided to give me the little gray stone with the raised white lines, as a token of the faith that I had given her.

five

THERE WAS A PLACE—left of the long slope of stairs leading to Widener Library, in the little belowground nook of the entrance to Pusey—where, immediately following the commencement ceremony, tucked away from the cheering celebrants and beaming parents and mortarboards falling from the air, hidden from her husband and my family, we'd agreed to meet, to steal a moment for ourselves.

When I arrived—newly minted doctor of government, still in my rented black gown with the crimson hood—she was already down the steps to Pusey, her back against the wall. I didn't see her until she was right in front of me: just a flash of a pale woman hugging herself as though she were cold. Before I could get a better look, though, she was already in my arms, her face pressed against my neck.

"Hey," I said with a laugh.

She was silent, holding me fiercely. I tried to step back to see her better but she wouldn't let go.

"What is it?" I asked.

"Nothing," she mumbled into my neck. "I've missed you."

"Well, I've missed you." Gently, I removed her arms from around my sides and stepped back. She did not look well. Her face was pale, the whites of her eyes streaked with red. I laid my hand against her forehead; she felt warm to me, possibly feverish. "Are you sick?"

"Maybe. I don't know."

"Have you seen a doctor?"

She didn't answer.

"Claire?"

"You'd better go."

"I can take another minute."

"No," she said firmly, almost pushing now, "you'd better go."

"Wait a second." I put my hands on her shoulders and suddenly the energy seemed to drain from her. "Now tell me what's the matter."

"It's just . . . this is hard, Julian. This is really hard."

I tried to think of something about the future that would soothe her; a comforting truth. But none came to me. "I know," I murmured. "I know."

Her grip tightened on my arms, but she said no more.

˙ ˙ ˙

I hurried back to the commencement area—where my father, by arriving four hours early, had managed to secure good seats.

By now, nearly all of the thousands who'd attended the

ceremony had dispersed to the undergraduate houses and respective graduate schools for the handing out of diplomas. Already the crimson-bedecked stage in front of Memorial Chapel stood empty as a prom hall at noon, and the festooned quadrangle with its hundred-year-old trees was but a sea of unoccupied chairs; the air, alive with jubilation just twenty minutes ago, felt sadly spent.

I saw my family: my mother, conspicuously angled with her back to my father, talking to my brother-in-law Ben (a computer programmer in Silicon Valley); and, a few feet away, my father and Judith standing in easy silence with each other.

As I approached them an old panic began to stir; ten yards away I paused as if catching sight of a ghost. Two years had passed since I'd seen my mother for twenty-five minutes in a New York coffee shop. Our last conversation—a New Year's Day phone call—had ended with my request that she not bring Mel, her husband, to Cambridge for my commencement. She'd hung up on me (I didn't blame her), and until just recently I had assumed she would boycott the event altogether. But here she was: hair dyed russet and cut in a Texas bob, waist a bit thicker—yet looking, even from this modest distance, visibly less careworn than when she'd been living with us. She claimed to enjoy her new life, and there was no reason not to believe her. What made the difference? It wasn't anger I felt at seeing her, or even guilt, but rather an anxious bewilderment at my inability to muster any happiness on her behalf.

"Well," called my father. "There he is. The man of the hour."

"Hi, Dad." I covered the last of the distance to them and my father squeezed my shoulder.

"Quite a day." His voice was flushed with pride.

Judith reached out for me. "Look at you!"

"Hey, Jude."

She never failed to laugh at this tired joke. We hugged long and hard, which was the only way my sister knew how to hug. She was the giver in the family, a bank vault of loving-kindness in a world of emotional penny-pinchers. Occasionally I found this frightening.

The hug ended only when Ben—decent, balding, brown-eyed Ben—cut in with a smile. He shook my hand warmly.

"Congratulations, Julian."

"Thanks, Ben."

Then an odd silence among the members of my family, as if a crow were flying overhead.

"Hello, Julian."

"Hi, Mom."

For a few wary seconds we stood sizing each other up. Until—two forces capitulating—we leaned forward and I kissed her presented cheek.

"Mel's feelings are hurt you didn't want him here," my mother said.

I stepped back.

"Mom," Judith warned. "You promised."

"Why not? Is this a temple? A place of worship? No, I won't be silenced. How often do I get to see my son, anyway? So I'm going to tell the truth. Feelings have been hurt. Feelings. My husband is a sensitive man. A good man. He doesn't hold grudges. Why should he? He was told he wasn't wanted here but still he sends his best to my son on his day of celebration. Why? Because you're my *son*, Julian. I thank God for Mel every day of my life."

"You just had to do it, didn't you, Mom?" Judith said bitterly.

My father cleared his throat. "Well, why don't we all get going? We don't want to be late. Where to next, Julian?"

But I was no longer there. I'd jumped ship. It was all Claire now. I saw her again as she'd just been, her troubled pallor and the fierceness of her embrace, her unhappiness. I began to imagine untold reasons, causes, illness or depression, things I'd done or not done, mistakes I'd made. I began to imagine loss. A feeling that threw a cloud over the bright day like a cloth over a portraitist's camera, leaving me enclosed behind the scene, suffocating in my own darkness, unable to focus on anything through the lens but the image of her suffering.

Abruptly I looked up. My family, four pairs of eyes.

"I'm going to have to meet you there," I said.

"What?" Judith said. "Why?"

"Meet us where?" said my father.

"A close friend of mine's sick. I need to get over to her house now and see her."

"Now?" demanded my mother.

"It's important."

"How sick is she?"

"For Christ's sake."

"What about your diploma, Julian?" asked my father.

"I'll meet you there. I promise."

"This is entirely disrespectful," my mother said angrily.

"No," disagreed Judith. "It's okay."

Then I felt Ben's hand on my shoulder. "Julian," he said calmly, "just tell us how to get there."

I ran through the Yard and out the gate to Mass. Ave., up the double-wide avenue, the hem of my graduation gown flapping behind me like a mourning skirt. Past Hemenway Gym and the Law School, Nick's Beef and Beer, Changsho Chinese Restaurant, left on Linnaean, right on Humboldt. When I finally stopped I was panting, standing with hands on my knees, damp with sweat. I pulled the gown over my head and bunched it in my hand.

The street was still. Trees grew tall on either side. The houses were big and handsome with lovely gardens behind. Professors lived here, lawyers, at least one Nobel laureate. In these gardens in June there were inflatable kiddie pools, telescopes for stargazing, tricycles on their sides, chemistry sets.

Their house was on the corner. Pale gray clapboard with black shutters. They had moved into it the week they were married. It had four bedrooms and two studies and a formal dining room and a living room big enough for the valuable paintings he already owned as well as those he intended to own, someday. There was a garden as big and lovely as any of the neighbors' gardens. In it was a single magnolia tree and the beds of irises Claire had planted late last fall, soon after the wedding. They were in bloom now. I had seen them.

I climbed the steps to the porch. On the days when he was

in Washington, when she knew it could only be me, she left the front door unlocked. *I want you to feel that you can walk in anytime. I want you to know that I'm always waiting for you.* Today, though, as everyone was aware, he was not in Washington. Today on the stage he'd sat with the other distinguished faculty in full view, his hood brighter and more honorific, it seemed, than anyone else's.

The door was locked.

I walked around the side of the house, past their Volvo station wagon parked on a rectangle of slate gravel, and into the garden.

The irises were purple and white. They stood straight and full in their neat beds. The magnolia was awash in white blossoms. The sweet fragrance reached my nose just as I saw her.

Three wooden steps led from the back door off the kitchen to the grass. She was sitting on the middle one, her arms resting on her knees. Her eyes were swollen and bloodshot. Her cheeks were blotched with color from where she'd been holding her face. Her only movement when she saw me was to lower her head.

I was on my way to her. Then I stopped. Looking down at my hand, I found the graduation gown bunched there like a black rag. I let it fall to the ground.

"Tell me," I said.

She shook her head. I had never seen anyone look as unhappy as she looked now, as sad and trapped.

"Claire, you're starting to frighten me."

"Julian, I'm pregnant."

She looked up then. Her face was brutally swift and clear. There wasn't time to imagine the joy of it being ours. Her expression told everything. It was broken, without hope, and I staggered back as if I'd been punched.

"Not his."

"Yes."

"How? How did this happen?"

"I don't know."

"What do you mean? Talk to me. How? When?"

"I missed my period." She paused to gather herself. "Last month, also. I hardly noticed then. But when it happened a second time, I panicked. I tried counting the weeks back but I couldn't make them fit with how long we've been together. I couldn't make them fit. I didn't tell you because I was afraid. I took a pregnancy test. It was positive."

"Those tests can be wrong."

"I did it twice. It was still positive." Again she paused, eyes narrowing as though she were groping in the dark for courage. "Yesterday my gynecologist did an ultrasound. I saw the baby, Julian. Its head and feet and hands. I saw its heart. He measured it and gave me the date of conception. It was April third, Julian. Two weeks before we saw each other that day in the Square."

It is a dream, a nightmare that keeps coming back. That day, street, garden. Noon, the sun high overhead. The perfect irises. The scent of magnolia. My graduation gown bunched on the ground like some corrupt flower. My unanswered question lingering in the air. Her hopeless face: she is crying again, sitting on the wooden steps.

Her silence is her answer. She is crying so hard now that

she's fallen over on her side, curled into a ball. I am on my knees on the grass. And still she hasn't uttered a word. Which is how I come to understand, finally, that she is going to have his child.

And so I do the only thing that seems available to me under the circumstances, if I intend to go on living. I get up and walk away.

PART
THREE

one

THE YANKEE CLIPPER rumbled out of South Station and began its long run down the Northeast Corridor. In New Haven
while the power was cut so the engine could be changed,
I waited in the airless dark with the other passengers—
students, businessmen, bleary-eyed young mothers taking
babies to the relatives. When the train moved again it felt like
a release, a slow breath toward life. Then we cruised until
Bridgeport; until Stamford. There, I saw commuters standing
on the cement platform, the mirrored peaks of office towers,
and, in my mind, the leafy trees that lined Willow Road.

The train pulled out. I was still on it. It was the end of June
and soon I was in Manhattan, the Upper West Side, and once
again my father was opening his door. He nodded, touched me
shyly on the shoulder, and asked if I was all right.

We fell back into it. Still in my head from that summer is the sound of his slippered feet going past my door on his way to the kitchen. Each morning he liked to be the one to make the coffee, set out the bowls and boxes of cereal.

Sometimes as we sat reading the newspaper I'd feel his gaze light on me from across the table. I would glance up and catch him staring. Then an expression of mild embarrassment would obscure the habitual worry on his face, making him appear, for a moment, years younger.

After breakfast one morning I was folding the bed back into a sofa when I felt his quiet presence in the doorway behind me. I had been staying with him longer than a month, and in all that time not once had we discussed the real reason for my leaving Cambridge so abruptly, despite my previously stated plans to remain there. I'd told him that I was hunting for a teaching job, and had already tapped all the possibilities in the Boston area. He'd accepted my explanation—or, at least, had decided not to question me about it; it was our common habit to respect each other's privacy. Now he handed me the last sofa cushion, helped me to make the room neat, and said consolingly, "A job will turn up. You just have to be patient."

"I know, Dad."

"I never told you this. After college, before I took the job with Addison, I was offered an assistant editorial position with Harcourt. Just three months into it there were cutbacks and they let me go. I felt ashamed. I was broke. I had to live with my parents for a few months, until the next thing came along."

"That must have been tough."

Gray light came through the sooty window that looked out onto the air shaft. We were standing together without making eye contact. This was our way. We were two men in a little room, and what bound our love, it seemed to me then, were not our successes but our failures.

"Well," he said. "See you at lunch."

He was turning away when he stopped, his back and head straightening—as if deep in the landscape of his memory he'd just spotted something moving.

"Are you still in love with her, Julian?"

"What?"

I had never told him about Claire. But he must have sensed something, if only half the story; in his face now I recognized the irrepressible hope that he felt on my behalf.

"Dad, she married somebody else. She's going to have his baby."

"I'm sorry," he mumbled.

Quickly he turned and left the room.

*   *   *

I dreamed about her. Lying in the dark on the sofa bed, weighing the unlikely odds of sleep, wondering if I'd ever see her again. Then the surprise of it, each time it happened. Sometimes the dream was so hushed and still it might have been invisible, and yet tiny fragments would drop off it, as though chipped away by the dull blade of my longing, and these I carried hidden in my pockets for days, to worry over in private. Like the moment when, sitting on the landing of the steps that lead from the back of her house to the garden, she turns to me and says she can't move, her legs won't work, she is too weak to make it down.

I do not ask her why; I pick her up. That's what I do. She is almost weightless. And I carry her, cradled in my arms, down the steps to the grass—until, all at once, the picture goes blank, I am awake, and those footsteps are my father's, here in the white light of morning.

t w o

OUT RUNNING ERRANDS on Broadway one steamy morning, I ran into Toby Glickstein, an old classmate from the Cochrane School.

"Missed you at the reunion," he said, shaking my hand.

Cochrane was the all-boys school on West Seventy-eighth Street, with a reputation for top-notch teaching and a student body made up of the city's smartest young Jewish princes in jackets and ties. Toby and I had been on the debate team together, as well as delegates in Model UN (Malta for me, Pakistan for him). Cool we'd never been, in truth—princes, neither. But academically we had thrived.

Still, that was ten years ago; I hadn't seen him since. Physically he'd changed little: short, with small feet and hands, close-cropped wiry hair, and freckles. An enthusiast and a thinker. A tendency to squint gave him the myopic air of an entomologist or a stamp collector.

We exchanged news about ourselves in the usual short-hand. I told him about getting my doctorate and my desire to teach, self-consciously making it sound as though I was currently weighing offers from several unnamed colleges in the Pacific Northwest. Then I asked him what he was doing with his life. Toby, it turned out, hadn't strayed far: he was the Cochrane School's deputy admissions director. Mrs. Hogan, the longtime director, was due to retire next year, he told me, and he thought his chances of succeeding her were good.

Once, caught in a stupid seventh-grade dare, I'd managed to slip a thumbtack onto a chair on which the dreaded Mrs. Hogan was just lowering herself. My friends and I waited breathlessly for her cry of outrage, but to our disappointment and amazement there appeared no sign—not so much as a twitch of her thin lips—that the woman had experienced anything at all. Later, however, seeking me out in the crowded hallway between classes, she demanded that I shake her hand like a gentleman. When I warily obliged, she gripped me hard. To my shock I felt the sharp point of the tack puncture the tender flesh between my thumb and forefinger. "That will teach you!" she hissed in my ear, a terrifying smile never leaving her lightly whiskered face.

"Speaking of retiring," Toby said, "did you hear we lost Maddox? He turned sixty a few months ago and announced he'd had it. Moved to Florida as soon as classes were over."

This was news. Bill Maddox had been a legendary teacher at Cochrane for some thirty years. Taking his class on the

American legislative process my junior year had been my first step toward a notion of what I might want to do with my life one day. The term had culminated in a trip to Washington, where Maddox, with his Georgian roots, proved to be incredibly well connected. His hands chopping the air, his good-ol'-boy drawl ringing through the corridors of the Capitol, he not only relished the chance to introduce us to the real-life figures who worked the levers of power but filled us with a reverberating echo of his own passion for the give-and-take of politics, the byzantine machinations and garrulous obfuscations of our great democratic experiment.

"Maddox was the best teacher I ever had," I told Toby. "Who could replace him?"

"Somebody good," Toby said. "I'm on the search committee and the pressure's heating up." He plucked a business card from his shirt pocket and gave it to me. "Keep in touch, Julian. And any ideas, let me know."

After he walked off, I stood looking at the card. It was beige, crimped in the center, still faintly humid from having spent the morning in his shirt pocket. *Tobias Glickstein*, it said. *Cochrane School.* There was a phone number.

I turned up the avenue toward home.

Recalling Maddox and his gift for teaching had brought back to me some vestigial memory of learning—a time of relative innocence when a fifteen-by-twenty-foot windowless room with a dozen desk chairs and a few pieces of chalk had seemed world enough for the full measure of my curiosity. A time when I believed I could learn everything that could be taught under the sun. Maddox, of course, knew better than this. He was not a mere politician, trying to snooker us with empty promises. Nor was he some ego-ridden Harvard biggie like Davis, who dealt only in the certainties of his own accomplishments. I remembered him as the rarest of birds: a teller of essential stories, a backroom bard in love with our wide eyes and our listening. His medium was democracy's sediment, the greasy workings, the engine under the hood and the unseen hands that had put it there. Over the years he'd fashioned this humble material into a glorious gospel, and like all true apostles he would not be ignored. His hands flapped, his lips smacked, his teeth flashed. He was tall and somewhat pear-shaped; he loved to bellow. Lightning-quick, he'd have you singled out, a thick digit (usually the middle one) jabbing at you from across the room: "Mr. Rose! Tell me a story about the longest filibuster in the history of the goddamn universe. . . . Mr. Glickstein! Talk to me about how LBJ mustered the count for the Voting Rights Act. If I'm not mistaken, it all began in the men's washroom. . . ."

Once, thrashing his arms as he acted out a paranoid rant that Nixon was said to have directed at an aide, Maddox accidentally gave a boy named Chuckie Klein a blow to the face. Blood came gushing out of Chuckie's nose. For a moment teacher and student appeared stunned, staring slack-jawed at the ruby stream puddling on the floor. Then Maddox coolly reached into his pocket and pulled out a handkerchief, none too clean, and, tossing it to Chuckie, resumed his lecture: "So there it is, gentlemen. Let no ignoramus ever try to tell you that politics isn't a battlefield."

When less than an hour later Toby received my call requesting an interview for Maddox's vacated teaching position, he said, "The thought occurred me, Julian, but you sounded as though you had lots of big-time offers out there. You sure you want to go for this? I mean, Cochrane's an excellent school . . ."

"I'm sure."

Next morning the interview process began. It lasted a week and all through it I held on to the outlandish fantasy that Maddox, out barbecuing behind his condo in Boca Raton, would somehow catch wind of my candidacy and feel inspired to fly back to New York to interrogate me himself. What a time we'd have! The gleam in the eye, the stories traded: "So, Mr. Rose, Harvard not good enough for you? The young pup returns triumphant, just as the old coonhound heads out to pasture?"

But Maddox never did materialize. Instead, for my troubles I found myself trapped in a small room with Mrs. Hogan.

The years had not been kind to her. She had shrunk visibly and her whiskers had multiplied, though her voice was the same steel trap it ever was.

"What a surprise, Julian, to hear from Tobias about your sudden interest in coming back to teach."

She hadn't forgotten about the tack incident, that much was clear.

In her office I noticed a ficus plant, several volumes of the *National Directory of Secondary Schools*, and framed photos of her husband, her two red-faced daughters, her Siamese cat. "Mrs. Hogan is a person too," I kept repeating to myself like a mantra, as the interview wore on and on.

And seated in one corner of my mind, dressed in the garish

checks and plaids that were his uniform of choice, Maddox softly drawled, "Well, son, you're up to your neck in it now." While in the opposite corner of my mind—the mind that seemed to be in the process of losing itself—simultaneously Davis appeared, dressed in one of his dark power suits, with his hands clasped loosely behind his back, and he too was talking to me, and though I tried to block out his voice, the words sneaked through anyway: "If you won't ask her for your-self, then at least do it for the *party*. Because I'll tell you, nothing makes the old boys happier than a pretty face. . . ."

In the end I got the job. I found a place to live too, and on the first of September my father and I rented a U-Haul and moved my things to a tiny studio apartment on West Ninety-seventh.

His housewarming gift was the corduroy sleeper sofa, along with other furniture odds and ends from his storage bin in the basement. With the help of the super of my new build-ing we got everything through the door and into the middle of the apartment.

The room was stifling; we were both drenched in sweat. At my suggestion we went around the corner to a bar on Amster-dam I knew, and sat in its stained shadows, drinking cold bot-tles of Tecate. A cool enough place to rest. Through the tinted front window we could see out to the street: a fire hydrant had been opened illegally and three giddy dark-eyed children were darting in and out of the gushing flood. Then a bus drove by, lofting a sheet of dirty water toward the sidewalk, and the kids scattered, laughing and cursing in Spanish.

Inside the bar, my father raised his bottle and tapped it against mine.

"To your new life, Julian."

I tried to smile. "So that's what this is?"

I could not remember ever being in a bar with him, sitting here like this in the middle of the day. After our exertions he looked depleted, wan, and I worried that helping me move in the heat had been too much for him. He wasn't a young man. A sudden image of him having a heart attack flashed before my eyes—he would be pale just like this—and then, in the cavelike surrender of the bar, I felt a nugget of helpless love for him break free of its hidden moorings and rise to the surface of my consciousness.

"I ever tell you about your mother's and my first apartment?" he said.

"No." He had told me once or twice, but for some reason, now, I wanted to hear him tell the story again.

"Across town, Eighty-ninth and Second," he said. "Well, it was major for us—our first apartment, and on the Upper East Side, no less. All those rich people! Of course the reality was a little different. The place was a hundred and ten bucks a month, which back then was a good chunk of my salary. And it was hardly bigger than your studio, except the landlord had decided to milk it for all it was worth by dividing it into four rooms." He grinned. Lifted by this local act of remembrance, color had returned to his cheeks and his posture had improved. "Four closets was more like it. We slept in one of them, cooked in the second, ate in a third. The fourth was going to be for you kids when you finally arrived."

Still faintly smiling, he took a swallow of beer. He looked

out at the street and the kids playing there in the flood of water.

When he turned back, his eyes were charged with feeling and his grin was gone.

"I remember measuring that room for a bunk bed," he said. "All we had was an old yardstick. I laid it on the floor, marked the place with my thumb and scooted it along. That's how we did everything back then. Eight and a half by five and a half, that room was. A closet. But big enough for a bunk bed. Big enough for kids."

He finished his beer. His eyes found mine in the smoky mirror above the backbar, and through the bottles of tequila and Cointreau and triple sec he saw me looking at him.

"That was my favorite room, Julian. My favorite room. Just knowing that one day soon you'd come along and sleep in it."

My first memory:

I am in a bathtub that is, to me, as big as a room. He is on his knees on the white tiled floor, smiling down at me, face like a moon, his elbows resting on the rim of the tub, his hands drifting in the warm water beside my legs and feet. Short dark hairs cover the backs of his hands: an underwater forest.

I reach out and grip his wrist with both my hands. "Hold my breath?" I say.

He grins. His teeth are white. He is bigger and younger and more hopeful than he ever will be again. "Sure," he says. "Hold your breath. But not too long."

With one hand he helps pinch my nostrils closed, to keep the water out. The other hand he puts behind my head. Shutting my eyes, I take a breath so deep it puffs my cheeks out into a single balloon. "Don't forget to come back," he teases, then lays me back like a holy child. The warm water closes over me. Once under, I let my eyes open. His face beams down at me through a penumbra of rippling light. His lips are moving.

"I see you," I think he's saying. "I see you."

This is the test I have conceived for myself, the only one that can tell me what I need to know. My cheeks are straining to hold enough life. As the oxygen disappears, my lungs replenish it with courage. My mind is everywhere, and just beginning. I am hearing the world as it might be.

I paid the check. He moved stiffly, his body already mapping tomorrow's soreness, joint by joint. We went outside, into the sticking heat and the smell of baked trash. The kids had gone, but the water was still pouring from the hydrant.

On the corner we parted with a brief hug. We would go to our own places now. I envisioned the cluttered heap of things sitting in the middle of my floor, the windows sealed shut with fresh paint.

three

A HAND WENT UP. Pale hand, short fingers, belonging to a small dark-haired boy with a purposeful but shy expression to his eyes, which, on this first day of school, he could not quite raise to meet mine.

A glance at the roll list in front of me and I came up with a name: David Glassman, junior.

"Yes, Mr. Glassman?"

"I heard you went to Cochrane yourself, Mr. Rose."

"That's right."

"How'd you like it?"

"Well enough to come back here and teach."

"How long ago was that?" asked another boy, whose tie appeared to be a swatch of hemp.

"Let's just say it was a while ago."

"Like how long? I mean, who was president?"

"Eisenhower."

A pause.

"Gentlemen," I said soberly, "that was a joke."

David Glassman grinned. He was the only one. Then I saw a couple of other boys smirk sideways at him, mocking him. Glassman observed this too; he swallowed his grin and ducked his head, turtlelike, down into his neck. Most damaging of all was the look on his face that showed implicit agreement with his detractors, even affection for them—the Stockholm syndrome, I thought, and instinctively my heart went out to him.

It was my first day. And on the first day of school—whether child or adult, student or teacher—in fear and trembling you received with inordinate gratitude what wisps of encouragement and generosity of spirit were offered your way. This wasn't ass-kissing but mutual recognition. In no more time than it had taken to call out the names and tell a thudding joke, I'd had a vision of a kid that matched in some restorative and hopeful way the vision I'd long harbored of myself: dark-haired and quiet, shy but confident, quick to duck his head but always listening carefully; always thinking. A boy who relied perhaps too heavily on the inventory of his brain as the sole means of getting across to higher ground. A boy who as he matured would grasp with scientific precision a large number of right answers—and yet who, for all that, would fail to translate those answers into the deeper poetics of selfhood. A boy who, having no real compassion for his own tender sensibility, was inclined to side with those who would denigrate it over those who would nurture it. A boy whose parents probably didn't love each other, whose family didn't feel like a family. A boy, in short, in search of a mentor or a big brother or a father. A boy waiting to be taught.

I began to speak to the class.

"This is a two-term course," I explained. "The second term will be called 'Effecting Political Change' and will be something of a kitchen sink of political topics. In one way or another we'll touch on elections, new communications technologies, voting patterns, media groups—whatever aspects of political life seem relevant to the changing world we live in. This is government and its workings as seen through the lens of political science, not history. But it's my belief—and it was Mr. Maddox's belief when I was his student here—that to speak about political science without first having a solid grounding in history is to speak first and foremost out of your asshole."

Laughter.

"Which brings us to the present term, which as you no doubt are aware is called 'American Political Institutions.' Here, we'll be concerning ourselves primarily with just that— the architecture and goals of the Constitution, the political and social environment that gave birth to it, the mind-set of the authors as we have come to know them. Aspects of Federalism. You all know what Federalism is? You've taken your basic U.S. history, I trust. Mr."—a quick glance again at the list of names—"Chen, would you please give me a succinct definition of Federalism?"

"Federalism was the approach adopted by the Federalist Party."

"Approach?"

"Um, doctrine?"

"Go ahead."

"I think Alexander Hamilton was the head of it. The idea was that the country needed a strong government and so it should vote for the Constitution."

"*Who* should vote?"

Brian Chen looked down at the cover of his notebook and sought to become invisible. David Glassman's hand rose a few inches, then stopped, at war with itself.

"Mr. Glassman, is that a raised hand?"

"The states," Glassman said. "The states should vote."

More smirking, from the same source as before.

"Is that amusing, Mr. . . . . Weisberg? The states are amusing? Which ones in particular?"

"Delaware," Liam Weisberg, a red-haired sharpy, shot back, uncowed. "It's smaller even than Central Park."

"Pejorative hyperbole will get you nowhere in this class, Mr. Weisberg."

"What's 'pejorative' mean again?"

"Disparaging or belittling."

"Well, George Washington was *from* Delaware and even he was pejorative about it."

"Is that so?"

"Yeah. My dad told me an anecdote about it."

"As I was saying, Mr. Weisberg."

"Sorry, Mr. Rose."

"The Constitution. Federalism. This is where we begin. Let's try to go back to 1780 and see if we can't imagine what government felt like then. Its effect. The footprint it left on the psyches of ordinary Americans. How much authority did government have at the time? Where was that authority located and how did it assert itself? Why might such authority be needed? Mr. . . . Jackson?"

A brown-skinned junior, tall and thin as a reed. "To control people? Otherwise, you know, all hell can break loose."

"Precisely. All hell can break loose. And what might that say about the nature of power in human hands?"

"It's a sign of human weakness," Glassman offered.

"I thought it was an aphrodisiac," Weisberg chimed in sarcastically.

"That's probably why you're in an all-boys school, Mr. Weisberg."

Laughter. Weisberg, to his credit, laughed the loudest.

"Wait a second," I said. "Let's stay with this. Power as a laboratory for human fallibility. Power also as a natural source of concern among a people, especially those Americans in 1780, who after finally liberating themselves from British rule were not necessarily keen to put themselves under a highly centralized authority again. Where is power to be observed?"

"In government?"

"Yes. Where else?"

"In families."

"Yes. Good. Where else?"

"Everywhere. Human nature."

"All right. Who here has seen the film *2001: A Space Odyssey*?" No hands went up. "Okay, so nobody's seen it? See it sometime, if you can. In the first scene a bunch of semi-prehistoric apes gathered around a watering hole are gnawing on a zebra carcass. Kind of like you guys here, in fact."

"If we're the apes, does that make you the zebra carcass?"

"Not bad, Mr. Weisberg, not bad. Now, to continue: the scene's sort of kitschy and amusing till a rival ape gang shows up wanting the food and water for themselves, and brutally attacks the first gang. What we then see, as Mr. Jackson so aptly phrased it, is all hell breaking loose. Bloody murder. As a metaphor for human nature at its most unbridled, this is about as good as it gets. Ape versus ape holding up a mirror to man versus man. Better even than all those old reruns of *Wild Kingdom*. Not a bad reason to start thinking about the role and function of government. After all, it's supposedly our brains that got us here, allowing us the rational capacity to control our otherwise animalistic tendencies toward the abuse of raw power. Checks and balances, in other words. Which brings us to the seventeenth-century English philosopher John Locke, whom you will all read more thoroughly when you get to college, I hope, and who among other things advocated the need for some restraining authority to keep that raw power in check against the bullies of the world. And there are still plenty of bullies in the world. If you don't believe me, just take a look any day of the week at the *Times* Metro section."

Brian Chen raised his hand.

"Mr. Chen."

"You mentioned bullies. Well, I was mugged last week."

"You were? Sorry to hear that."

"They took my watch," Chen said. "And fourteen dollars."

"That's terrible."

"I've been mugged three times in the last five years," another boy said.

"Which brings us," I persisted, "to Madison. James Madison. Anybody? Mr. Glassman."

"The fourth president of the United States and one of the authors of the Federalist Papers."

"Correct. And Madison, you can be sure, had read his Locke. He'd read Locke's *Second Treatise*. He'd read a great many things. He knew Locke's writings on the state of nature intimately, and drawing on them, and on his own observations as a political thinker in a newly formed nation, he was able to dream up the notion of using the idea of human fallibility, human weakness, as a virtue within a new and necessary document—the Constitution—that would address and codify the relationship between the people and the power they had entrusted to their government. It's a beautiful thing, this system of checks and balances. The three branches—legislative, executive, judiciary—each working as both initiator and ballast. . . ."

Suddenly, outside our classroom, a clamor had begun, the hallway rumbling with footsteps and voices. My momentum broken, I glanced at the clock on the wall: the period was over.

"Okay, I guess that's it for today." I felt the disheartening change in the room—the communal distraction, the itching to bolt. A couple of students had put down their pens. "For Thursday, read the first chapter of *American Government* by James Q. Wilson and John DiIulio."

"How do you spell that?"

They were closing notebooks, stuffing book bags.

"Look it up on the syllabus, Mr. Weisberg."

In a minute they were gone, all of them, Weisberg and Chen and Jackson, David Glassman too, packed up and eager to join the boisterous river of youth flowing to other parts of the building, other teachers, subjects, words, dreams.

Standing in the empty classroom, I felt the shock of the vanished hour, the relief of having navigated it, and the hollow sadness of depletion.

four

FOLLOWING TRADITION, at the end of term I took my class on a trip to Washington. The highlights were a tour of the Capitol, a lengthy observation of the House in the throes of procedural debate (an amendment to an existing logging bill), a fifteen-minute meeting with Senator Daniel Patrick Moynihan of New York, and a somewhat longer meeting with Representative Barney Frank of Massachusetts.

The boys were curious and enthusiastic. Our second night we ate a celebratory dinner at a chain steakhouse. As the chocolate sundaes arrived, Liam Weisberg stood up, tapped his glass with a spoon, and announced his candidacy for president in '92. He was aware that it was a little early in the process—there was a year to go yet before the '88 election—but, he said, he wanted to let us all know now, so we'd have a chance to get in on the ground floor, so to speak, while decent Cabinet positions were still available.

"That's very thoughtful of you, Mr. Weisberg."

"In return for a perfect grade, I'll give you Health and Human Resources, Mr. Rose. Whaddya say?"

I laughed. "Weisberg, you're a little Caesar in the making."

"Caesar knew how to handle his PR, Mr. Rose, I'll say that for the guy."

"Julius Caesar was stabbed to death by his most trusted aide, Mr. Weisberg."

"Bullies!" Brian Chen declared in a jovial voice.

Chen's face, I suddenly noticed, was the color of rhubarb; so, for that matter, was Weisberg's. I wondered if they hadn't sneaked a couple of drinks somewhere before dinner.

"Sort of, Mr. Chen."

"How about me?" David Glassman asked. "What position do I get?"

"Missionary," Weisberg shot back.

General laughter. Ducking his head, Glassman took a bite of sundae and did not speak for the rest of the meal.

We returned to our hotel. By eleven o'clock sharp the boys were in their rooms for the night. I went to my own room and turned on the TV and found Larry King interviewing Susan Estrich, the manager of Dukakis' bid for the Democratic nomination. Dukakis hadn't failed yet. He was still climbing the mountain, still rising. The earth from where he stood must have looked flat, despite what he'd learned to the contrary in grade school; he could reach out and cover it with his hand. Such was his confidence at the time. And Estrich too—smart tough-talking commander of the minions—shared in the sense of imminent power. She was brazen in the face of King's self-satisfied mien.

I turned off the TV and lay there—fully dressed, shoes on—in the hotel quiet. Sleep anytime soon was out of the question.

It was not a real quiet in that generic room, but a pervasive humming. As if there existed somewhere close by a generator, a strange white-noise machine designed to drown out all the televised lie-mongering and whining mea culpas and pandering.

I got up and left the room, intending to go to the bar for a drink. As the elevator doors opened on the lobby, I almost ran into David Glassman.

"David! What are you doing down here?"

His head ducked. "I . . ."

"It's after curfew."

"I know, Mr. Rose. Sorry."

He ducked his head again, and this time I felt a flash of annoyance. I suppressed the urge to point it out to him, to explain how a tic like that—a kowtow in miniature—might express weakness or even servility to other kids, and how under certain circumstances kids could be as power-mad and ruthless as adults. Hadn't he read *Lord of the Flies*?

"Everything okay, David?"

"Sure, Mr. Rose." He was staring at his feet. The elevator doors started to close but I held them.

"David, look at me."

The head turned up. The eyes were bloodshot and the nostrils mildly inflamed. He'd been crying.

"You're a lousy liar, Glassman, you know that?" I said as lightly as I could, stepping out of the elevator. "Come on, I'll buy you a soda."

Wordlessly he followed me across the lobby.

A brief journey—but even so, time enough to reflect on whether the student was feeling relieved or merely dutiful at the prospect of a tête-à-tête with his teacher, however sympathetic; whether, for that matter, the teacher genuinely thought he could help the student with his problems (whatever they might be), or whether this was just another example of the rampant egoism of the lonely.

We went in. A hotel bar, half past eleven at night and the tables all full. Not just the seat of government, then, this town, but the mother lode of convention centers. Did people never sleep? Did they not have families to go home to? All these indefatigable male conventioneers in wrinkle-free gray suits and white shirts hunched over stiff drinks, groping for one more handful of nuts. All these tired women in heavy makeup and starched blouses and Colonel Sanders ribbon ties, whose permanent-press smiles evoked the last steps of a forced march that had begun eons ago in some other desert. A scene, as they say, to make you weep. Except that as we entered the bar a couple of heads turned in our direction, and mirrored in their curious stares I caught a glimpse of the little docudrama I was unwittingly directing: a man and a boy, at night, entering a bar. A mistake. Clearly the boy was too old to be my son. What, then, was happening here? Nothing good, declared the silent, judging faces.

I pushed on anyway. Though now I was angry with myself—it was sheer stupidity not to have considered appearances.

And it was too late. I hadn't thought ahead, hadn't noticed the stares in time. And the last thing I wanted to do was add to David's problems and his pain, his clearly advanced if not yet fully articulated sense of being inadequate in the world. No, I wanted to say to him: The burden of being intelligent and shy and young is that you will always know, cannot *not* know; have grown up in a fiction of perpetual responsibility, believing that whatever cracks in life you find must be *your* cracks, that anything at all can be your fault. I wanted to tell him that what he didn't see couldn't hurt him, whereas what he did see would be with him for the rest of his days. And he would see a great deal, always, except perhaps his own worth.

We reached the faux-mahogany bar. There were two empty stools at the end. I slid onto one of them, and David climbed onto the other and perched there awkwardly. All of a sudden, he looked excruciatingly young.

The bartender sauntered over. Gray-haired, with a plush walrus mustache and a thick pitted nose that no doubt in its time had borne witness to entire epochs of pre- and post-convention despair, joy, and camaraderie. His eyes shifted from me to David, then back to me, before he asked what I'd have.

My order of two Cokes seemed to reassure him. He brought the sodas without comment, and went back to the other end of the bar.

"Now," I said, turning to David. "Do you want to tell me why you were in the lobby half an hour after curfew?"

"I'm sorry, Mr. Rose."

"I know you are."

He took several gulps of Coke. I waited.

"I was using one of the pay phones," he said finally.

"Why?"

"My parents made me promise to call." He paused. "I didn't want to do it in the room, Mr. Rose. In front of anybody."

"I understand. Is something happening at home?"

He wouldn't look at me.

"David?"

"They're getting divorced," he said softly, looking at the bar.

"How long have you known?"

"Since last weekend."

His gaze was fixed on his hands, which were wrapped around the glass on the bar; he was staring at his hands as if there were something in them that he was in the process of recording for posterity.

"It's my mom who wants it," he said. "She says she loves somebody else."

He was quiet then, staring at his hands; I could hear him breathing. There was acne on his forehead, and he hadn't yet grown into his nose. But he held himself like a man. It was all inside him, whatever it was.

I put my hand on his back. More than one head in the room turned our way, but the stares no longer made any difference to me.

For a few moments longer David held himself still. Then,

bit by bit, he began to cry. He cried quietly, just as he was, sitting on the tall stool, his hands gripping the glass of soda.

From behind, in the cheap murky light of the bar, nursing your third drink or your eighth, you wouldn't have heard him. You might have mistaken my young friend for an adult, a slight small-boned man, possibly a drinker. You would no longer have discerned in him the student, the growing boy, the hungry seeker of knowledge who until just a few days ago, a few minutes, had remained an optimist in spite of himself. This new pain was all confusion to him, a note struck in the darkness: knowing its source had changed nothing, shed not a single ray of light.

five

SHE KEPT COMING BACK. She was never far away. Washington
or New York, hotel room or cheap studio, Riverside Park or
Central, take-in Chinese or hot dogs on the corner, James
Madison or John Locke, Mrs. Hogan or Mr. Maddox, Glassman or Jackson or Weisberg or Chen, my words or theirs,
reading or teaching, teaching or struck dumb. It made no difference. Every day she came, and every night. I was a blank
screen and she was the only movie, and I watched her and
watched her and watched her.

s i x

THE FOLLOWING SUMMER, while running for the highest office in the land, the short dour governor of Massachusetts ill-advisedly placed an olive-green, one-size-supposedly-fits-all Army helmet on his large head and climbed into a tank. At that moment he lost the presidency, which he had desired for as long as he could remember.

Hours later, with the first clips on the evening news, the whole thing was over—vanished in a buffoonish mishap, an unwitting joke, a pantomime of such hubristic and small-minded desperation that somehow it would succeed in erasing all other impressions of the man. Gone forever was whoever he had been. This was what he was now.

November and the general election still lay ahead. Those final weeks must have seemed to him like a slow but certain public drowning.

At Cochrane, a new year began. I wasn't a rookie anymore; walking down the hallway between classes, during lunch, you'd hear it: "Hi, Mr. Rose!" "Hey, Mr. Rose!" "Mr. Rose—my *man!*" The sheer numbers of students, their raw energy, backpacks stuffed with enough hope and anxiety to fuel a shuttle launch.

It's the paradoxical reward of teaching that the job is never finished. No one, especially the brightest, will ever know enough. You yourself can never stock the larder of knowledge full enough to guarantee continual nourishment throughout the long winter of uncertainty that is living.

On top of this, perhaps, must be counted the old adage that teachers remain eternally young because their students never age. A time warp, in other words. Except that I did not believe it.

In my minuscule apartment there was a single mirror the size of a sheet of notebook paper. Big enough to shave by. Big enough to reflect back at me those few visible surfaces—a relatively unlined face, a long-fingered hand—capable of carrying on this charade of youthfulness to the outside world. At my age the skin was still resilient, if no longer exactly fresh. It made for the most natural of disguises.

The heart, of course, was a different story.

I tried dating a couple of times. But as had been the case in Cambridge, these attempts at romance lacked conviction, and were short-lived.

I took Carol, a redheaded English teacher, to an Italian restaurant on Columbus, then back to my apartment, where we sat on my sofa drinking wine and talking desultorily about school and the students we shared. Not a terribly demanding date—though not so simple, either, as it turned out. I couldn't find the words or guts to tell her that most of what we said to each other sounded disturbingly secondhand to me, echoed by the memory of other, more resonant conversations; or that the toss of her head, the lifting of her hand to her face, too often struck me as shadowy reminders of moments already past. There were no original gestures left, I wanted to tell her, but didn't.

And then, at some point, I simply began to shut down. It was involuntary; as though I were the last of my species, defeated by the grind of existence, fatal flaws made glaringly evident under evolution's dispassionate magnifying glass. Excusing myself, I went to the bathroom and stood leaning over the sink. That was all. The tiny mirror, showing me myself, did the work of an entire wrecking crew.

When I returned, Carol was gone.

seven

In February, for my thirtieth birthday, Toby Glickstein threw a party in my honor.

That night it snowed heavily. Toby lived up near Columbia, in a rent-controlled apartment passed on to him by an uncle. I walked up West End Avenue, the snow sifting down between the residential buildings in fat adhesive flakes; the city windless, muted, yellowed and shadowed by streetlights. The sidewalks nearly empty: a different place. The street, otherwise obscured, revealed itself as two furrows of oiled black made by the tires of a recently passed car. Nothing else went by as I walked, and gradually the furrows took on a velvet whiteness, and soon disappeared.

"Jesus, Julian," Toby said, opening the door. "You look like a fucking snowman. Well, happy birthday. Put the coat in the bathtub, please."

In the living room eight men about my own age were huddled around bowls of tortilla chips and salsa. I knew this crowd. We were all Cochrane almuni of a certain ilk. Many of us had grown a bit taller since the old days, but neither contact lenses nor Clearasil nor hair gel could hide the fact that somewhere in the past we'd been geeks.

I shot Toby a raised eyebrow. He followed me back into the apartment.

"Well, *you* try rustling up some women on such short notice," he said defensively. "Anyway, don't knock it. These guys are the last line of defense between you and another night flying solo with Captain Kirk."

"Nice try, Tobe, but I don't have a TV."

"You think that's something to brag about?" Toby said. "That's pathetic, pal. Now how about taking off the coat? You're dripping on my carpet."

We rallied. We drank—red wine, beer, and bourbon. We stuffed ourselves with Chinese food from the Moon Palace and traded ten-year-old wallflower gossip as if it was hot currency. There was Muller, Goodman, Krebs, Piombo, Wolff, Scheinbart, Pleven, and Yang. Krebs was trying to make his first film, Wolff was a freelance journalist, Pleven was in computers, Yang was a lawyer, and Goodman was an oil and gas analyst for Salomon Brothers. Improbably, Piombo had written a children's book that was being published in the fall (he confessed to having intended it for adults). Scheinbart and

Muller were between things and discussing the possibility of some kind of joint venture, possibly a yoga studio. This idea was greeted with derisive hooting by all.

After a couple of hours of this, after cake and tone-deaf singing, I snuck off to the bathroom, simply to be alone. I'd been having a decent evening. But beyond the daily routine of the classroom, I guessed, I'd fallen out of the habit of being around a social group for any length of time.

I closed the door and sat down on the edge of the tub. Beside me lay my heavy winter coat, where earlier I'd put it to dry. The wool was still damp. The snow that had covered it was strangely vivid to me, despite having disappeared. In my mind I saw it still falling, felt it settling once again on my head and shoulders. I put my face in my hands.

I was thirty years old. I needed to stop remembering, looking over my shoulder, being dragged from shore by a swirling tide of feeling for a woman who was gone and would not be coming back. Gone. A mother now, I had to presume. I didn't know whether she'd had a girl or a boy, but I imagined a girl made in her image, and I saw this child walking, almost stumbling. . . . And Claire picks her up—

"Julian?"

Toby's voice, through the door, followed by a tentative knock.

I jumped to my feet. "Just a minute."

He knocked again. I flushed the toilet for the sake of appearances, turned the tap on and off.

"What is it?" I demanded, opening the door.

Toby's eyes were bloodshot with drink. "You okay?"

"Fine."

"You weren't puking, were you?"

"No."

After a moment his face broke into a lopsided grin. "Good. Because we've got company."

I followed him out of the bedroom and down the hallway. In the living room three women stood surrounded by eager, nervous men as at a high school dance. Two of the women were laughing. The third, standing slightly apart, was Marty Goodman's sister, Laura.

She was pretty, if quietly so, with short dark-blond hair, gray eyes, and small, finely made features. Years before I had known her in that way—if you were a pimpled, late-blooming boy imprisoned in the dungeon of adolescence—you inevitably knew the elder sisters of your friends: across a hopeless chasm of immaturity. A year older than us and several inches taller, Laura Goodman had belonged to another, better race. Once while visiting Marty in his parents' palatial Central Park West apartment (a bunch of us, including Toby, had gathered to play a marathon game of Risk), I'd had a glimpse of his sister in her room, sitting on her bed with her back against the wall, reading *Jane Eyre*. Looking up from her book, she caught me spying on her through the half-open door. And there followed—or so I'd imagined—a shared ephiphany of eros, during which she saw through the humble chrysalis of my present physique to the gallant winged man within. I'd felt readier than ever to fly.

But then she shut her door, and that had been that.

All this I wanted to recount to her now that we were adults. But she hadn't been at the party more than a few minutes before she put on her coat, clearly intending to leave. On an impulse I asked her where she lived; when she said the Upper West Side, I offered to accompany her. To my surprise, she accepted.

I walked with her back down West End. The snow had stopped, the sky was a frozen pond tipped above us. Our breaths fogged in the night. But the sidewalks were no longer pristine: boot prints and dog piss and soot. A snowplow came grinding up the avenue, thrusting mounds of gray slush against the sides of the frozen, parked cars. Then the tar of the street was visible again, wet and glistening.

I told her about the last time I'd seen her, fifteen years ago. By the time I reached the part about her closing the door in my face, she was laughing.

"You were all such pests!" she said.

"Thank you."

"You know what I mean."

"You bet I do."

"You were more interesting than the others, though," she added thoughtfully. "I remember you."

Subtly encouraged, I told her what else I remembered. The *Chorus Line* poster on the wall above her bed. The shelf of books about horses and the light blue bedspread with dark stripes and the old stuffed horse with the missing eye. How when she read a magazine as opposed to a book, she'd sit hunched over with her legs crossed and the magazine in her lap, turning the pages noisily from the bottom. All of it meaningless except that it should be recalled now, years later, by two different people.

"Yes," she agreed, looking me in the eye. "Different."

Outside her building, within view of the uniformed door-man, she let me kiss her. Our breaths blew smoke. The surface of her lips was like polished stone. But past that I tasted in her an abundant warmth.

I had been celibate for too long. Untouched, a tribe of one, muttering my own language, ritualizing myself to no avail. Not caring or wanting or having. The months simply passing.

Now, through the bulky layers of our clothes, in a public street, I felt the first resonant intimations of Laura's slender body, and pressed myself against her like an animal.

She pressed back.

eight

FROM THAT NIGHT FORWARD we were a couple. I would return home from teaching and find the red light blinking on my answering machine. (Her modesty evident in this too: she always opened her message with, "Hi, it's Laura," as if in the intervening twelve hours I might have forgotten the sound of her voice.) Or I'd walk straight to her one-bedroom apartment on Eighty-ninth and Columbus, to which just a few minutes earlier she'd returned from her administrative job at Lincoln Center. Often she greeted me at the door still dressed in her cold-weather work clothes: white or blue blouses and trim gray flannel pants, a navy cashmere blazer and black ankle boots. Plainly elegant, well-made things were what she liked. She had grown up with money, though most of the time she took pains not to show it. This was the locus of her private contradictions: she wasn't vain in the least but she dutifully took excellent care of herself, as though she instinctively felt obliged to uphold the standards of appearance she'd been raised with. Once a month she went to a chic East Side salon to get her hair cut. Opalescent half-moons floated on her perfect, unpainted fingernails.

She was slender, small-boned, physically and emotionally discreet. From my adolescence ogling her down hallways and through half-closed doors, across vast rooms, I'd imagined her as a cold and willful queen. But I was wrong. Laura turned out to be gentle, kind, on occasion thoughtful to the point of passivity. It was five weeks before she would undress in front of me with a light on in the room (and then she rushed quickly into bed, like someone hurrying naked through the cold). When we made love the first time and she came, in the dark, in her own bed, her arms wrapped as far around me as they could go, her brief, poignant cry held a note of surprise or confusion, as if she'd just discovered that passion was really only another form of vertigo.

In the spring I moved in with her. I was a hermit crab, ditching my one-room apartment like a spent shell, scrabbling sideways with vigor. No crying or weeping, no memories to speak of. And my furniture, the corduroy sleeper sofa, my mother's old chest of drawers, heavy as a yak—all this went onto Ninety-seventh Street one morning, and by nightfall was gone.

She lived, surprisingly, in one of those recently built yuppie towers, a high-rise sided in toneless brick—though otherwise chock-full of amenities, such as an in-house gym, designed to appeal to the legion of young bankers who had flocked to the neighborhood in the last few years. Still, way up on the fifteenth floor, it wasn't so bad. Laura's apartment faced west, and received plenty of afternoon light.

There was a comfortable sofa and a leather reading chair. There was her impressive collection of opera CDs and her books, novels by the Brontë sisters and James and Ford Maddox Ford, the stories of Chekhov and Alice Munro and William Trevor, the poems of Emily Dickinson. There was her equestrian library, still intact as I remembered it, how-tos on English riding and show jumping, an encyclopedia of equine body types, a catalogue of rare handmade saddles. On these titles and others the dust jackets had been worn from countless childhood handlings to a clothlike nap, the very feel of the past.

I added my belongings to hers. She encouraged this. She did more than make room; she opened her life wide to me. It may sound ridiculous to talk about manners in this day and age, but I believe that Laura's manners were as important and as fine an expression of her true nature, her tender modesty and thoughtfulness of spirit, as any speech or promise she ever made. She did not tell lies, either in gesture or in word. She did not flirt or tease. There was a reason why animals, dogs and horses above all, trusted her implicitly, often would come forward from wherever they were playing or running or feeding to thrust their wet noses against the palm of her hand, or sometimes simply to lean into her.

A good person, in other words. Someone who, despite her own intrinsic reservations and fears, with courage tried to give all of herself, to love with a full heart while holding nothing back.

nine

ONE EVENING IN MAY my father stepped through our front
door bearing a bouquet of white chrysanthemums. He was
dressed in a tie and tweed sport coat, and seemed as nervous
as a schoolboy.

"So," he said carefully, "how are you?"

"I'm all right."

"You look all right."

We nodded at each other, then away. He came forward,
still holding the flowers, letting his eyes roam the living room,
taking in the books on the shelves (Horses? I could almost
hear him thinking; horses are so East Side), the stacks of mul-
tidisk opera CDs, the costly leather chair. Signposts, I assumed, ways of reading this new life of mine. He'd never been
here before, never met the woman I now lived with. In fact,
these past months I'd hardly seen him.

"Laura's just getting out of the shower," I said. "Can I get you something to drink? A glass of wine?"

But he was too absorbed in what he was seeing to hear me. He was standing close to the CDs; something there had caught his attention. I followed his fixed gaze to the top of one of the stacks and a cover photograph of a striking, dark-haired woman.

"She came to the Met," he murmured.

"Who did?"

"Callas," he said more firmly, without looking at me, still lost in his own world. "December '56, *Lucia di Lammermoor*. She already owned opera then. You can't imagine the sound of that voice at its best. A voice that could stop time. I waited hours in line just for standing room. Beside me in the stall that night was a woman about my own age. Magnificent. Dark hair, huge dark eyes. I told her she looked like La Divina herself. The performance hadn't started yet. We were packed into standing room like cattle, right next to each other, but she wouldn't even give me the time of day. Looked down her nose at me, with that haughty eye of the Jewish princess saving herself for better things. I recognized that look, all right. My God, though, was she something! Still, it wasn't just anybody singing that night. It was Callas. And when the music started, I forgot all about that woman next to me. Callas sang the first aria. And soon people, grown men and women I'm telling you, people were crying at the beauty of it. Tears were rolling down faces. Underneath the music you could hear the weeping like a dirge. Like being sung to by a voice too beautiful to be human or real. Then she finished, Callas finished, just the first aria, and there was a pause like a single cumulative breath, a pulse, and then the audience—three thousand men and women, the rich sitting, the middle class standing, the poor at home listening on their radios—the audience couldn't contain itself. Oh, it was bedlam, total goddamn rapture. And the woman next to me, that cool beauty next to me, your mother, she was weeping too, and she took my hand. Just reached out and grabbed it. Because of the music. Because of that voice. It was the greatest moment of my life."

My father looked up and found me staring at him.

I stood there, wanting to know where that man had gone. The man who was the first to applaud after a performance, who wept at the sound of the human voice, who knew his desires, who wasn't afraid of being noticed. A man who was *visible*, in weakness and in strength. A man to pity and yet to admire, who'd risked and lost but who at least had wanted, a wounded veteran of love. Where had he been while I'd been growing up? As though, like a miser, he'd hoarded all the best for himself.

From the back of the apartment Laura's footsteps sounded against the bare hardwood floor. We turned just as she was entering the room.

I cleared my throat. "Dad, this is Laura Goodman. Laura, my father, Arthur Rose."

She came forward smiling, her short hair still wet from the shower, slicked back from her face. Her dress the same soft gray as her eyes, falling just below her knees. A single strand of pearls around her neck, their unadorned radiance amplifying her smile and her good intentions, which she presented to him now with innate grace, crossing the room and kissing him on his cheek, welcoming him.

"We wanted to get everything in order first," she told him, "before we had you over."

Her warmth worked on both of us, plucked us from the heavy grip of the past with nimble feminine fingers; she raised us up. I felt it happen. And watched him rise to the occasion too, my father, shedding the losses at least for the moment, blushing and smiling and saying that he was happy just to be here at all. Her charm the magic elixir we'd so badly needed— suddenly he was some goofy kid, not the tired man who'd spent his life editing college-level textbooks on behavioral anthropology, the Great War, the rise and fall of ancient Greece.

He remembered the chrysanthemums. "These are for you."

"Thank you, Arthur. They're beautiful."

The flowers she arranged in her grandmother's Tiffany vase while I poured the wine. Then a tour of the apartment, though it wasn't big and not much touring was needed. I stayed in the kitchen, putting olives into a bowl, breathing in the smell of Laura's roast leg of lamb (her mother's recipe), polenta, cherry tomatoes sautéed in butter. No meal like this had ever been cooked in my studio on West Ninety-seventh. They were in the bedroom now, she and he, the sound of the closet door opening, her ironically concise architectural description ("Closet"), then footsteps again and her sweet voice: "I wish we had two bathrooms but we don't."

"You can borrow one of mine," replied Arthur Rose a bit giddily, "I can't seem to use them both."

Laura laughed generously at this odd little joke. And out in the kitchen, relieved and happy and almost unrecognizable to myself, so did I.

· · ·

After dinner, Laura remained behind to start cleaning up as I walked my father down the long hallway to the elevator. Already my mood was descending from the high of the meal in ways I couldn't put my finger on. His too, perhaps. We were alone again. The bright green carpet, the uniform lighting that would never be quite right—one of those buildings that are killing the souls of our great cities, block by block. Doors and doors to either side as we walked; and through many of them, and louder than you might imagine, came the boxed vibrations of televised voices, canned laughter, screeching cars and shattering windows. Such hilarity and drama as to make our actual lives seem absurdly small if we weren't careful.

We reached the elevator, and I pushed the call button.

In a voice of carefully restrained optimism he asked, "Do you think she might be the one, Julian?"

"I don't know, Dad."

Like a Greek chorus on acid, the dissonant voices continued to reach us through the neighbors' closed doors. There was no sign of the elevator, and I jabbed the call button with my finger. He waited a few moments before broaching the subject again.

"You want her to be, though, don't you?"

"Of course I do. I wouldn't have moved in with her if I didn't."

He nodded. Thoughtfully, he ran his hands over the sleeves

of his tweed jacket; I could see him thinking. He seemed suddenly restless, perhaps reliving the dinner and envisioning my future: Laura's graceful manners, the kiss she'd given him, the delicious food she'd made.

Suddenly his hands went still, he let them drop to his sides. They were a reader's hands, an editor's, the nails bitten down, a smudge of blue ink on the left thumb and another on the ring finger. His gold wedding band still there, the last shining emblem of all the hope he'd ever had for himself.

He cleared his throat. "A nice apartment," he said. He nodded vaguely while staring at his feet. "A home."

A comforting verdict for us both; but a melancholy expression had taken hold of his face. Without knowing why, I felt certain he was thinking about my mother.

Just then, far down the elevator shaft, I detected the first sounds of the approaching car.

"All her books," he murmured to his feet. "Her records, hats, her umbrellas. . . ." He shook his head in helpless denial. "How could she have left so much behind? That's what I can't understand."

"Dad, don't."

He looked up. His pale eyes still locked and blurred on some distant point, which was the inscrutable heart of another human being. He couldn't understand how his love had failed to keep her. Spurred by an impulse, I reached out and took his hand. At my touch his eyes appeared to regain focus, and with the effort his stubborn memory released him back to this place and time, and to me.

The elevator arrived. I kissed him on his cheek, held on an

extra moment or two, let him go. Then he stepped into the brightly lit box and the doors closed over him.

She was in the bathroom, out of my sight. The door open, the tap running, the sound of falling water broken intermittently by her hands, which scooped and splashed.

In the next room I sat on the edge of the bed, holding a shoe. The other shoe was still on my foot. She was saying something, but because of the water all I could decipher was the vague murmuring of her naturally quiet voice. Then the water shut off, and she emerged wearing a white robe, drying her face with a towel.

"Did you hear what I said?" she asked lightly.

I told her no.

"Did tonight feel different from the other times you've introduced your girlfriends to your father? Or the same?"

"There haven't been any other times."

A look of sober incredulity crossed her face. But it was the truth: I'd never introduced Claire to my father; and none of the others had mattered enough. I bent down to untie my shoe.

Passing in front of me, the lemon verbena scent of her French soap wafting behind her, Laura went to her side of the bed and from under her pillow pulled out the white cotton nightgown that she'd folded and placed there that morning. With her back toward me, she let the robe fall on the bed. Her pristine nakedness freshened the room like a flower, and I sat up. Then with a swift practiced motion, she slipped the nightgown over her head and covered herself.

I had the second shoe off. Getting up, I set the pair together on the floor against the wall, for tomorrow.

"Weren't you ever in love?"

I turned around. Laura was looking at me with an intense vulnerability that I'd never seen in her before and that erased in one glimpse whatever lightness of tone the conversation had begun with.

This was new territory for us. We were both private people, a couple who'd arrived at living together by way of fewer promises than most, and fewer probing questions too.

"Once," I said.

"When would that have been?"

"When I was at Harvard."

"What was her name?"

I didn't answer right away, and Laura's penetrating eyes never left my face.

"Her name was Claire Marvel," I said.

A single, slow nod, as if the name itself had some significance for her.

"What did she look like?"

I shook my head.

"Was she beautiful?"

"Yes."

"How long were you together?"

"Not long. For most of it we were friends."

"But you loved her."

I paused. "Yes. I loved her."

"How did it end? Assuming it ended."

"It ended, Laura. She married somebody else."

"Are you still in love with her?"

"How can you even ask that question?"

Her voice hardened. "Are you still in love with her, Julian?"

"No," I said. "No."

Moments passed. Laura dropped her eyes. Then, as though winded, she sat heavily on the bed.

In a drained voice, her hand aimlessly smoothing the duvet, she said, "I guess I'm going to have to think about this."

"There's nothing to think about," I said. "I'm with you now. We're together."

"That's a nice thing to say, Julian. It's full of good intentions. But I guess I'm not really sure that's what I heard in your voice."

She got under the duvet. She turned on her side, away from me, and brought her knees up until the shape of her body beneath the covers was a small, hardly noticeable thing, no bigger than a girl's.

She closed her eyes. "Would you turn out the light?"

I did as she asked; the light went out. And I stood blinking, almost panicked. In the boundless dark the room no longer seemed familiar. I could not even find her.

"Laura."

She didn't answer.

"Laura, I love you."

I waited but there was no answer. Just her silence like a long, slow drop. She was breathing there but I couldn't hear her; she was listening. I felt close to tears, and I groped through the darkness for the door.

A sound stopped me: her hand lifting the bedcovers. Then her whispered voice:

"Darling, come to bed."

In the middle of the night, lying sleepless beside her, I had a vision.

It was a vision of beginnings and endings; a gossamer net of intertwined hopes cast so wide that it held worlds, and in those worlds was my own.

A vision of what would come to pass, up to a point.

On a crisp blue day in autumn, on a bench by the dog run in Riverside Park, I would ask Laura to marry me. And she would say yes.

On a warm clear day the following spring, on the lawn behind her parents' house in Westchester, with my father acting as my best man, under a chuppah as round as the sun, I would break a glass and we would be married.

Afterward I kiss my wife, whose smile this day has a wattage that is entirely new to me; literally, she glows. I kiss her again. And later, after the cutting of the cake and the start of the dancing, as with some difficulty I am explaining to her appalled great-aunt on her mother's side that, in fact, I have never visited Israel or set foot on a kibbutz, Laura appears. "Excuse me, I need him for a minute," she says, and whisks me away, out through the side of the enormous white tent, across the lawn, past the swimming pool, into the house and up the stairs and along the hall to the corner bedroom that has always been hers.

The door closes behind us; for the first time we are alone together as husband and wife. And I am aware that whatever she might have done as a child, she did in here; whatever she might have thought, she thought in here. My wife. I don't know what this private history means or what consequences it will bring, but suddenly I feel the immense unimagined weight of it and how, today, it has been entrusted to me for the rest of our lives.

"I wanted to see this with you," Laura says, and leads me to the window.

There below us is the tent. Its flaps are tied open and we can hear the music flowing out of it, can see into the luminous interior where all the people of our shared lives are dancing to a mediocre wedding band, our friends and family holding each other, embracing, murmuring into each other's ears, telling jokes, laughing, raising glasses, celebrating us even though, for the moment, we are not among them. And watching, I smile. It is beautiful and innocent and generous and kind and above all hopeful and before this scene Laura and I are like two momentary angels, given this rare chance to witness our own good fortune on earth.

Among the guests is David Glassman, by now three inches taller and a freshman at Swarthmore. A little less shy, it appears, a bit more grown into himself—at one point he's even spotted taking a turn on the dance floor to Stevie Wonder's "Signed, Sealed, Delivered I'm Yours" . . . .

Then the vision tilts slightly, time regains itself; it is long before all this, it is only next month, and David is graduating from the Cochrane School. With a knot of pride in my chest I watch him receive his diploma, and the prize for Most Distinguished Long Essay. I applaud as loudly as any uncle when his name is called. And afterward at the reception, when he brings his parents, who are barely on speaking terms, over to meet me, I shake their hands and tell them what a son they have here, a smart, good son, and how privileged I feel to have been allowed to teach him. My throat seizes up with feeling, and for a moment I am too moved to speak. . . .

Then the vision tilts again—it's just a vision after all, it's not life—and the reception is over, the echoing hall is empty, everyone has gone. But the feeling remains, such hope mingled with such sadness, a fragile net of all desires past and present. . . .

I was tired then, and finally I slept.

PART
FOUR

o n e

I WOULD TELL YOU that it was a good marriage. I would tell you that for eight and a half years Laura and I were more than merely peaceable companions. I would tell you that we were husband and wife, sharing a life together, books, food, music, theater, friends, quiet nights. That we talked to each other every day, recounted, explained, discussed, advised, comforted, gently humored. That we rarely had serious arguments or complaints. That at night when we touched each other, it was with ever wiser and more understanding hands. That a loving trust was our currency, our savings and our gold, the essence of all that we had made together, and until the end neither of us willingly squandered it.

It would all be true.

I would tell you that after almost seven years of marriage

we decided to try to conceive a child. That Laura was by then thirty-nine, and I was thirty-eight, and though we'd been discussing the issue for several years, we kept putting it off for professional reasons, Laura's mainly. That during those years of talking about it, while most of our friends were having children left and right, Laura was promoted three times at Lincoln Center, eventually being named director of promotion. It was only then, she said, that she felt she'd earned the right to take a year off to have a child. Though from that moment onward, she looked ahead to motherhood with a quiet but abiding passion.

I would tell you that in my own way I eventually grew to want a child every bit as much as Laura did. It just took me longer to know it. Surrounded by teenage boys all the time, lecturing and quizzing and supposedly molding them into the adults of the future, I spent my days in a romper room of fatherly intimations. These were children. They came from all kinds of homes and families. Their individual needs differed no less than their names, faces, smiles. Some students wore their spirits on their sleeve while others kept them locked within. There was a secret password for each, had to be, if only I could figure it out.

I would tell you that David Glassman was long gone from these waters, being then a doctoral student in history at the University of Chicago. Every so often I received an e-mail from him. He was doing well, living with a girlfriend. The program was good—though the teaching, he kindly suggested, had yet to reach the level of inspiration that he remembered so vividly from his days at Cochrane. His parents both had remarried; he had a three-year-old half sister now. "I guess this is the modern family," he'd written dryly in his last message. "Which, if you're me, kind of makes you think twice about the whole notion of human progress."

Where David had been in my life there was now a lingering feeling, a need to care for and instruct, to watch out for, that was too deep to be simply reactive; it was, I only gradually intuited, biological, perhaps even spiritual.

And so I'd tell you that when Laura and I finally began trying to conceive, we did so in earnest, without reservation, we did so with hope. We consulted books, followed the calendar, checked her temperature five times a day, gave up alcohol and coffee. The days were a series of physiological signals to be read and acted upon; the human body turned out to be at once cruder and more mysterious than I'd imagined. Still, it was boss, channeling its unsentimental demands through my wife. More than once I received a lunchtime call in my office telling me, as it were, to get home and fire up. Which, of course, I did.

Together and separately, we turned our faces toward the future.

And I would tell you that when, after a year and a half of trying, we still hadn't conceived, it was with a growing sense of dread that we consulted a fertility specialist. Tests were done. After a week of anxious waiting, the results came back: egg and sperm counts both appeared normal, the doctor assured us. We should just keep at it. Sometimes it took as long as it took, especially at our "advanced" ages.

That day, without talking about it, Laura and I returned to

our apartment and went straight to the bedroom. We would make love, try again. It wouldn't work, either, this time, but we couldn't know that. It was the effort that counted now, or so the doctor had encouraged us.

What we felt that day, I believe, each in our own way, was gratitude. A reprieve had been granted. No, more than that: sitting in the waiting room at the doctor's office, dreading the irrefutable evidence of the test results, my longing to be a father—to be something more than myself—had finally been revealed to me. Here in the opportunity about to be lost lay the seeds of the life I'd always wanted, and had not lived.

IN DECEMBER 1998, I found myself in the Metropolitan Opera House, standing over a brushed-aluminum drinking fountain fifteen minutes before the start of James Levine's star-studded production of *The Marriage of Figaro*. A well-heeled opening-night crowd filled the passageway, conversing in hushed but excited tones and strolling over the thick crimson carpet. Laura had gone ahead to our orchestra seats. Stepping away from the fountain, I'd just noticed an ugly water stain on my new silk tie when from behind me a man muttered sarcastically, "Well, well."

The clenching of my heart told me who it was. I turned around.

Dressed in black tie, Carl Davis looked statelier and more self-assured than I remembered him. If anything, the added years seemed only to have increased his regal hold on himself. He was tall and still handsome, with those eyes of such a hard cerulean blue that behind the rimless glasses they glimmered like fragments of iced sky. The silver head was truly leonine now, indomitable; not even six years of a Clinton presidency had dimmed this Republican star. It might have been the second coming of Kissinger: a man perversely and continuously elevated in the world's eyes not despite, but because of, his moral failings.

"How long has it been, Julian?" he asked in the same biting yet refined voice, rhetorical as ever.

"Twelve years," I answered coldly without hesitation. And even as I uttered them, the words triggered the simple, staggering awareness that if Davis were here, then in all likelihood Claire would be too. She might be within sight. Might even be approaching at this very moment. My heart began to pound, and I scanned the passageway for any glimpse of her.

"Twelve years," Davis repeated with elaborate slowness. His stentorian voice reeled me back to him—just as, with the unerring marksmanship of a sniper, his own gaze dropped to my water-stained tie. A small, brittle smile appeared on his lips. "And what brings you here?"

"Mozart."

"Still the young wise-ass, I see."

"You're not remembering, Carl. I was never a wise-ass. That was my problem."

The smile vanished, the eyes seemed to darken.

"So what happened to you, Julian? Charlie Dixon says you dropped off the face of the earth."

"I don't imagine Dixon gets out of Cambridge much."

"I'll make sure to pass the kind words along to him."

"I've been in New York, Carl. All these years. I'm a teacher."

"A teacher? Really. And where might that be?"

"The Cochrane School."

"The Cochrane School?" At my news a complacent satisfaction spread over him, softening his mouth but making it crueler. It was the look of a smug winner, and I wanted to knock it off his face. "Sounds highly rewarding," he remarked, his voice dripping condescension.

"It is."

I bit my tongue then; there was no point to this. With anger and apprehension and hope I turned to watch the people filing by, strolling down the long, sloping aisles to their seats. And then Davis shifted his feet like a boxer who's got the fight in the bag but still wants one more punch.

"Well," he said, and there was a finality to his voice (there always had been, I thought). "I think that about covers it. No point in dredging up old disappointments." He paused and with a decisive gesture lifted his glasses and resettled them on the bridge of his nose. "I'll make sure to give your regards to my wife."

"You do that."

He walked away then. I strained to follow his tall, silver-capped figure with my eyes until, too quickly, he was swallowed by the crowd. There was no sign of her.

For some moments I stood where I was, in a moving sea of strangers. I couldn't keep myself from thinking that even here,

among his own kind, Davis distinguished himself like a king—
which fit in some way the hushed, luxurious procession, and
the muted tuning of the instruments from the orchestra pit,
and the lush carpet that gave to all privileged enough to walk
on it the soundless tread of royalty.

ı   ı   ı

In a kind of daze I made it to our seats. Laura was there, leaf-
ing through her program. She asked me where I'd been for so
long—but at that moment the lights went down and the audience fell quiet, and I used this as an excuse not to answer her.

With the silent marking of Levine's baton, the music began. The overture. Inside it the instrumental refrain of the entire opera, to be heard again in the second act, the third, the
finale; in your head as you walked home in the snow or lay
dreaming in the bath; in the weeks to come as you scratched
yourself or shaved or drank a glass of wine, as you made love
to your wife—these exuberant, comical, bittersweet, absurd,
love-besotted threads of simple notes that, woven together in
just this way and to this higher purpose, formed an eternal
tapestry of experience.

I looked at Laura. This opera was her sentimental favorite. She could recite much of da Ponte's libretto by heart
in Italian, knew the machinations, the timing, the quicksilver
entrances and exits, the hide-and-seek. She was sitting forward, listening intently, eyes glued to the stage, anticipating,
like someone about to open a present, the parting of the gold
curtains.

Then it happened. The curtains parted. I looked from

Laura to the stage. Time became something else, became music and story: *A partly furnished room, with an easy chair in the center. Figaro with a measure in his hand, Susanna at the mirror, trying on a hat decorated with flowers.* Figaro calling out numbers: five . . . ten . . . twenty . . . thirty . . . thirty-six . . . forty-three. Susanna saying no, the room won't do, not for a wedding bed, not with the Count next door waiting to pounce. Figaro singing his plan to foil the Count. . . . Oh, it was farce, it was tragedy. The costumes and disguises, the misguided messages, the chronic lack of seeing, the voices calling to one another, the misunderstandings and false recognitions, the broken hearts that certainly will mend. The foolish Count wishes his wife were somebody else.

Then my mind went off it, tumbled off it like a boy off a bicycle. I lost the music and the story. As though my ears suddenly went deaf and my eyes, blinded by the light of the stage, turned inward to where my deepest and most impermeable thoughts resided, and soon were seeing only what was imagined there. And what was imagined there was not these characters in costume. It was not my wife, whom I loved, sitting beside me and mouthing the words.

Claire's here, I thought. She's here, somewhere close, sitting in this same darkness.

three

I GOT TO MY FEET as the houselights were rising for intermission. There was still scattered applause as I reached for my overcoat on the back of the seat. Laura looked inquiringly at me, and I murmured that I wasn't feeling well. My chest felt uncomfortably tight, my face hot. Cold fresh air was what I needed, some atmospheric jolt that would knock every last memory and feeling out of my head.

Then Laura offered, "I'll come with you," and reached for her coat too.

Through the buzzing crowd I slowly navigated my way up the aisle, Laura following. We reached the already jammed passageway and I was forging across the flow of traffic toward the staircase when I heard Laura calling me. I looked back and beyond the moving net of people saw her standing beside a trim well-dressed man in his fifties. She motioned for me to come over.

"You remember Colin Weeks," she said as I joined them.

I looked at the man.

"It was Colin who took the gamble and hired me all those years ago," Laura said.

"Hardly a gamble," Weeks commented pleasantly to me. "And it couldn't have been that long ago—Laura still looks twenty-five. Hello Julian, Colin Weeks. I think we met last year at Amanda Baird's."

I had no recollection of him. His hand had come out and I shook it. Then he politely asked how I was enjoying the production. A question to which I responded with an answer so terse and beside the point that it was followed by an awkward social pause, a pocket of dead air, which Laura tried to fill by observing that she thought Barbara Bonney's voice more than equal to the hall. To which Weeks thoughtfully replied that Bonney possessed a beautiful vocal instrument, there could be no doubt about that, but as for its capaciousness for opera, in his mind the jury was still out.

ı ı ı

I mumbled my excuses, left them talking. Down the wide, curving staircase. I pushed through the glass doors onto the plaza and a gust of freezing air smacked me in the face; instantly my cheeks stung and my eyes began to water. Nearby, a handful of opera fanatics stood huddled in front of posters announcing upcoming productions. I walked past them, buttoning my coat and turning up the collar. Ahead lay the fountain, lit as well as any Parisian monument, around which, on occasional balmy evenings in summer, a jazz orchestra played ballroom and swing tunes and couples of all ages danced under stars they could not see. Laura had never been able to persuade me to do this. I wasn't a dancer, I'd explained numerous times; I hadn't even danced at our wedding.

The plaza was nearly empty now. I came to the fountain and tilting my head one way, the water looked a cheap swimming-pool blue; tilting it another, it was gold I saw. My breath steamed into the night. Through the heavy slabs of stone and the soles of my best shoes the cold pressed up into me. The fountain flowed and sprayed, creating a mist rainbowed with light. Around it where the water had splashed onto the stone there were bluish gleams of thinly iced puddles. I remembered dancing once, in another country. How slowly we'd moved. I could name every song on that album, and the order of the songs, even though I hadn't listened to it since. I remembered how her head had seemed to support my shoulder, rather than the other way around. How once I'd looked over at our reflection in the windowpanes and seen us moving together, suspended on glass, the image grainy from dust, yet luminous from within like coupled ghosts.

I turned around and there was the Met—acres of gold-lit glass. The light spilling far out onto the plaza. And standing in it, now, a familiar silhouette.

Claire came forward, away from the light, her heels knocking cold stone. With each stride she became less of a shadow. And my heart began to step with her, to climb a ladder of feeling long unused, like something stored and forgotten in an attic. First her pale face, emerging like an apparition. Then her white throat disappearing into the depths of a black overcoat. Her hair as long as it had ever been and brushed down her back. Her eyes never leaving my face. She came forward and stopped in front of me and now the distance between us, after eleven years, was down to a yard.

"Where do we begin?" she asked in a quiet voice.

My mouth was too dry to speak; I shook my head.

"Does that mean we don't begin? Or that you have no idea where to begin?"

"I don't know what it means." My voice sounded rusty to me, weak.

"That makes two of us." She frowned, as if unhappy with how this had sounded. Her anxiety appeared to be growing rather than lessening.

"It's all right," I said. Then I said it again.

My words seemed to calm her. We stood looking at each other, our breaths tiny smoke signals forming and dissipating in the air between us. Then she tried again.

"He said you were a teacher. What kind of teacher are you?"

"High school. Political science and history."

"Do you like it?"

"Yes."

"Then I'm happy for you." Her voice was low and steady but her eyes had begun to glitter with what might have been tears, or light reflecting from the fountain behind me. "Are you married?" she asked.

"Yes," I said.

I watched her take this in; she hugged herself.

"Children?"

"No." I hesitated. "Not yet."

"Do you—"

"I think we've covered me."

For the first time she smiled. "Oh no," she said with a flash of the old irony. "We could never cover you."

We stood smiling at each other. And then, after a while, we looked away.

"Now you," I said.

"Me?" she replied dismissively. "I went back and got my Ph.D."

"Good for you."

"I went back and resurrected Burne-Jones to the best of my ability," she said, her tone darkening with every word. "You try to show people what beauty is, how it's more alive than we are, the best of ourselves. You want to spread the gospel like some sort of prophet. But after a while you start to feel you're shouting into a vacuum. You're quite certain that nobody out there is listening." A wave of the hand, and then she was done with herself. "C'est tout."

"You've had your reasons," I said.

"I don't know about that. Housewife isn't much of a reason."

"There's being a mother."

The words came out of my mouth sounding reasonable and not especially embittered. I felt almost proud for having forced myself to say them, as if here, finally, was evidence that I had not been trapped in time.

But then I saw the effect my words had on her: she'd gone still and expressionless.

"I'm not a mother," she said quietly.

I stared at her, my heart like a bird grabbed out of the air.

"I had a miscarriage that first time," she went on in the same quiet voice. "Then twice more."

"You didn't tell me."

She shook her head as though helpless about the past, but said nothing.

I turned away from her. Out of the corner of my vision the fountain appeared as a burning pyre. I tried to breathe but could not seem to get enough air.

Turning back, I saw that the glitter in her eyes had returned; she was trying to wipe it away with her hand. Some tears fell anyway, soundlessly, picking up reflected light, painting her face in pale licks of color. In a stricken voice she said, "I'd already hurt you too much. I had to let you go."

I held up my hand to silence her. I couldn't stand to hear any more. Her mouth opened but she made no sound, and then she covered her mouth with her hand, as if to stanch whatever thoughts were on the verge of speech.

"I have to go," I said. "My wife is waiting."

Her chin lifted. Her tears were falling freely now. I lowered my eyes and walked past her toward the opera house.

Four months later she was dead.

four

IT WAS TEN O'CLOCK on an April morning. Laura had left for work an hour before. I was sitting at the dining table reading the *Times* when the intercom buzzed and the doorman announced that Kate Daniels was in the lobby.

A moment's hesitation as my brain sought to place the name of Claire's old roommate, whom I hadn't seen in a dozen years. But only a moment: the snap of recognition brought with it a clear picture of Kate's strong face and chlorine-tinted hair, and then the once-familiar sound of her husky voice.

*   *   *

She stepped out of the elevator, turned, saw me standing at the end of the hallway. We stood looking at each other. An uneasy smile showed on her face—the expression of someone determined to walk the plank and trying to seem enthusiastic about it—then withdrew. She shook her head, admonishing herself.

"I should've called first."

I told her not to worry. She came down the hallway and we hugged. Her hair was short and already gray, her body slimmer and less obviously athletic than I remembered, though still fit. On her way through the door she stopped to scrutinize me again.

"You look good, Julian. A little skinny maybe, but good."

I left her in the living room and went to the kitchen for coffee. As I poured her a cup and refilled my own, a sad self-awareness reared its head: sometime during the winter, without ever discussing it, Laura and I had stopped following the advice of the how-to-get-pregnant guides, despite the fact that we were still ostensibly trying to conceive a child. We had an appointment scheduled with a new fertility specialist in two weeks. But we were drinking wine and coffee again, Laura no longer checked her body temperature with any regularity, and our lovemaking had dwindled to hardly more than once a week.

I carried the cups back down the hallway and into the living room. Kate was standing by the window with her head down, deep in thought. As she looked up, her unmasked expression showed a mix of grief and apprehension that I didn't understand, but that already was infecting the room.

"You're probably wondering how I knew you'd be home on a weekday morning," she said.

I smiled and shrugged. "It's spring break. But actually, I'm wondering a lot of things."

"It was an educated guess. I'm a teacher too. Public

high school, Bethlehem, PA. My alma mater. I teach social studies."

"How'd you know I was a teacher?"

There was a pause. She wasn't facing me directly but obliquely, still half angled toward the window. "From Claire." Kate watched me. When I remained silent, she added, "In a letter."

"How is she?" I asked, hearing my own dull voice in my ears.

Taking a deep breath, Kate turned to face me. "She's dead."

I didn't hear her at first. Or I must have heard her, but I didn't feel anything.

"Julian," Kate said gently, "Claire killed herself."

Within my body there was no sign of what I knew I'd heard. A grievous dislocation was what it was. As if her words had not been what they'd appeared to be, as if it was all some trick. I stood waiting for the real words, which would carry the real meaning. Hoping to feel something. And then, with brutal and unsentimental swiftness, it came. Nausea flared in my stomach and my face went cold.

"She was in France," Kate went on grimly. "The police found her in a river not far from the house where you two stayed. There were things in her pockets. Heavy things. The French police say she drowned herself."

"When?" I heard myself ask.

Kate gathered herself. Her eyes, which had been cast down as she'd been speaking, now rose to meet mine. "They found her body ten days ago. She was living there. She'd left Carl just before Christmas."

She waited, visibly expecting a question, some reaction. But I could not speak.

"I may be the only person who knew where she was," Kate went on. "She wrote me from there last month. To tell you the truth, I was surprised to hear from her. We'd sort of fallen out of touch the last couple of years. Not a lack of closeness, more like drift. Carl and I had our problems. Then out of the blue I get a letter from her with that address on the back. The Lot. When I saw it I figured she and Carl were on vacation. I remembered how you and she went there together. And I thought it wasn't right for her to take him to that place, even if they were married. I never liked Carl. Still, she married him, and for a while I tried my best to be a good friend about it."

She paused again, trying to straighten her thoughts.

"The letter was dated March eighteenth. It was on thin blue sheets of airmail stationery and she filled most every inch of five pages. Just seeing her handwriting made me smile. At that point I had no idea she'd left him, or the country, or any of it. Then I read the letter. It was warm but strangely matter-of-fact about events. She'd left while he was on one of his trips to Washington. Packed what she could carry in two suitcases and abandoned the rest. Never looked back. Didn't leave him so much as a note. Almost makes me sorry for him. In the letter she said it wasn't planned, she just knew she had to leave. By the next morning she was on the train from Paris. By that evening she was in a little hotel in the Lot. She found that house you stayed in, sitting empty, and five days later she was living in it. Managed to track down the owner and persuaded her to rent it. It was cheap because there wasn't much heating.

She moved her suitcases over there and within a couple of weeks she'd gotten sick. She thought it was just a cold and didn't pay much attention. Anyway, she was alone and didn't know anybody and didn't want to know anybody and there was no one to call. Turned out it was pneumonia. She didn't say much about it in the letter except that she was very sick and it lasted five weeks and that the owner of the house, who lived not far away, turned out to be very kind. 'Saved my life' were her exact words. 'Saved my life.'"

Kate's mouth and eyes tightened. "Oh, fuck it. I'm talking too much about too many things that don't matter now."

"They matter," I said. "I need you to keep talking."

Our eyes met.

"Please."

She took a breath. "There's not much more. She was writing the letter about six weeks after the illness. She'd gotten past it, was someplace else, maybe she didn't know where, but things were a little better than they'd been, and certainly not worse. It was almost spring. And she had a friend, or kind of a friend, in the old woman who'd rented her the house. She was lonely, but free."

Abruptly Kate's face bunched in anger. "Don't listen to me. Those aren't her words, they're mine, and I don't have a fucking clue. Here I am again trying to explain her to you like some kind of expert. I didn't do too well the last time, did I."

"You did fine," I said. "You were a good friend to her. You're still a good friend."

She shrugged weakly, as though drained.

"Tell me the rest," I said.

"That was about the end of it. She said Carl didn't know where she was and she didn't want him to know, so please not to tell anybody that I'd heard from her, or give anybody her address. She said she'd write again when she could. She said she was sorry about being so out of touch but that unhappiness and mistakes had just about turned her to stone. She hoped I could forgive her. She hoped everyone could forgive her. And then just 'Love' and her name. And then after her name there was a last part about you. It wasn't a P.S. It was more than that. It was all by itself at the bottom of the page, practically the only words in the whole cramped letter with any space around them, just floating there like an island. She said you were a teacher in Manhattan and wondered if I might look you up every now and then and send her word about you. But only so long as I promised not to tell you that I was doing it for her."

In the afternoon, Kate left. She was taking the train back to Pennsylvania, where she lived in an apartment with her long-time girlfriend. There was a big dinner at her parents' that night, including all her brothers and their wives. "Marcy and I are just another couple," Kate explained dryly. "We just happen to be better at sports."

We stood on the street corner, searching for a taxi, talking about trivial things. For three hours we'd sat in my living room trading memories of Claire. For this is what you do with the dead: resurrect them moment by moment, hoping that the edifice you're constructing might one day house their spirit;

yet knowing it will not. The rest is faith and pain. We'd sat lay-
ing the foundation for how we would always talk about her.
And then we'd grown tired, and wordlessly agreed to move on
to other subjects.

A taxi arrived. Kate and I hugged, and I watched her
drive off.

I stood on the street a while longer. Today, in April, the sky
was clear, but there was a chill in the air that cut to the bone.
I glanced up at the building I'd lived in for nearly ten years and
saw how it was ugly and blocked the sun, throwing a perpetual cloak of shadow over the avenue and the people who went
about their business there.

In front of me a livery cab slowed, hunting for a fare, and
I angrily waved the driver off. He flipped me the finger and
drove on.

I turned and went back inside the building.

Of the hidden things, the secret hands, the private knowledge, the memories that were all spirit, like sunlight trapped
in a glass—I'd told Kate nothing. How could I have? And
with what words, anyway? Claire was the only one who'd ever
known how much I'd loved her. She was the only one who was
ever meant to know.

f i v e

"JULIAN?"

Standing in her white nightgown at the edge of the darkened living room, Laura seemed almost a figment; only her voice was clear. It was the middle of the night. I peered at her from the chair across the room, where I'd been sitting for I didn't know how long.

"Are you all right?" she asked.

I felt unable to answer her. In the dark I reached down for my glass on the floor and took a gulp of watery scotch. The sound of ice cubes ringing against glass.

"Julian."

"Go back to bed, Laura."

"No," she said. "I won't."

She flipped a switch on the wall and the room was flooded with light.

I sat furiously blinking, trying to shade my eyes with my arm. Gradually my vision adjusted and my arm came down. Laura stared at me from across the room. It was not the tall glass of scotch that had fixed her attention, I realized, or the heavy wool sweater that, groping in the dark of our bedroom, I'd thrown over my pajamas. It was my face.

"I've never seen you cry before."

"Leave me alone, Laura."

She seemed momentarily stunned by what she was witnessing. Then, visibly arriving at some decision within herself, she came farther into the room. I ducked my head down—an image of David Glassman—and moments later felt her hands on my shoulders trying to hold and soothe me. But I would not be touched. I shrugged her off and without a word she moved away; her footfall faded down the hallway while I remained where I was, not stirring, feeling the ache rising in my chest and throat and eyes. It was the darkness I wanted again. And then I heard her coming back.

With grace and tender practicality she brought me a box of Kleenex. She waited patiently on the sofa a few feet away while I wiped my swollen eyes and blew my nose. When I was finished, though, it was a denser silence that came scudding into the room with us. We sat in its enormous shadow.

Finally, she drew a long hard breath. "It gets lonely out here, Julian. You must know that."

"I'm sorry," I mumbled, looking at my hands.

"I don't want your apology. I want you to talk to me."

"It's not that simple."

"Yes it is," Laura said urgently. "Yes. It. Is. You're my husband. I love you. And I want you to talk to me. That's how simple it is." She leaned forward and grabbed hold of my wrist and shook it. "Talk to me, Julian. Something terrible's eating you inside. And I'm supposed to watch it happen? Stay here and keep quiet? Wait for you to remember how much you need me? Well, forget it. I'm not blind, whatever you may think. And I'm not deaf or dumb, either. And my patience is not infinite."

The room was still.

"A friend of mine killed herself," I said.

Slowly, Laura released my wrist and sat back.

"Which friend?"

"You didn't know her."

There was a long silence.

"Which friend?" Laura repeated.

I rubbed a hand over my face. "Claire Marvel."

She stiffened. It had been ten years since Claire's name had been uttered in our house, but on my wife's face now I saw immediate recognition, as if the name had always been present.

For a while neither of us spoke. From the street far below there came a faint reverberating din, a garbage can being knocked onto its side. My mind, seeking escape, dully attached itself to this far-off noise. I imagined a homeless man sorting through the spilled refuse, searching for bottles and cans.

Then, quietly, Laura said, "I'm very sorry. She must have been in agony to do what she did." She reached out and pulled a tissue from the box. She seemed to need to do something with her hands and she folded the tissue in quarters and placed it on the coffee table between us and did not look at it again. "I saw you talking to her that night at the opera," Laura said. "I saw you out on the plaza. And I knew who it was."

Her voice was hardly a voice anymore; I couldn't hear her in it. An urge to reach out for her rose in me—but by then her expression had already changed, hardened, and a bitter and righteous anger lit her eye.

"That was the only time I saw her, Laura."

"Don't tell me that," she snapped. "In your heart, Julian, in your real heart, you've never seen anybody but her. You've never truly loved anybody but her. Certainly not me. Not like that."

She got to her feet. With grim determination she crossed the room. When she finally turned to face me she was on the verge of tears.

"You and I have been trying to conceive a child. For a long time now, a long time—" Laura's voice fluttered, threatening to break; she waited, a fist pressed to her mouth, for her self-control to return. "We've put our hearts into it. More than our hearts. We've been trying to make a life together, to bring another life into this world. And for what reason, if not for love of each other? Tell me that, Julian. For what reason?"

six

BREAK A PERSON'S HEART and you become a kind of amnesiac killer. All the empathy you possess is momentarily held in abeyance while you address yourself wholeheartedly to your own emotional survival. You're just doing what you have no choice but to do, you think. You're just living.

Then it's over, and standing amid the wreckage of your life you remember.

Laura and I tried to go on together.

In the morning she went to work earlier than usual, and returned later, often eating dinner with colleagues. During the rare hours when we were awake in the apartment at the same time, she spoke to me when necessary, was polite as always, but otherwise kept to herself. It wasn't hostility, it seemed, so much as exhaustion tinged with an almost spectral premonition of grief; a process of emotional damage assessment as a prelude, I sensed, to mourning.

I spent more and more time at school. There was no teachers' meeting too routine to attend, no student concern or academic question too minor to try to assuage or answer. As if time had suddenly turned infinite; as if there were no reality but the present. Which was ironic, in a way. Because what I felt like, without understanding or shame, was nothing so much as a shattered hourglass, its sand leaking onto the ground.

seven

ON A CLOUDLESS SATURDAY in June I sat with my father on a bench overlooking the Riverside Park dog run. The dog run consisted of no more than a narrow strip of field worn to bare earth. Over it, watched by their owners, about a dozen animals of various shapes and sizes ran in a knot of swirling trajectories, chasing each other with unbounded joy. A light scrim of dust rose from the ground. The drone of unseen traffic carried from the Westside Highway.

My father wore neatly pressed khakis and a short-sleeved shirt frayed at the collar and a beige hat against the heat of the sun. A black eyeglass case bulged in his shirt pocket, and the gold clip of a Cross ballpoint glinted there too, for doing the *Times* crossword.

At seventy-five, he was feeling all right. Perhaps better. For someone who'd never exercised in his life except to walk the seventeen blocks to his office, and then, post-retirement, to the movies and on Sundays to Zabar's, his heart was in decent shape. There was a slight chronic wheeze in the lungs suggesting, his doctor had said, some diminishment in respiratory capacity. And there was the prostate exhibiting a bit of age-typical swelling. But his physique was surprisingly trim. And the inevitable map of wrinkles had had the paradoxical effect of adding interest to what admittedly had been a bland face. His eyes, pale as moonstones, seemed still to be searching, however cautiously, for clues to the bigger puzzle.

It wasn't that he'd forgotten my mother, or ceased wishing she were part of his life. But in recent years some semblance of peace had come to him. It had come slowly, surreptitiously, from the ground up, as ivy climbs a wall. Until one day he stared out through the weblike mystery of its growth at a landscape that no longer frightened him. Suspicion fell away, leaving him lighter on his feet. Somewhere along the line he'd simply stopped trying to plug the myriad gaps in his understanding of her heart. She was another person. And what for years had felt like a searing judgment on his soul he now viewed rightly as some brute manifestation of personal choice. It wasn't the choice he would have made, God knew, but he could accept it. And somehow that acceptance, however humble or hidden, had allowed him to regain his dignity.

I was thinking intensely about him. And then, abruptly, I was back in myself; an unwelcome shift prompted, somehow, by the familiar barrenness of the dog run. Everything green and living had been worn down to dust.

Lately my insomnia had returned full force. My trouble wasn't in falling asleep but in staying there. Wake at three in the morning, every morning on the dot, and the remaining hours are a tundra, blurred at the edges by fatigue and a vague disconnected panic; something to be crossed slowly in the dark, a long trudging toward sunrise. All the regrets you can't allow yourself to think about are strewn like stars in the sky above you. All you know is that you must not look up, must not think, or you will never make it across.

But Laura was a good sleeper, a profound sleeper. Watch her in bed at night, from lights-out till the first rhythmic bars of her somnolent breathing, and you'd witness a beautiful paradox: a surrender that was also an embrace. Once, early in our marriage, I watched her fall asleep smiling—not from anything to do with me, I felt sure, but from something private and inexpressible, like a sky diver's thrill in falling alone through the ether. From her expression then you might have started to believe that my wife's real story lay precisely in that moment of commingled loss and gain—the invisible X where the quiet girl gives up the safe act of quietness and claims the passion of her hidden self. But you'd have to look hard for that story. You'd have to want to know the state of her soul. You'd have to wait for the moment of surrender and embrace, listen to her breathing, study her face as it relinquished the burden of consciousness. You'd have to be devoted enough to give that moment of her private desire your total imagination. You'd have to love her as if she were the love of your life.

Out on the field somebody hurled a tennis ball. Two black Labs shot off after it in pursuit. The ball sailed through the air, bounced high, and both dogs ran under it and lunged at the same instant, mouths primed, sleek as panthers in the heat-glazed air. They missed each other by inches. They missed everything, and while they were barking at each other the ball rolled away and was retrieved by a dachshund.

"What do you know," my father commented dryly. "The little guy won."

For an hour we stayed there, not saying much.

Some of the dogs, who would have gone on happily playing all day, were too soon taken away by their owners. New dogs arrived, dragging their humans behind them, living for the moment when the leash would be unclipped and they could run free, out into the thriving, sniffing, barking maelstrom of their own kind.

It made me feel young again, and old. I remembered walking in this park as a little boy, holding my father's hand. The field covered with grass back then. A Great Dane loping across it. I point to the immense beautiful dog, black as anthracite and running like a foal, and try to say something. But I am speechless. It isn't fear. I point and point. Until, frustrated by my inability to articulate the wonder I feel, I burst into tears. "What's this?" says my father lightly, crouching down and putting his hands on my shoulders. "What's this? My little guy," he says.

Now he said, "You seem unhappy." He spoke slowly, carefully measuring his words, looking out at the dog run. "Actually, you've seemed unhappy for a long time."

I stared at him.

"It's just my impression," he added, still facing straight ahead.

"There was a woman in Cambridge," I said. "I was in love with her. You asked me about her once, and I told you she'd married somebody else." I paused. "You may not remember."

"I remember."

"She killed herself."

He turned to face me then. Color had risen in his cheeks. And I sat waiting for him to say something, while out on the field the dogs scurried and ran and played, nipping at each other.

My father remained silent, though, and finally I began to give up on him.

Then, as I was turning away, I felt his hand on my shoulder. He squeezed hard and for a long time, and the pressure that rose at the bottom of my throat was almost unbearable.

In a tight voice I said, "I don't think I'm going to get over it."

He nodded, looking me in the eye. "Do you *want* to get over it?"

I thought about this, and then I shook my head.

"What are you going to do?" he asked after a while.

"At the end she was living in a place in France where we were together. Where we were happy." I felt the pressure rising behind my eyes and I paused again, swallowing repeatedly. "I think I need to go there."

"For how long?"

"I don't know."

"Have you told Laura?"

I shook my head.

"This will be tough on her," he said. He'd loved Laura from the beginning.

"The whole thing's been tough on her."

The dachshund was leaving. He followed at his owner's heels, trotting with head up as though wearing an invisible cape.

"There goes the little guy," said my father softly.

His smile was thoughtful and sad. Most likely, I thought, he didn't know the comfort he gave, just sitting on that bench with me. Though I hoped he did.

IT WAS A BRIGHT SUNNY AFTERNOON and I was afraid of myself.

After dropping my father at his building, I didn't go home straightaway. For a while I aimlessly wandered the Upper West Side, staring into shopwindows. Later, passing the cineplex on Eighty-fourth and Broadway in the late afternoon, I noticed that a teenage horror spoof I had no interest in seeing was about to start, and I bought a ticket and went in. Two hours went by in a goofy haunted summer camp of screams and fake blood. It was almost a relief to sit in the darkness believing I knew what to do.

I returned to the apartment in the early evening. I let myself in and stood by the door, looking across the living room.

Through the windows the view carried west over rooftops to the Hudson and into New Jersey. At the cusp of the horizon an orange sun floated, radiating a garish wash of color over the factories and abandoned terminals that reached all the way to the river. The room was on fire with that light, and in it now my heart felt constricted, on the verge of suffocation. Thinking I was alone, I let a sound escape, something between a groan and a sigh.

"Your father called a little while ago," Laura said.

Startled, I looked down. She was sitting on the sofa, watching the sunset as I was. She hadn't turned around. It was just the back of her head I saw, a silhouette speaking with her voice. The voice not fully realized yet, as if she'd already spoken the words in her head and was merely repeating them secondhand, offering an objective report. Giving me the news from there, I thought sadly, just as I'd taken to giving her the news from here. News for news. This was what it was down to.

Slowly I walked around the sofa and sat on the leather chair.

"What did he say?"

"He said he wanted me to know he loved me like a daughter. I told him I felt the same way. It was a little awkward at the end, though. You see, he thought you'd already come back and told me whatever it is you have to tell me."

I could see her face now, her cheekbones dimly reflecting the conflagration outside. I could see her eyes but not their expression.

"I'm sorry," I said, regretting the words the moment they were out of my mouth.

"You're *sorry*?"

The room was still. The sun continued its imperceptible decline. The light deepened: rose, burnt umber, tangerine, blood.

"Do you remember my grandfather?" Laura said, and abruptly her tone was almost blithe, though hard as a bullet. "He was the one in the wheelchair at our wedding. Kidney cancer. Grandpa George, the grand old prince of Wall Street. Maybe you don't remember. He died two months later. Well, here's what you probably never would've known about him, even if you'd cared. The kind of thing you wouldn't know unless you'd been married to him. Poor old George was a stinking bastard. He ignored my grandmother for fifty-five years, never gave her a dime of love, never said please or thank you or isn't that a nice dress or I like your hair that way. Hardly ever kissed her. Hardly ever even spoke to her except to say his shirt wasn't ironed properly or the roast was overdone. She spent too much of his money. She looked big in the hips. She looked scrawny. She was too loud. She was too dull. He'd be overheard asking her rhetorically why he'd married her in the first place. The girls had been all over him in college, she should remember. He'd been a big goddamn deal. But he'd married her, picked her, chosen her, and she should thank her lucky stars, shouldn't she."

She paused. The words had come all in a rush to the surface, and now in the still room I heard her breathing.

"He died on the operating table," Laura said. "The last kidney wouldn't cut the mustard. He died like anybody else, maybe worse. He saw it coming. Grandpa George was shrewd when it came to looking after himself. His posterity mattered to him. Maybe this was what he was thinking about as they wheeled him out of his hospital room on a gurney. My grandmother walked alongside, holding his frigid hand. You know the last thing he ever said to her, just before they rolled him into the elevator? Probably the last word he ever uttered. Just one. He was always efficient, my grandfather. One word sent out to do the job of a lifetime. 'Sorry,' he said. He was sorry. He told her he was sorry, and then he died."

I looked up. The sun had fallen behind New Jersey, the colors were just about gone. We were turning into shadows where we sat.

"Laura—"

"I'm not finished yet," Laura said. "I've been quiet. You think I'm quiet, and I am. But I'm tired of being quiet. I'm tired of being so quiet that sometimes you forget I'm even in the room. I'm tired of giving you so much room that after a while you don't even see me. Do you ever even ask yourself what that speck is in the distance? It's me, Julian. It's me. Even though I'm right here next to you. And I am tired of walking alone through a desert. It's too hot during the day and too cold at night. I am tired of being held up to the standard of somebody I never met and who isn't even on this earth anymore. I am tired of being made to suffer for the fact that you can't remember if she loved you enough. What's enough, Julian? Will anything ever be enough for you? Well, I won't be made to feel any longer that I'm not enough. I *am* enough. I am more than enough. If not for you, then for somebody else."

She was crying. Her arm came up to shield her face and she curled up on the sofa, trying to make herself invisible. It was more than I could bear to watch. I got to my feet and went to hold her. She tried to push me away but I forced my arms around her and her crying grew louder. Her body was shaking against my chest. And then my own tears came and we were holding each other with a fierceness we'd never known during the long calm days of marriage, and her fists were drumming on my back and her mouth was at my ear, murmuring in a voice racked with sadness that she hated me, that loving me had never been her choice.

PART
FIVE

o n e

THE SAME COUNTRY and not the same. Summer now, not spring. The same rental car—a Peugeot—and nothing like the same; all the models of everything had been changed. In thirteen years the French government had extended the autoroute through much of the Quercy, shortening the trip from Paris by an hour. Unless you happened to be me. If you were me, peering anxiously through the windshield with the road atlas on your lap, you'd get lost somewhere in the Paris banlieue and the trip south from the airport would take two hours longer than it took that other time, back when the map was written with the names only she knew how to pronounce.

Not everything was different. Tiny cups of bitter coffee along the way, a croque-monsieur. Around Châteauroux, the open fields of turned soil and vibrant yellow and cool green be-

ginning to lose ground, gain complexity, geometry, grow humps;
become the Limousin, old hill country of stone walls and
red-tiled roofs. Then off the autoroute, onto the small roads
that curved and dipped. Low hills already parched and half
browned under the full blaze of summer, Roman-nosed sheep
packed like salmon in meager wedges of shade offered by the
odd plum or walnut tree, swallows perched on telephone lines
like unused punctuation. The few cows paragons of bovine
stillness. The valley and the narrow gray-blue river, the miles
of jagged limestone walls, the hamlets and their simple white
signs, the market town with the half-timbered facades in the
square, the food shops where she'd shaped her tongue around
the words and made them delicious.

I followed the river out of town until I lost sight of it. I
climbed the road that wound up the side of the mountain.
And then in my mirror the wide valley and the river were
splayed out again.

My breath had quickened and I was beginning to sweat. At
the top, on the plateau, I turned left, away from the single-
lane road flecked with sheep droppings that led to the house
where once, thirteen years before, Claire and I had stayed.

The nearest village sat on top of the mountain three kilometers away. Undoubtedly a place of significance once, with for-
tified walls built straight into the mountainside and long views
of the valley. Though by now irremediably shrunken, several
sizes too small for its own history, its constituent parts re-
duced to an épicerie with a FERMÉ sign hanging on its glass
door, an auberge with eight rooms, and a pack of scrawny dogs

who began barking at the sight of my car. There wasn't even a café.

I parked in the tiny square beneath a brutally pruned chestnut tree and entered the Auberge du Soleil.

Behind the desk, leaning on it as though for support, stood a solidly built old man. He straightened up when he saw me.

"Monsieur, bonsoir."

My French was halting at best. I asked for a room.

I was in luck, I understood him to say. Usually this time of year there were no vacancies. But a cancellation had opened a room. One of the better ones. Avec la vue, he said, though the price was of course reasonable. And might he ask for how long I would be staying?

I said I didn't know. Exhaustion was taking over; it was difficult to speak any language. When he took my credit card he inquired whether I had ever been to the region before. Once, I mumbled, a long time ago. He waited for me to say more, but I shook my head and opened my hands in a helpless gesture, and on a chair nearby a gray scruffy dog woke from its nap and regarded me with interest. Then, with slow measured steps, the man helped me with my bags up the stairs to my room. There was no elevator.

The room was small: a bed, a chest of drawers, a chair, a sink hardly deep enough for both hands, the toilet and bath down the hall. He turned on the light and opened the shutters. The yellow walls were decorated with framed photographs of the town, its stone fortifications and magnificent views, and of Rocamadour and the celebrated statue of the Black Virgin that Claire and I had never seen.

The man and I stood there, gazing around the room and

out the window at "le point de vue." Dusk was falling. Across the valley lights had come on, winking at us like earthbound stars. He asked if there would be anything else. He appeared reluctant to leave. His manner was formal but friendly, unsmiling but intensely solicitous; inspired, it seemed, not so much by the business as by the company. Now and then he rubbed his hands together as if simply needing to feel them. They were used hands, hard-worked and thick-skinned, the color of old teak, and in the quiet between us the sound of their moving against each other took on, somehow, the properties of eloquent speech. I began to feel oddly moved by him. In the deep weathered creases of his face and the watery focus of his eyes I sensed something forsaken, a faded resignation like a vow endlessly kept but no longer reciprocated.

"J'espère que vous serez bien content ici, Monsieur."

I was too tired to respond. Still, I was grateful to him for saying it. And when, with a last rub of his hands and a nod of his head, he left me to myself for the night, I felt his absence and was sorry he was gone.

Then I sat down on the bed, and within moments sank into a dreamless sleep.

t w o

BY ELEVEN, when I stepped from the cool shade of the auberge, the small village square was already an oven. In the fierce sunlight I stood blinking and partially dazed. There were no people that I could see. The heat of the paving stones reached up through the thin soles of my shoes, and the constant buzz of flies made it sound as though somewhere a power line were humming.

Nearby there were three stone houses of indeterminate age, shutters closed against the glare. The middle house had a wide downstairs window—a vitrine, unshuttered—and seemed a shop of some kind; but there was no sign, nothing to see inside but a single ladder-back chair, a rusted watering can, and a very still black-and-white cat that, had it not opened its eyes to watch me, I would have thought was stuffed. I turned away.

Across the square two narrow roads met. One headed down into the valley; the other was a short dead end leading to a cluster of old stone houses, bisected by a cobbled walking path, the whole framed by the ancient fortifying wall at the edge of the promontory.

As I stood there a thickset woman carrying a heavy sack of flour on her shoulder trudged past. She wore a brown housedress and dusty black shoes, and her shoulders were broad, and her footsteps echoed dully off the paving stones. She turned onto the cobbled path and disappeared from sight.

Rousing myself, I walked around the side of the auberge to the épicerie. Today the sign on the glass door said OUVERT. I went in. A tiny one-room shop, its floor-to-ceiling shelves crammed according to some arcane theory of practical juxta-position: boxes of rat poison beside cans of green peas, cartons of long-conservation milk next to dark and dusty bottles of Cahors. Behind a makeshift counter a doorway was hung with a fly curtain of green plastic beads. The place was empty; there was no bell to ring. I was thinking about leaving when I heard footsteps—and then through the fly curtain stepped the old man from the auberge, a blue smock covering the clothes he'd worn the night before. Around him the long strips of beads shimmied and ticked. Inclining his mostly bald head and half opening the palm of his hand in the direction of the shelves, he greeted me.

"Monsieur?" he said.

I asked if there was coffee.

"Oui. Voilà le café." His palm opened fully as he politely directed me to the packages of coffee on his shelves.

I shook my head. "Ah, non." I tried to mime a tiny cup of bitter coffee and my sipping it with pleasure—coffee already prepared. In the middle of my performance his mouth appeared to consider a smile, but wouldn't commit.

"Attendez," he said finally, and disappeared back through the curtain.

I waited. I didn't mind. It was almost cool in the shop, the shelves with so many ordinary things to look at and name. You could not be lost here.

Then through the glass door I saw the old man's scruffy dog trotting across the square, intent, his nose pointing with the certitude of a compass arrow. This wasn't a village to him, but a kingdom of infinite possibility. Inexplicably, I felt a stirring in my chest. Then the old man reappeared, for some reason walking backward, the long strands of beads parting before him like a dime-store sea.

He turned around. His eyes were generous. On a round waiter's tray were two tiny cups of coffee on saucers.

"Et voici du café," he said.

We stood in his shop drinking the coffee.

His name was Delpon—which in the old tongue of the region, I understood him to say, meant "bridge." He'd been born not ten kilometers from where we were standing. An uncle and an older brother had been in the Resistance during "la Guerre." The brother was dead now fifteen years. His wife, too, was dead. Ma pauvre femme, Delpon said, a phrase of irrefutable simplicity.

He asked if I'd come to the Lot as a tourist, for the Lot was beautiful indeed and there were many tourists in the region during the summer, English and Americans mostly, but some Germans too. A Japanese couple was said to have passed through at one time, but that was just a rumor, said Delpon, for he had not seen them with his own eyes.

He waited, swirling the dregs of coffee around the bottom of the cup to soak up the remaining sugar and then finishing it in a swallow.

I inquired if by chance he'd met an American woman during the winter. It would have been in December, around Christmas. An American with long brown hair who stayed at an auberge in the area, and who then lived for a few months in a small house in the next hamlet.

All this I asked in my slow, halting French and it took a while.

Delpon set down his cup. He saw that mine was empty too, and with a surprising lightness of touch he lifted it from my fingers and set it on the tray. His expression had changed.

"It was here," he said in French. "She stayed here." Slowly, a gesture of respect, he took off the blue shopkeeper's smock, folded it, and placed it on the counter beside the tray. He put his hand on my arm as if to steady me, and then added gently, "She is dead, you know?"

I said I knew.

He shook his head at the pity of it. "She was beautiful." He paused. "It was clear," he said. *C'était clair.*

Outside a car drove by, heading down into the valley. Appearing from nowhere, the village dogs charged after it barking, but quickly halted. It was just for show. They came trotting back, meek as rabbits, and soon disappeared again, each to his own corner of the kingdom.

"And the house where she lived?" I asked.

"A simple house," he said. "Typical of the region. At the moment not occupied."

"And the owner?"

"A local woman. I have known her many years. She was married to an American, but he died. She lives by herself on the other side of the river."

"What is her name?"

"Madame Conner."

The name sounded in my memory: the wife of Leland Conner, Lou Marvel's childhood friend. So the property was still in the family.

"I would like to see the house," I said. "If possible."

Delpon looked at me. The little shop was quiet and filled with things of all kinds. Outside the sun was high and in the white heat not a soul could be seen. His eyes with their own losses seemed to read mine without effort.

"I will see what can be done."

three

THREE HOURS LATER there was a knock on the door of my room.

"Yes?"

First just his head peered in, then the rest of him followed. The blue shopkeeper's smock was gone.

I set down the bulky manuscript I was reading. It was David Glassman's dissertation on the history of political radio in America.

"Am I disturbing you, Monsieur?"

"Not at all, Monsieur."

Delpon stood in the room, softly rubbing his hands together, his expression grave. "I have spoken to some people," I understood him to say. "More exactly, I have spoken to the husband of the woman who on occasion has done some sewing for Madame Conner. And he has spoken to his wife, who informed him that Madame Conner has been away all this month. She is sorry to say she does not know where Madame is or when she will return." His hands stopped rubbing and parted, embarrassed to be empty.

"Thank you," I said.

He bowed his head and I saw his eyes fall on my large suitcases in the corner of the room. After a moment's reflection, he added, "Might I offer you a glass of wine, Monsieur Rose? It is made by my son-in-law—" His lips pursed ever so slightly, perhaps suggesting that his son-in-law was not everything he had hoped for. "But in any case, I believe you might find the wine passable."

"Thank you, Monsieur Delpon. It is very kind of you. Perhaps later. At the moment I must go out."

The single-lane road, the glistening sheep turds left that morning. At the edge of the hamlet an ugly, recently built house made of cement, stuccoed brown. Then the old stone houses. An upside-down wheelbarrow in the grass. A sloe-eyed donkey, his muzzle poking out from under the low-hanging branches of a plum tree, shrewdly contemplating the pool of his own shadow. An elderly man in blue workman's jacket and large wooden shoes hoeing a rectangle of garden, slowly straightening himself to stare at my car as it passed.

It was still the last house, sitting slightly apart from the rest, behind a low wall. I stopped the car and got out and stood there. My heart suddenly calm to the point of numbness, and strange to me. Then I let myself through the gate.

The house was shuttered and locked as I'd expected it to

be. Apparently, no one had been there for some time. The parched grass reached to half a foot. The air vibrated with bumblebees, and butterflies sketched drunken lines of color against the cloudless sky. Clinging to the walls above the stone bench were the roses I remembered, already too late in the season, the pale pink flowers pinched by the killing heat until they looked like the delicate, unhappy faces of French schoolgirls. There was no scent left.

I turned away toward the barn. The double doors were unlocked and I eased them over the warped floorboards and stepped inside. Arrows of white light pierced the gloom through the roof holes, churning the heavy trapped air in the intense heat, illuminating swirling dust motes like colonies of tiny, swimming creatures.

That was all. I remained there, staring into the shadows and light. Then I went out, closing the doors behind me. I walked back to the house and sat on the stone bench. Around this particular place the air seemed to crackle with unseen life. Lower down the valley, a sheep bell sounded like a tin can being struck with a spoon, followed by a chorus of forlorn bleating.

I tried to think about Claire, but couldn't.

Eventually, I must have dozed off.

I dreamed I was drowning under a mile of black water with my mouth wide open. How I'd got there I didn't know. I was calling out, calling out, but making no sound. The sea was filling me.

Dazed and sweating, I woke. My head had fallen back against the blue shutters and my mouth was open as in the dream. But here was the real day—light-filled, hot, and buzz-ing with life. And beyond it a sound, a childish giggling. Star-tled, I looked there. Two young girls stood on the other side of the stone wall, observing me from a safe distance. Seeing me awake, they abruptly fell silent. And then, holding hands, they ran away.

four

A WEEK PASSED, followed by another. Madame Conner did not return. The little house in the next hamlet remained shuttered and locked. The weather stayed hot and dry. And soon enough I had become a fixture at the Auberge du Soleil. This was not hard to do. Despite Delpon's initial indications to the contrary, there were few other guests. I rarely saw another person there other than Delpon himself, rarely heard another voice besides his or mine. A quiet, forgotten place.

I took to using the lobby as my own reading room. It was there I wrote David Glassman a letter telling him that I thought his dissertation publishable, that it was something I would have been proud to have written myself, that he was someone I felt lucky not only to have taught but also to call a friend. You have already gone far, I wrote, and will go farther.

I told him not to forget to have a good time on the way. As for myself, I added, I was currently in the French countryside. I didn't yet know what my plans were.

And it was in the lobby of the auberge one afternoon that I read a note from Laura:

Were you ever really there? Even on our wedding day, holding each other in my bedroom? This is what I keep asking myself. It's a terrible thing not to believe the one you love. And still this wishing and wondering, damn you, what it might be like to have you whole.

As I finished reading, Delpon emerged from the spartan rooms behind the counter where he lived. He nodded at me and went out, the scruffy dog whose name was Max trotting after him, nails ticking against the tiles; the sound reminiscent of the ticking of the beaded fly curtain Delpon had stepped through on my first day in the épicerie. Such was the strange circular nature of my impressions those days. I didn't know what they meant. I was a plane caught indefinitely in a holding pattern, circling, waiting for permission to land.

The house was closed. There was nobody in it. There was nothing to do but sit and wait. If this was grief, I thought, I despised it, and myself too. There were moments every day when I was afraid I might burst into tears, and other, more numerous ones when I seemed incapable of any feeling at all. It was as if I had come all this distance looking for Claire only to get further away from where she'd been. I could not seem to find even my love for her now except in dreams and day-

dreams, which inevitably were morbid and sometimes frightening and came like ghosts out of the walls of my memory,
darkening whatever rooms they entered and then disappearing
without a trace.

I sat holding my wife's letter, wondering how, if ever, I
might uncover in myself a person complete enough to go back
to her.

At dusk I stood with Delpon outside the auberge, drinking the
sharp-toothed red wine made by his son-in-law.

Neither of us spoke for a time. In the two weeks we'd
known each other he had taught me how to be easily silent
with another man. He had seen my wedding ring and my suitcases, and no doubt from my manner and my questions about
the American woman who'd lived nearby he had drawn his
own private conclusions about what I was doing alone, week
after week, in the Auberge du Soleil.

"The wine is young," he said now.

"Young but good," I said.

"Passable?" The hint of a smile.

"Passable."

His son-in-law had a problem with debt, I'd understood
him to say, but otherwise was not a bad fellow. There was
a daughter, divorced, in Paris. There were three grandchil-
dren, two girls and a boy. Everyone lived elsewhere. He worried about the daughter, who was not happy. He'd asked if I
had children and I'd told him not yet.

While we were standing there the valley darkened. In the

corner of the square a streetlamp turned on automatically (Delpon made a disapproving noise with his lips). And then into the translucent fan of its light small bats came swooping and the village dogs, Max among them, arrived and began darting in and out, like fish in the shallows.

I asked him how long he and his wife had been together before her death, and he answered without hesitation. "Fifty-eight years."

"How did you meet?"

"She passed by one day on the back of her father's tractor. I was standing practically where I am standing now. She had a scarf over her head, red, but anyway I could see some of her hair. It was long and dark, her hair, and when she saw me watching she touched it—" He brought his thick, hard-worked hand up to his shoulder. "They were going to the market in Bretenoux," he said. "That tractor was not so fast. I followed behind all the way to town, ten kilometers, and when her father was not looking I went over and talked to her."

Below us, past a stone wall, snaked the paved road on its long descent into the valley. A car was driving down it, the yellow headlights sweeping over the wooded mountainside, dusky poplars and oaks, throwing shadows colored with the sepia of time.

Delpon drained his glass. "One does not forget," he said quietly. "My God, one does not forget."

He whistled for his dog then, and turned back into the auberge.

five

I WENT TO SEE THE HOUSE AGAIN. I went twice, and both times it was the same. And then one afternoon I went again and saw that the shutters had been opened.

I stood outside in the tall grass. With the shutters folded back it seemed a different house, awakened, claimed, neither Claire's nor mine. For weeks I'd been waiting for Madame Conner's return, I had thought; but now that the waiting might be over it was clear to me that I had made a grave miscalculation. I did not want to see another person in this house. I did not want to find another person's clothes hanging in the closet or a toothbrush in a glass or a dish in the sink. I did not want to have my face rubbed in the fact that in the end I owned nothing of my past except my own fragile idea of what had occurred. That what I had believed in as our history,

Claire's and mine, what for years I had privately endowed as some inalienable right, was just a fiction, a floating dream no more real or lasting than a reflection glimpsed in a dusty windowpane, here played out on a stage that had been occupied by others before us and now, evidently, was to be occupied by others again.

These were my thoughts at the time. I stood with them for a while, feeling strangely chilled in the hot day; and then I approached the door and knocked. My palms had begun to sweat and my breath had quickened. No one answered. The house appeared empty, and I knocked again. Then, with a glance back toward the road, I tried the door. The latch gave and the door opened and I stepped inside. Daylight entered with me, breaching the room, flooding around my body and throwing my shadow onto the worn straw matting. It was the same matting I remembered. At the edges it was in tatters, and the newspaper stuffed underneath for insulation was in various stages of decomposition: smells of wood pulp and lichened firewood and cobwebs and burnt ash and shaded stone. In the stone was the winter held over, cold and damp and unforgiving, oblivious to the heat outside. I felt chilled again, and couldn't seem to get enough breath. To the left, the long summer light shone through the glass panes of the door to the terrace, its ribbons bright and empty of anything but dust. A few logy flies careened through the air, while countless more lay dead on the floor beneath the windows.

I went into the kitchen. And it was all the same, down to the strip of flypaper hanging in the corner. As I stood there among the old appliances and pieces of chipped china, a kind of panic began to rise in my chest.

I went out and climbed the steep, creaking stairs to the second floor. Where it was the same: the bathroom with nothing in it, the narrow room with the pitched roof and the single bed, the larger room with the French windows and the double bed. The mattresses bare and stained. There were no blankets, sheets, towels, books. There was nothing left of her.

I went back downstairs. I didn't know what to do with myself now, and I stood again in the center of the big open room, remembering the first time. After the night and day of travel, she had stood right here, turning so as to see everything, her arms outstretched as if for balance, her face filled with rapture, wonder, awe. At what? I wanted to know now. At dead flies and rotting papers and warped floors and cracked mirrors and pounds of dust. At this dull, ordinary house whose walls enclosed nothing of the feeling I remembered, and all of the neglect.

It was then that my gaze landed on the wall cupboard by the entrance to the kitchen, and out of the gloom a memory broke like a beacon. I went to the cupboard and opened it. A strong smell of must rushed up my nose. I stood looking at a stack of familiar LPs, and at something else wrapped in a faded, moth-eaten blanket. I pulled back an edge of the blanket and read the name: PHILLIPS.

It was when I lifted the turntable from its resting place that I found the only signs left of her in that house: two spiral notebooks. One older, its cover stained and worn, immediately recognizable to me as the impromptu anthology she had made of her father's remembrances. The other notebook more recent, its cover unblemished. She had filled only about a third of the pages, I saw, but those were densely written.

My hands trembling, I sat down to read.

January 6, 1999

This is to you. I'm shaking a little at the moment, but that won't last, I'll calm down eventually. I don't know why it's so frightening to write words I know I'll never send, you won't ever see them, they're for me and I feel the need to talk to you and it is everything.

Every day for almost fourteen years I've talked to you in my head. Every day we've had conversations, whispers, Socratic dialogues, and there have been monologues and soliloquies and pieces of poems and snippets of songs, even silences, long ones, the kind that speak, and you are good at them and I don't mind. In my most private thoughts you never left.

And so I write.

January 10

This afternoon a woman from the hamlet came by with a basket containing two turnips, four potatoes, and five fresh eggs. Fifty-ish, with good strong farming hands and that local accent straight from the troubadours, a decent woman even if beyond her charitable instincts she was mainly interested in snooping around my life on behalf of the rest of the neighborhood. (Neighborhood? This is the Land That Time Forgot.) She assumed I was British so I gave her a cup of tea, which was about all I had to offer anyway, I haven't had the strength of mind to buy groceries. I think about it, but then almost immediately a lethargy comes, despite the freezing cold, a lethargy or something heavier, a steel net, and there's no point then but to lie down under the crushing weight. I'm getting very good at lying down. Still, it's a different weight, and a different darkness, than the migraines I used to get. You don't know about those. My first came about a month after you left Cambridge.

Carl had invited a couple of professors and their wives to dinner. I didn't know how to cook but I was supposed to learn, but I never did learn, not really. While the chicken was roasting we had drinks in the living room, where there was the usual talk about Iran-Contra and Carl was wearing a pink shirt and silver cuff links and his face was red as he talked, going on about Reagan and what a visionary he was and how reviled by his enemies, and I was just sitting there thinking quietly about you and the baby I was carrying. Trying to weigh you in one hand and the baby in the other and make the balance come out right, as if I were a scale, true and old and wise, one of those scales from the Bible whose arms were believed by some to represent God's arms and His divine justice and so could shed light and determine fates. But it was just me, you see, and I wasn't doing very well, was more or less paralyzed with grief. I couldn't think about you because if I did I'd start to cry, and crying wasn't allowed in that living room or that life, not by the rules I'd set for myself. So I tried to concentrate on the baby, tried to feel the baby, the baby was sacred, the baby was who I had. But I couldn't feel the baby then, it wasn't moving or kicking, I could sense its nascent weight but not the life inside it. I felt utterly alone then, is what I'm trying to say, and it was terrifying.

There was a dull pounding in my head, focused behind my right eye, a dull pounding like waves, a rough sea, if you're on the other side of a high dune and can't see it but know it's there and coming. And light, spots and streaks at the corners of my vision. And nausea. I got to my feet. Carl stopped talking and looked at me, they all sat gawking at me like baboons, and I was holding my head in my hands and could feel the waves pounding and coming closer and see the light flickering at the edges, giving everything I looked at a nasty little halo. And I thought, The chicken will burn, the potatoes will burn, and I could have laughed. Then the waves crashed all together and I stumbled from the room, swimming in the pain. But I wasn't sorry, I knew I was free, if only for as long as the pain lasted. Nothing else to think about then, or to regret. I went upstairs and locked the door and lay down in the dark with a damp cloth over my eyes.

That was the first time.

January 11

Snow. Nothing to say.

January 14

The power's out, don't know why. I'm writing this by the fire and there's not enough wood, everywhere but right here the house is dark and freezing. A little while ago I went upstairs with a flashlight to get some blankets, and on the way down lost my footing and almost fell.

Now I have a blanket on my lap, another around my shoulders. The dust makes me sneeze, I feel strangely hot in the head, the sky outside is black, the sun hasn't showed itself for days, the moon is a fucking coward.

January 16

Fever today, chills, not so good, thank you. Writing this from bed, blankets piled high, thinking, Stupid, stupid to have come, ashamed to see myself like this. Always prided myself on courage and intelligence and wit, but there's none of that in evidence now.

Once, about a year after you'd gone, I went to New York for the day. Took the train down by myself, just to be somewhere near you, and sat in a coffee shop, then Central Park, looking for my nerve. Never found it until too late. Saw multitudes that day, none of them you.

My unsent letters could fill a book.

More snow. Tired now.

February 5

A woman has saved my life.

Corinne Conner owns this house. Her husband Leland and my father knew each other for nearly fifty years, you may remember. Well, Corinne's still here, though she lives in another house now, down in the valley. She was stopping by, checking up on the new tenant—around here doors are never locked—and says she found me upstairs in bed mumbling to myself like a madwoman. (I am a madwoman, couldn't she tell?) My temperature was 105 but I don't remember. All I really remember is the sense of existing in a bubble, neither gripping the world nor being gripped by it. Something had got away from me and I was watching it go, that was all. It wasn't difficult. It was easy.

How she got me down the stairs and into her car I'll never know. She's not a big woman. I'm not sure of her age but my guess would be seventy. The nearest hospital is an hour away and I spent a week there, and then they sent me home with Corinne to recuperate. She lives alone in a house across the river because Leland died a few years ago and they never had children. She gave me my own room and I'm there now, my coughing filling the house. I've lost a lot of weight and she keeps making hearty soups and stews trying to fatten me up, but my appetite isn't coming back. She went to the other house for some of my things, including this notebook, so here I am—awake, skinny, alive, writing these words and wondering what it would have been like to keep letting go. I wouldn't be sorry, I think. I wouldn't miss you then. But I owe a great deal to this woman I hardly know, and don't want her to realize that now the fever's gone and the weird dreams have receded and I'm thrown back on my old self, I'm starting to feel desperate again. That I was saved but not born again. Medicine hasn't figured that one out yet. It's still me here, with the content of my character, such as it is, held up to the ruthless light: what I've done and not done, the choices I've made, inexplicable mistakes. I don't think I've ever missed you as much as I do right now. Dip a hand in me and you'd bring it up holding your picture in a thousand pieces, all the minutes hours and days I was lucky enough to have with you, and I don't know, I still don't know, if that's reason enough to keep holding on, or reason enough to let go.

February 10

Today Corinne drove me back to the little house. While I was staying with her she had someone come and fix the heating here (she says she blames herself for my getting sick), so now the three radiators are faintly warm to the touch instead of ice cold, and she's given me one of her husband's sweaters, which I'm wearing. It must be thirty years old but the wool's still oily and pungent, as if the sheep it came from all those years ago were somehow still alive.

Tomorrow I'll wake up and not hear Corinne puttering around her kitchen, talking to Gaston, her Belgian shepherd. She calls him her joyous shadow—ombre joyeuse—and that's exactly what he is. While I was still drifting in and out that first week I'd hear her murmuring to him, and once in a low voice when she thought I was asleep she sang him a song about a hedgehog.

She has soft white hair cut short and beautiful hands. Lines at the corners of her mouth make her look uncertain and severe at the same time, though I don't believe she's either of those things. Her eyes are bright and large and with her hands they do much of her talking.

Every so often I'd wake up and see her standing at the foot of the bed just watching me, and it would be like waking up into expectation, a space already cut to my size, and then I'd realize I'd been talking in my sleep. I've never asked what I said and she's never volunteered it, but I think we've grown close so quickly in part because of my communicating like that, telling her the un-conscious things that I'd forgotten myself or was afraid to believe in or maybe never really knew.

One time I woke and she was there, standing very close, look-ing at me with a peculiar intensity. "I was seeing your father," she said. "I was seeing Louis."

She told me then how she'd been twenty-five and waitressing in the auberge in Carennac when two good-looking "Améri-cains" walked in for dinner one night and started paying court to her. It was Leland Conner who had the perfect French and gen-teel manners, but it was my father—handsome, witty, a "smiling pessimist"—she fell in love with. They began an affair. He was open about the fact that he had a job waiting for him back in Connecticut and was only visiting for a month, but after a few days the passion between them was so strong Corinne believed he would change his plans and stay. She was wrong. He went back to Connecticut, took his job, and later met my mother. Corinne nursed her hurt for a long while, and Leland offered consolation. He was patient, even reverent, and he was loyal. She made a de-cision to grow her heart toward a different sun, she said, and gradually that's what happened. It was a decision, she said, and then it was her life.

I have the notebook in front of me now, the one filled with my father's memories. He made a decision, too, all those years ago, and here's what it says, all it says, about that:

> *Corinne—French, beautiful. Walked the causse w. her.*
> *Married. Still think about.*

Sometimes I imagine there's a great rope circled around all of us like a noose. We don't know who controls it, but when by an invisible hand it tightens, the circle grows smaller and we're thrown in against one another—sometimes fatally, sometimes ecstatically, sometimes for life, with our arms open. But then when the rope loosens and the circle grows wider again, grows huge, the forces that have pressed us so closely together turn opposite. We fall back, fall a little way or a long way, depending maybe on how far we traveled in the first place, and when we come to our senses again we're in the outer reaches of a much larger world and alone, like Ovid exiled to the edge of the Black Sea, humbled now by how small we are and how far we've fallen, hungering for the old crowded intimacy, and endlessly surprised by the love we've known.

The only good thing about your not being here is you can't leave.

February 12

The sheep are sent out no matter the cold or rain. A man from the hamlet—husband of the woman who brought me the eggs, I think—tends them. I've glimpsed him through the window *in the distance, early morning or late afternoon, walking in the early darkness, conducting the animals with a long stick like a wand. They don't know enough to run away. Where would they go, anyway? Doesn't he have a son to help him? All the young people have left for the cities, or at least the towns. It's six weeks since my arrival and I've never seen his face.*

February 16

Rain four days straight, rain down the chimney and the fire hissing like a snake. Too much darkness coats everything with the same brush until there are no variations or discrepancies, and the spirit goes numb.

February 17

The pen isn't mightier than the hand that holds it—there's my little epigram for the week, good for me. See how my words are drying up, shriveling, growing weightless; any stiff breeze will scatter them, and that'll be me they find out on the causse one day, hunting wild-haired for my lost words among the stones of the ruined walls.

March 9

Lost heart there for a little while. Forgive me. But here I am again, the hand steadies and grips, the pen moves.

Yesterday morning the sun shone. Corinne showed up unannounced in her pale blue deux chevaux and declared she was taking me to town for market day. I didn't want to go, but there was hardly any food in the house and I hadn't seen another human being for almost a week and the sun was out and she wouldn't leave until I agreed. So I ran a brush through my hair and changed sweaters—from heavy sheep to light sheep—and we went. An hour or two of sun had stripped the gauze off the valley, leaving blues and greens, the limestone luminous, the river rippling with light. We drove along in silence until Corinne announced that she'd been telephoning for a week, had I been away? I said no, the phone must have been broken. With a pointed look she said, But certainly it's fixed now? And I said, Yes, it's fixed. And then—I couldn't quite believe myself—I smiled at her, I didn't know where it came from, I couldn't remember the last time I'd smiled. It just happened, and we drove on to town.

You remember the livestock farmers in their royal blue smocks and black berets and knee-high rubber boots gathered at one end of the square, over by the river, auctioning cattle and sheep. Behind them under the plane trees a couple of games of boules going on, and in the middle of the square the café with the dilapidated pinball machine and the teenagers half crazed with boredom, and the Produits du Quercy shop with the fancy tins of foie gras and bottles of eau de vie. Also—one performance only—a ground-floor apartment through whose open window I happened to spy a woman in a head scarf sweeping her living room while happily belting out, in heavily accented English, the theme song from Titanic.

Everywhere stalls were set up where people sold clothes or cheap luggage or housewares or produce. Corinne and I strolled among aubergines stacked like fairy-tale artillery, shimmering trout in beds of crushed ice, disks of cabécou on wax paper, round flour-dusted loaves of bread. Dogs trotted at our feet and the cobblestones ran with water, voices rang out saying Fish or Cheese or Bread, a man in an apron dispensed wine from an oak cask into dark green bottles that customers brought from home. Corinne went purposefully from stall to stall, buying what appealed to her, and I bought nearly as much as she did. On this day my appetite had finally come back, she saw, and every so often she'd turn and look at me with approval.

March 14

Today I walked to our ruined fortress. It took me a while to find it. First I went down a path that led to somebody's house, and a small boy with a dirty face opened the door and stared at me without saying a word. His expression was so solemn and his face so dirty I thought maybe he was an orphan, but then just as he was closing the door he said Bonjour in a small high voice, and I said it back.

When I finally found the right path, I looked for the donkey we saw that day. How long do donkeys live? She was gone, of course, and where she used to stand the grass was up to my knees and full of nettles.

The ruin was deserted, just as it was that day. I came to the spot overlooking the valley where you lifted my hair and put your hand on the back of my neck, and today it was clear again, the view was no different, and behind me the fortress seemed no more or less of a ruin than it had seemed then. To a ruin thirteen years is nothing, I imagine, except the added weather. Walls don't collapse in thirteen years, or stones bleach in the sun. It's a slower clock, more patient, and it'll be ours too eventually. But until then, wherever we are or aren't, I'd rather feel the time than not, I'd rather know what thirteen years without you really feels like than take the long view, the historical perspective, the clock set to eternity rather than the days as I have counted them. I'd rather be weak than strong, if strong is being a wall that takes four centuries to fall down and another four centuries to turn white. I have fallen down and turned white and it didn't take as long as that. I know exactly how long it took.

March 19

After dinner at Corinne's last night we were sitting by the fire with Gaston stretched out on the floor at our feet when she reached down and put her hand on his head. Just put it there. Feeling her touch, he looked up as if expecting something, or as if he was listening very hard to something she was saying without words, and gazing back at him she said softly, Je te donne la main, Gaston, I give you my hand, and with that he lowered his head and went to sleep. The house was quiet then except for his breathing and the fire and the wind outside.

Soon afterward I began to talk about you for the first time, and once started I kept going, and Corinne sat and listened.

March 24

Not yet warm in this part of the world, but less cold. The days are not the battle they were. For stretches, even, they are no battle at all, and I find myself infused, inexplicably, with a heart-

fulness that just might be hope, tilting at sunspots where, ever since you left, only darkness ranged.

March 26

The plan was not to send these. The plan, you understand, was that these were for me, and not for you. But forgive me, my love, I'm beginning to question the plan.

I woke a little while ago, picturing you reading these words. Picturing you with the clarity of one who knows your image, your face and body, better than my own, and wondering what you'd think after reading my words to you, and what you might do.

Perhaps nothing. That's the risk if I send them, such a huge risk, it feels.

In my head now is the image of Burne-Jones' picture of a young woman holding a ball inscribed with the medieval proverb, "If hope were not, heart should break."

How strong our hearts have turned out to be, Julian! How strong, and strangely hopeful, and mysterious.

March 29

Spring has come early, the thaw in the mountains has begun, the Dordogne is running high. I walk everywhere and for the first time am glad not to have a car. I've figured out a walk from my house to Corinne's—down the sheep path about a mile and across acres of fields to the river and over a little crumbling Roman bridge and then a last half mile to the wall enclosing her plum trees, where Gaston greets me without fail and barks me in as though I were a visiting dignitary. In the dusk he looks like my shadow. If dinner runs too late or the weather turns, I stay the night in the room where I recovered from my illness, which is starting to feel like my own room. The walls are pale blue, the bedspread is yellow, and outside the window is the small orchard of plums, and the whiteness of their blossoms.

April 2

If I could give you anything, it would be my eyes opening this morning in my own house, which is yours, too. From the bedroom window I watch the sheep going out. Their steps are lighter now; all winter when they had nothing but stubble to eat they trudged like condemned men, but no longer. The new grass springing up everywhere is delicate, almost translucent, and they dip their heads, chewing steadily. Below them the fog, suffused with sunlight, is lifting, turning into sky, the river gleaming through it, centering the valley and telling me where I am.

I am here. The dark raked earth around the walnut trees whorled like a giant thumbprint; the moss-covered roots and black humus in the stands of scrub oak; the underground streams and caverns; the goats perched on rocks; the hens testing the mud; the Romans gone; the Gauls dead; the shepherd with his wand saying Go, go and Come, come.

Far too late I walked away from the life I had, the marriage I had, missing you too much to go on, regretting everything and expecting nothing. It wasn't courage but necessity. Now these riches have found me here, and I want to give them all to you.

seven

THAT WAS THE FINAL ENTRY.

I sat unmoving with the notebook open against my chest. I felt as if through hearing her voice like this a great rock had been levered off me and I was lying now in the crater of its impression, the ground still cool where the weight had been for so long.

After a while, I got up and went out to the terrace, wanting to see what she had seen on her last day.

It was early evening and the declining sun cast a lustrous glow over the valley. I stood taking long drafts of air. Birds were singing in the stand of old oaks just below the house. Beyond was the bare, raked field of walnut trees, and beyond that a grass-covered sheep path, and then the slope of walled pastures to the river. In the distance the river's surface was slate and blue with a fine misting of gold. Nearer, I could see the sheep massing in one corner of the fields, and hear their childlike bleating and the tinny, irregular rhythm of their bells. A man with a long stick was calling to them. In the transforming light the stick seemed to dance like a wand, and the sheep wore veils of gold on their newly shorn backs. I watched as they filed through an opening between two walls and onto the path that wound up through the hamlet, the dusky shuffling of their hooves and plaintive sound of their cries rising steadily up the valley like a mourning procession.

I stood seeing all this as she had seen it. And then I went through the house and out the front door and up to the gate, where the sheep were passing. Here on the paved road their hooves clicked like a constant hail of stones. They were close to home now and had begun to hurry, throwing off their attitude of somnolent mourning and filling the air with occasional bleats of expectation. The man followed the rear of the flock. He was silent now, no longer needing voice or stick. From ten yards he offered me a nod, sober though not unfriendly, and then he too was past and the sheep were well up the road toward his farm. Soon the road was empty. The hamlet was utterly quiet except for the cawing of a crow and the distant tonk of a bell. And I stood at the gate, not yet ready to go inside, the notebook still in my hands.

Not long afterward a car approached, coming from the village. It slowed to a stop in front of the gate, and a woman dressed in beige pants and a black cotton shirt climbed out. She was thin and striking, with cropped white hair and fine-boned hands. She stood observing me across the hood, her large dark eyes moving slowly from my face to the notebook in my hands, and back to my face. Strong lines at the corners of her mouth gave her an initial expression of severity or hardness. Then that shifted, and her eyes were lit with recognition and deepened by intense feeling; her mouth softened.

"So, it is you," said Corinne Conner.

e i g h t

WE SAT IN FRONT of the cold fireplace like two people who had known each other a long time, and she told me many things. She spoke a strongly accented English, and she told me about being the first person in the house after Claire's death, and how she had found the two notebooks on the floor by the bed and recognized the handwriting inside and then taken them home with her. She described the arrival of the husband soon thereafter, his arrogance and bad manners that would be remembered in the region for many years to come. He had stayed in an expensive hotel in St.-Céré rather than in the village nearby, and had chosen to speak only to the police, rather than to any of the local people who might have corrected his false impressions of the nature of her death; and so, because of this, no one but the police had chosen to speak to him. Then, two days later, he had departed, taking with him back to America her body and her things and his misconceptions, her heart still, as ever, unknown to him. And then the house was as empty as it had been before her arrival, nothing left of her but the notebooks, which Corinne had read and then read again.

"I bring them back to the house," she told me. "Her letters to you. She did not have time to send them. I put them in the closet, the old place, to save for you if you come. I know you will come, because about you I have this sentiment that we are not strangers. And then yesterday I return, and Monsieur Delpon tells me you are here. So I open the house and wait. I do not want to hurry you. And now you are here, knowing the words she wanted you to know."

She fell silent. The open room was a patchwork of shadows. And up by the road, as I sat waiting for my voice, a three-wheeled truck was heard puttering through the hamlet, and an old woman called out a greeting.

Finally I said, "So you don't believe she killed herself any more than I do."

Corinne Conner's eyes cut through the shadows with sudden light, and she shook her head. There was compassion in her gaze, perhaps affection. Slowly, she got to her feet.

"Come," she said, "and I will show you."

In her car we drove back through the village. Delpon, standing with a glass of wine outside the auberge, solemnly raised a hand in greeting as we passed, and we nodded in return.

Corinne followed the road that led down the mountain. She drove slowly and we hardly spoke, and all around us the light kept seeping away. We crossed the river on a one-lane steel bridge, and then by degrees the road began to rise with the bowl of the valley, and in a little while she turned onto a rutted dirt lane lined with poplars that circled back toward the river. At the end of the lane was a stone house three or four hundred years old. It stood on a slight incline adjacent to a small plum orchard, and its front windows glistened as though oiled by the last of the day's light.

As we got out of the car, a large black dog came bounding over, barking and sniffing at my legs. Corinne half raised her hand and instantly the dog quieted and stood back, his velveteen muzzle tilted up, something very like a smile spreading across his face: joyous shadow. Then Corinne, offering me her arm, led me beyond the house in the direction of the river. Against my side her limbs suggested a matchstick fragility, but her stride and voice were firm. The dog followed at a short distance.

Reaching the edge of the plum orchard, we stopped.

"Claire came here often," she said. "She did not have a car, you understand. She did not have money. She came by foot, in all weathers. The long walking she adored. Voilà sa route."

Her free arm swung out, a finger extended, drawing, in the magic hour quickly filling with shadows, an invisible map, a way. Left of the plum trees, along a perpendicular stone wall stark as a jetty, down the gradual slope and over the dark tiled roofs of other houses (one already a ruin), there shone, like a mirror flashed in code, a stitch of the river. Then, gently ascending, my eyes followed her finger up the far side—over empty walled fields and pockets of trees and acres of grass greener at this hour than at any other—rising finally to the sheltered hamlet where, standing apart, gray and blurred, I saw the house and barn that I knew.

I asked her how Claire had crossed the river.

Corinne's arm moved two inches to the right, her finger marking the river. "There is a metal bridge for the cars, the one we came over. But Claire detested its ugliness and noise. So, un jour, she finds for herself another route, this way—" The arm swung again, now to the left half a foot, the place there hidden behind a stand of trees and the one ruined house. "Here the river is not so wide. There is a very old bridge made of stones by the Romans, in bad condition, with signs of warning from the département saying attention, do not walk, en réparation. This is what Claire liked—the chance to have it for herself."

Corinne's arm had begun to tremble in the air, and she lowered it.

"I was expecting her for dinner. She was coming by foot. Half the hour, maybe the hour it takes. And each time she brings me always these things, petits cadeaux—bottle of wine, sometimes books, stones she finds, n'importe quoi. Objets trouvés, like a conversation between us. Because it is in these small things, these beautiful small things, that I see her best. You understand? Son âme, tout ce qu'elle était."

Corinne paused, her head turning, and in a moment the dog had appeared at her side—so quickly that I had no idea where he'd come from. He stood still, leaning imperceptibly against her legs as if to shore her up. She began to stroke his back.

"I wait, but she does not arrive. I telephone but there is nobody. Éventuellement I begin to look. Je la cherche. To the river I take Gaston. I find the place there, la route qu'elle préfère, the stone bridge where it crosses and the fast water just beneath. The light is like this now, not so easy to see. The bridge I know well. I have lived here all my life. There are the signs of warning as before—attention, en réparation— and the river at this time of year is fast, plein, dangereux. Too much rain from the winter and the water so high under the bridge. Stones wet, mouillé, not for crossing. And on one edge I see that a piece is missing. Next to the sign that says attention is a hole where before there was stone. I tell Gaston to stay and carefully I go on the bridge. And it is true. On one edge the stone is gone, fallen into the water. And I begin to understand. I remember how her pockets are heavy with the things she brings me always, and the water is high and fast like this, and the darkness. And no one to help her."

Corinne stopped petting the dog and her shoulders slumped, and now she looked old.

"C'est tout," she said in a voice full of sorrow.

"What about the police?" I asked.

"The police?" Suddenly her voice was hard and she turned her eyes back to me. "He comes the day after to talk to me, l'agent de police. To say a farmer has found the body, floated almost to Carennac. To ask me stupid questions of his own imagination. Was Claire happy? Was she sad? Does she drink too much wine? A boyfriend who does not love her? And I say to him, 'Pourquoi? Pourquoi vous me demandez ces questions?' And then he says, 'Parce qu'elle s'est suicidée.' He says this to me as he sits in my house. About the accident, the bridge that falls away into the water—nothing. The idea of her misery is what he likes. He says to me how they find all these things in her pockets—heavy things, two books, bouteille de vin, piece of stone, et cetera, and how this proves her wanting to drown herself. And I call him a fool. What kind of wine? I ask him. Maybe it is one I talk about with her before. What kind is this stone? Is there not maybe a picture on it, a shape, something maybe she brings to show me? It is beauty she loved, the taste of life. She could not get enough. It is more of life she wanted, not less. But of course he does not know what I am talking about. He does not listen. It is not written sur son papier. He does not know why I am crying. To him she is just a body—un objet trouvé, without desire."

It was dusk, the day deepening to its end. Lights were shining now from most of the houses. But by the river the ruined dwelling remained cloaked in darkness, and from one end of the valley to the other the tight walled fields appeared as smoothly impenetrable as floodplains at midnight. The hamlet, the house and barn—all had vanished.

"Listen," said Corinne urgently, taking my hand. "Listen to me now, Julian, and always remember: c'était un accident. Un accident. There was so much more Claire wanted. And already when she fell, she was coming to you."

nine

THE WOOD IS IN THE BARN. The sheep are in for the night. At day's end I stand on the terrace of the house we once shared and watch the valley born again with the lights of other lives, as the gray-blue river that is Claire's spirit grows silvered and yet still more luminous. Until as evening comes, her glow finally starts to fade, and I let her go.

a c k n o w l e d g m e n t s

I am particularly indebted to the following people:

My agent, Binky Urban, whose support and wisdom have guided me since I was twenty-one, and always will.

Nan Talese, for being that brilliant, old-school editor writers dream about but almost never meet in real life.

Ileene Smith, whose razor-sharp intelligence as a reader is matched only by her generosity as a friend.

Beatrice Rezzori and the Santa Maddalena Foundation in Donnini, Italy, for the chance to work undisturbed in a place of great beauty, peace, and inspiration.

Ed Maddox and Zach Goodyear of Choate Rosemary Hall, who long ago showed me what it means to be a good teacher.

And finally, my wife, Aleksandra, who gave me the knowledge, and the desire, to write a love story.

BICYCLE DAYS

When Alec Stern arrives in Japan, he discovers a land of opportunity, where an impressionable young man fresh out of college can find, in one stroke, a new job, a new family, and a society that lavishes attention on Japanese-speaking *gaijin*. Yet, even as he claims a place in this new world, Alec is haunted by memories of the one he left behind—a world which disintegrated with the breakup of his parents' marriage. In this incandescently observed novel, John Burnham Schwartz introduces readers to one of the most appealing protagonists in contemporary fiction while enchanting them with the keenness of his eye and the aptness of his voice. Through its exquisitely rendered scenes and vividly imagined characters, *Bicycle Days* surprises and enlightens us as very few books do.

Fiction/Literature/0-375-70275-X

RESERVATION ROAD

A tragic accident sets in motion a cycle of violence and retribution in John Burnham Schwartz's riveting novel *Reservation Road*. Two haunted men and their families are engulfed by the emotions surrounding an unexpected and horrendous death. Ethan, a respected professor of literature at a small New England college, is wracked by an obsession with revenge that threatens to tear his family apart. Dwight, a man at once fleeing his crime and hoping to get caught, wrestles with overwhelming guilt and his sense of obligation to his son. As these two men's lives unravel, *Reservation Road* moves to its startling conclusion. This is an astonishing tale of love and loss, rage and redemption, that is as suspenseful as it is emotionally compelling.

Fiction/Literature/0-375-70273-3

THE BUFFALO SOLDIER
by Chris Bohjalian

Two years after the deaths of their twin daughters, Terry and Laura Sheldon take in a foster child. His name is Alfred; he is ten years old and in their small town, he is the only African American. As Alfred cautiously enters the family circle, Terry and Laura struggle with their grief, and with the pain of Terry's adultery. Meanwhile, Alfred befriends a neighbor who inspires him with stories of the buffalo soldiers, the black cavalrymen of the old West. With his trademark emotional heft and storytelling skill, Bohjalian creates a moving and morally complex portrait of an unconventional family.

Fiction/Literature/0-375-72546-6

LOVE AMONG THE RUINS
by Robert Clark

When William Lowry writes to Emily Byrne, "I don't know if you know that you know me," the seventeen-year-old hardly suspects that his life, along with the rest of America, is about to change forever. But the day Emily receives the letter is also the day that Robert Kennedy is shot. In Minnesota, even during the tumultuous summer of 1968, first love cares little for matters of time and place. The young lovers decide to escape to the wilderness to start anew. Left behind to grapple with the shifting mores of the nation, their parents must search both for their children and their own lost innocence.

Fiction/Literature/1-4000-3030-7

HONEYMOON
by Kevin Canty

The characters in Kevin Canty's new collection are people we all know. People who are perhaps ourselves, searching, often in the wrong places, for something meaningful, real, or at least, for a moment, right. Here are couples like Vincent and Laurie, who must confront the inevitable end to their ill-timed romance. There is also Olive, a recovering drug addict, who finds herself in an illicit relationship with her nephew and his problems. And a chubby young boy nicknamed Flipper who finds unexpected comfort in the company and forbidden gifts of a pregnant teenager.

Fiction/Short Stories/0-375-70800-6

PALLADIO
by Jonathan Dee

In her small hometown, Molly Howe is admired for her beauty and poise, until a secret is exposed and she is ostracized. She escapes to Berkeley, where she meets a young art student named John Wheelwright. They embark on an all-consuming affair, until the day Molly disappears—again. A decade later, John is lured by the eccentric advertising visionary Mal Osbourne into a risky venture that threatens to eviscerate the entire advertising industry. And much to John's amazement, one of the many swept into Osbourne's creative vortex is the woman who left him devastated so many years before.

Fiction/Literature/0-375-72641-1

SHELTER
by Jayne Anne Phillips

In a West Virginia forest in 1963, a group of children experience an unexpected rite of passage. In this shadowy, suspenseful narrative, Phillips unearths a dangerous beauty in this primeval terrain and in the hearts of her characters: Parson, a mysterious drifter; two young sisters, Lenny and Alma; and a feral boy called Buddy. Together they come to understand the importance of compassion, as lies, secrets, erotic initiations, and the bonds of love between friends are transformed in a wilderness undiminished by societal rules and dilemmas.

Fiction/Literature/0-375-72739-6

ALL I COULD GET
by Scott Lasser

Barry Schwartz had it all: a strong marriage, two children, and a job that let him ski a hundred days a year. But at thirty he decided it wasn't enough, and headed for Wall Street to make his millions. With the voice of a born storyteller and an intimate knowledge of the trading floor, Lasser captures Barry's new life: the hardball diction of Wall Street and the social pressure to get ahead. *All I Could Get* pits ambition against happiness to make shrewd observations about human nature and the cost of the American dream.

Fiction/Literature/0-375-72787-6

VINTAGE CONTEMPORARIES
Available at your local bookstore, or call toll-free to order:
1-800-793-2665 (credit cards only).